FLEECED
CUT FROM THE WRONG CLOTH

a novel by
George H.R. Goldsmith

Fleeced

Copyright © 2016 by George Goldsmith

All rights reserved. No part of this book may be used or reproduced in any matter without prior written permission.

Tellwell Talent
www.tellwell.ca

ISBN
978-1-987985-85-6 (Hardcover)
978-1-987985-86-3 (Paperback)
978-1-987985-87-0 (eBook)

This book is dedicated to my wife Catherine.
Her support and motivation were keys to its getting
written, and she suffered elegantly and with a wonderful
sense of humour through the torture of the process.

Fleeced is a work of fiction inspired by experience, triggered by events, and tempered by many insights of friends and expert associates. The first inkling of the story came years ago when I read Tom Harpur's excellent book "The Pagan Christ; but the trigger was the 2009 excommunication of a Phoenix-based nun who faced grey-area issues and was judged harshly by black-and-white thinkers.

Many helped with facts, editorial review, and "realmarketing" (my term lifted from "realpolitik") so essential to those of us who must self-publish. These include Tony Afecto, Steve Ackerfeldt, Linda Ahmet, Cindy Anderson, Marie Andryjowycz, Bill Ardell, Henri Arnaud, Brad Ashley, Elad and Sasha Barak, David Bell, Peter Blaiklock, Joan and Richard Boxer, Diane Brooks, Wes Brown, Mary and Terry Bryon, Brenda Buckingham, Jeremy Busch, Brendan Calder, Robin Campbell, Steward Campbell, Leonard Cappe, Don and Martha Carr, Frank Caruso, Mario Causarano, Diane Chabot, Peter Clark, Nancy Codeanne, Donna Cohen, Chris Coombs, Jim Coutts, Joan Curran, Allison Dellandrea, Jon and Lyne Dellandrea, Meredith Dellandrea, George Denier, Nick DiRenzo, Colleen and Mike Dolan, Jack and Sue Duffy, John Earle, Lihi Eder, Eric and Kristie Ehgoetz, Diane and John Elder, Tina Epps, Mike Fedchyshyn, Dusanka Filipovic, Jonathan Fine, Ken Florence, Rivi Frankle, Fred Fuchs, Matt Gassenbeek, Charles Goldsmith, Bob Gorrie, Elaine Gray, Lorne Greenspan, Tony Griffiths, Gordon and Wendy Hall, Deborah Hall, Liberte Halkidis (for whom one character is named), Rob Hamilton, Bob Harper, Mary Hayes,

Grant Haynan, George Hood, John Hughes, Judy and Warren Hurren, Heather Kaye, Doug and Peggy Kelcher, Claire and Stirling Kenny, Roger Kenrick, Suzanne Kernahan, Rudy Koehler, Jacques Krasny, Joel Kulmatycki, Beverly Larkin, Mark Ledwell, Helen and Larry Leduc, David MacCoy, Murray Makin, Uwe Manski, Melissa McGuire, Lance McIntosh, John McKay, Joanne McKenna, Sue McKee, Bob Mitchell, Bill and Sharon Moriarty, Joan Murphy, Rob Nihil, Frank and Martha O'Connor, Karyn O'Neill, David Pace, Cathy and Wally Palmer, Lawrence Partington, Jane and Stephen Pasquale, Emil Petko, Alan Pyle, Emily and John Osborne, David Pace, 1ohn Robertson, Kirstin Rochford, Judy and Tim Rodenbush, Rhea Roebuck, Don and Joyce Rogers, Ben Rovinski, Kara Russell, Jim Saloman, Alan Schwartz, Martin Sear, Brian Shaw, Leslie and Tony Sinclair, David Smith, J'aime Spork, Lee Strickland, Greg Sutherland, Yvette Sutherland, Ed Swerhone, Shaul Tarek, Margot Taylor, Norm and Wendy Trainor, Sharyn Varty, Frank Vasilkioti, Sybil Veenman, Deborah Vittie, Marni and Roland Wieshofer, Lee Williams, Rochelle Zorsi.

Errors are mine. Please forgive any omissions.

CHAPTER 1

In the jungle at the end of the garden, the violent feeding chain prepared for the day shift. These were honest labors.

Sarah tossed in predawn darkness, threw off her bed sheets, arose to meet nature's call, then slid quietly downstairs. She planned to start the coffee brewer, then perform personal ablutions before a day of teaching and caring for the sick, the lame, and the math-mystified.

Sidestepping the creak of the third step, she muttered an obscenity about darkness, unsteady stairs and old wood, then immediately crossed herself in apologetic outreach to her heavenly father.

On the main floor, Sarah noticed light under the once-was study, now seconded to dormer. A recent arrival had upped the head count to one person over capacity in this hellish Eden. The latest addition was Sister Therese, forced to Florida by a medical condition requiring more warmth than Rome offered.

Assuming the light meant Therese was awake, Sarah knocked to offer a "Good morning." No answer. She knocked again. No answer. With deliberate palaver, she opened the door. All her senses assailed, she stopped in horror.

Blood. Dead eyes. The smell of shit. Silence. No breathing. Inhuman pallor. Inert. Lifeless.

There lay Therese, dead as a mackerel. Stabbed by a knife still buried at an oblique angle. Sarah's first thought was Golgotha.

Light-headed. Sweat. Her heart smashed frantically in her chest, pounded in her ears. Tremulous. Fascinated. That thing; the knife. It was jammed straight into what used to be the dead nun's crotch, sticking obscenely from her ravaged vagina.

Alien-like and outside her own body, Sarah floated, horrified, removed. Transfixed, she studied the scene in shock.

Therese's wide-open, lifeless eyes mutely screamed the terror, the pain, the humiliation of her last living seconds. Dark red blood had pooled and begun coagulating around the cruel obscenity left in her. An arc of pubic gristle blotched the corpse, spilled to the bed and floor. Cloying sickly-sweet dankness of blood, headiness of morbid tissue and stench of involuntary post-mortem bodily issue pervaded, assailing Sarah's senses, brain, soul. She opened her mouth to scream, then dammed it to stifle the vomit.

She wrenched her eyes away for modesty of the dead woman.

But the corpse and phallus were magnetic. Living and dead eyes locked for the eternity of a minute. The dead ones penetrated with onus, obligation, plea.

Nausea abated. Fear subsided. Sarah knew her own awful death was not imminent; coagulation meant the killing was hours old, the doer now gone.

"Jesus, it's a cross," she muttered, then crossed herself for saying and considering the sameness of the murdering knife and the cross of salvation. God's interjection triggered reversion from her near-catatonic state; Sarah returned to her body, to the present, and her mind began to work.

Oddly, her first deliberate thought was the computer. The thing never left the dead woman's side. It was clearly important. Was she killed for it? Because of it? What should she, Sarah, do now?

Within minutes of the grizzly find, taking just enough time in her own cell of a room to blow her nose and calm her heart, Sarah tapped on another door, that of Mother Superior.

Light knocks to no avail, Sarah let herself in to avoid waking the others in panic. Heavy regular breathing informed that so far as Sarah knew only one murder had occurred.

The matriarch displayed more panic than Sarah had, seizing initiative only after, and precisely as, Sarah ordered her; see the body, call the priest, call the police, tell the nuns.

With the respite of transferred obligation, Sarah submitted to emotion in the privacy of her own room. Lying prone abed, seeing only the vagina mutilating cross of the knife, she allowed herself to weep. She wept only for a couple of minutes, then willed herself from the selfishness of such personal release; a luxury for which she and the convent did not have time.

In a trance, Sarah began girding herself in the old style. The outdated habit every nun owned but no longer wore which was the armor of black serge, underskirt, overskirt, and tunic. She rolled up her flaming red tresses and crammed them into the white cotton cap, made severe by the bandeau, turning her image to monotonous and stale. The scapula over her head, pulled down tight, locked in place with the Spartan woolen belt. The wimple completed her transition to medieval.

Thus attired in the retro armor of her calling, Sarah sallied forth, door-by-door to check for causalities and whispered disclosure to each sister, all of whom had had an uninterrupted night. Each looked starkly blank as Sarah delivered the news, then silently closed their door.

With all accounted for and informed, Sarah raced back to the crime scene. Mother Superior Marie stood sobbing over the corpse. A cadre of nine nuns became ten, each dressed exactly as Sarah. They surrounded the deceased, each kneeling in feverish silent prayer.

No priest.

Sensing Sarah's presence, the ten rose from their prayer and Therese's sightless challenge, looking passively to Sarah, so that she might direct them.

CHAPTER 2

Ted Coulson loved his early repast. The sun had risen but not too many humans had. In another hour the place would be crawling, but for now, it was his. The early Florida sun offered gentle warmth that would later turn to swelter. Sitting alone at Jimmy's wharf-side diner, breakfast inhaled, he now reached for the highlight: the daily Sudoku puzzle. "Ah, 'Diabolical!' – my favorite," he muttered into the background chatter of pelicans and gulls. Ted had already been up for hours; first playing catch with the fish, then going from cover to cover of both the Miami Herald and USA Today, and now, finally, his pièce de résistance. A pelican perched ten feet away studied him as Newton did that apple.

Ted had been coming here to Ophrah for years now. It was his haven. No Miami. No traffic. Just the fish. And his sister. More correctly, the sisters.

Ophrah existed because of fishing, wilderness tours, the US Corps of Engineers, drug control and enforcement, and a botanical outpost at the University of Miami. The Orandu, a spring-fed river to the north, provided fresh water sufficient to the needs of the some 3,000 people that called Ophrah home.

Unemployment here never got much below 25 percent, every family had at least two guns but no dentist, and most of the indigenous population hadn't read anything longer than a menu. Ophrah boasted itself to be the world's best wilderness outpost, but tourists didn't seem to care, and the town slumbered in a kind of expectant mediocrity, waiting to be discovered, waiting to be saved. It would have been different if it had sand for a beach. The sea qrapes that would save the land might very well kill the town.

For ten years Ted had made this pilgrimage. He came for two weeks of fishing and visiting with his sister, and now really all the sisters. They had become his family. He ate, prayed, and lived among them. Occasionally they had called upon him in Miami in his official police capacity for information, advice, assistance, or help on behalf of those in crisis. "Time off purgatory," he thought each time as he cheerfully complied. But that was a dog's age ago, as Ted was now in his eighth year of retirement.

Ted was a lonely man. He had no real friends, and no family other than his sister, Sister Mariah, and no interests to bring him into contact with others. His time in Ophrah was the least lonely of his existence. It kept him going.

Deeply into his puzzle, the first siren went unnoticed. The second crashed the game. The third wrenched him to acute awareness. "What? Too many zebras for something minor. Kind of close to the convent. Better have a look," he thought. He heaved his 265-pound, fifty-three year old, out-of-shape frame into motion and lumbered toward his fate.

In minutes Ted was on the scene, and sure enough, there were the black-and-whites, parked helter-skelter, doors ajar, all three of them. *This must be about everyone on duty! Christ! Someone must have died!*

Hackles raised, Ted crossed what would become the perimeter; succeeding only because the yellow barrier tape wasn't yet in place. Perversely, Ted felt good, alive, back. A crime scene was home, his comfort zone.

He knew where the perimeter would be set, how the detectives would soon take over, then cede it to the CSIs who would scour for hours in a relentless search for the minutia that make cases. They would most likely come from Naples, maybe Miami, or perhaps Tampa.

He knew the detectives would view him as suspicious.

Eleven ashen-faced penguins surged toward him, swallowing him into their midst. "What's with the outfits?" he wondered.

Notwithstanding the obvious, which was crisis and loss, Ted felt alive, excited, and needed to help the police with the case and his girls with their ordeal. Instinctively he knew, based on twenty-five years at Miami homicide, that he was senior in skill and experience to everyone now on the scene. Eight years of retirement fell away in an instant. He was back.

When the answer to his first question was, "It's Sister Therese, she's been murdered," his reaction was smiled relief that one of his personal flock hadn't died.

That smile was unobtrusively noted by detective Sergeant Liberté Alvarado, of the Town of Ophrah police force.

The detective approached Ted, and as she did, despite all else that was going on, Ted sized her up. He noted a nice face, workable chest, the wide "good for babies" hips he found so enticing. He thought her a bit short, apparently fit but prone to weight gain and later-on dumpiness, maybe forty-five at the outside, and purposeful, but somehow not quite comfortable in this situation. She wore slacks. Ted preferred his women in skirts.

Before he could disengage from his penguins, the object of his assessment arrived and offered an outstretched hand.

"Hello. I'm Detective Liberté Alvarado. I'd like to ask you a couple of questions. First being, 'who are you?'"

"Sure. Ted Coulson. What happened?"

"Mr. Coulson"

"Please, call me Ted."

"OK Ted. There's a deceased nun here named Sister Therese. She died violently about four hours ago. Ted, if I may say, you kind of stick out in this crowd."

He looked blank, then gave a half-smile kudos for her apparently unintended joke. Her steel-trap mind noted his ability to see humor, and to have appeared amused earlier.

"Ya," said Ted, "See that woman over there, on the far right? She's my sister. Mariah. I come here every year. Fishing. These people are my family. I mean, she is my family. I live here. Well actually, in the cabin out back."

Liberté guided Ted to a chair in a manner that suggested she wasn't so much asking as telling. "I need you to not talk to the witnesses. Do you understand?"

She plunked him in the targeted chair. "Stay put, sir. I'll be right back. Can we get you something? Water?"

"Sure, but really you don't need to. My prints are on file. I'm ex-Miami homicide. I've been at a lot of crime scenes, ma'am. I can probably help you with this. For now you don't need the prints, but the water would be nice. Thanks."

Then she was gone, and he was left to watch. As she left, she talked briefly to a "Uniform" who then hovered by Ted, leading him to the correct assumption that he was in a sort of temporary protective custody. A dark thought flashed through his mind, "I wonder who they are protecting from whom?" But more than anything, Ted held a blind faith in the system within which he had toiled for his entire working life. He would give her answers, she would see that he was innocent, and then he could help her to catch the real killer. He thought that would be fun. She was sort of attractive. Who knew?

This woman, Liberté, returned with his water and then excused herself. She did not return to him for just over an hour, but for most of it, she was within his eyeshot or earshot, so he got to watch in growing amazement.

There was no team as such, just this one woman. She had four Uniforms with her, one watching him, one outside maintaining the perimeter, another studying every door, window and ounce of earth for clues of entry and departure, and a fourth who did this woman's every bidding.

He watched as detective Alvarado sent each nun to her room, and then interviewed each separately. It would have taken forever because she made copious notes, except each had almost nothing to say. Ted was able to glean only that everyone in the house had been asleep for the event, and that the body had been discovered by the young one, Sarah.

Notwithstanding the trauma of the moment, or perhaps because of it, he noticed Sarah for the first time, as a woman and not as a nun. This was ironic since the traditional outfit Sarah now wore did more to hide her than any of the modern smock outfits ever had. Maybe it was the jolt caused by the death, but at that moment he could feel the vitality of his old job and the stimulation that brought to him. Maybe it was how Sarah seemed to have changed. The girl was, well, regal, magnetic, compelling. Not just tall, she was six feet if not an inch over, and erect. She didn't so much walk as glide. Her gaze, while kind, penetrated. One felt examined, probed, exposed under that gaze. Maybe it was the eyes that were a deep, remarkable blue. Contrasted against her blue-veined marble skin and her flaming red hair now hidden, they were intense.

He couldn't take his eyes off her. He was, he realized, a little excited. He loved strong, dominant women, but always from a distance because he was also cowed by them. Ted caught himself in a momentary fantasy of gaining this woman's attention. Immediately ashamed, he began a silent round of prayer, using his fingers to count. While he felt he should pray, he didn't want to become a spectacle, and so left the rosary in his pocket.

While praying, Ted kept an eye on the proceedings. He noted that each nun had been Dapper-tested for gunshot residue. After processing, each had then been evicted to the back yard, where he guessed they would just mill about until bussed to the police headquarters for videotaped statements.

Apparently the only thing the nuns had been able to add was that a computer was missing. Therese took the thing with her everywhere she went, and spent almost every waking hour using it. It should have been in her room, probably on the desk and most likely tethered to an electrical outlet. But it wasn't.

He was surprised that no one from the diocese, no priest, had showed up. He heard some chatter about well-wishers dropping gifts, mostly flowers, at the front gate, and wondered anew at how news, especially bad news, traveled.

He watched as much as doors and walls would permit, as Liberté seemed to stalk the dead woman's body searching for anything that could be called a clue. He sensed she wasn't getting much.

The detective took as much time with Sarah as with the rest of the woman combined. She made poor Sarah retrace her steps to discovery and thereafter, at least ten times. Just before checking Sarah for gunshot residue, she had sent Uniform number four on an errand of search and discovery in Sarah's room. It was apparent that the nuns were all "clean." He had seen, or rather heard, sparks when the cop had referred to Sarah's attire as "kind of medieval" and the nun had spat back that modern America with all its security might be leaning in that direction. Well, thought he, some spice. This feisty little thing had struck a chord in him. He liked Sarah, and felt filthy for doing so.

Finally, it was his turn. As the detective approached, she handed a bagged Blackberry cell phone to Uniform number four with instructions that the call history and calendar be fully documented, stat.

She then coiled into the chair across from him. "So Mr. Coulson, er, Ted, you live here?"

This was his moment. He explained he was a retired homicide detective from Miami and that he was impressed with her performance so far, although shocked at the lack of resources given her. She thanked him, and he continued to explain. He told her about Mariah, the fishing pilgrimages, the old service piece, a Glock 22 she would find in the cabin. He mentioned the fact that just last evening he had gone to the shooting range for his weekly target practice, and yes there would be residue, that he had a key to the main house but in ten years had never used it, that he slept in the cabin, that he had been up at four to go fishing, that he had raced back because of the sirens.

Ted shared his take on the missing computer; that it was most likely the target of the raid, and the brutal violation a ruse. He told her that crime solving is like Sudoku, "Good players follow each new fact as far as it will take them before moving on," and "Every new fact requires a new assessment of all unknowns." She had actually seemed a bit testy and only wanted to know if he had a computer, and could he please show it to her and turn it on. He had found this a bit annoying. By now she ought to have seen the light and understood how helpful he was being. It was proving difficult to get this woman to understand how smart he was and to make her like him.

A little desperate to get through to this new challenge, Ted had reached back into history and told her about a case from his past, where the dots hadn't fit together until viewed within context. That, as in Sudoku, the key is the pattern. From what he saw, this had been planned and it was about the computer. Based on that case of several years ago, he predicted another killing and that by now the murderer, himself a patsy, would already be dead.

He took her to his cabin, gave her the Glock, and was then ushered out where he remained under the silent guard of Uniform number three. When she emerged from the cabin, Liberté wore the latex gloves common to detectives, medical practitioners, and sex trade workers. Ted found it kind of exciting. She instructed Uniform number three to collect the bagged and tagged items of laundry: clothing, bedding, towels…and Ted's personal computer. She asked Ted to confirm the clothing he had worn last evening at target practice, then asked him to strip and surrender all the clothes he was now wearing. She also took his cell phone.

By now the CSI team had arrived from Miami. Ted looked them over in search of a friendly face, but a lot happens in eight years. There were no people he could call later for an off-the-record update.

"One more thing, Ted," began the police detective, "Are you close to Sister Sarah? Is there anything that you want to tell me now?"

"Nothing. I mean she's here. But no, nothing special. Why?"

"Well Ted, I find you interesting. Forgive me for jumping steps, but right now all I know is that I have a dead woman in there and a man with a gun out here. So far, all circumstantial, both means and opportunity. Not good if I find a motive. Tell me, Ted, what would you see?"

He realized he was being tested. "Uh-huh. I would see it the same, Liberté. But my gun didn't shoot that woman. I didn't shoot that woman. Do what you gotta do. Just remember the rules of Sudoku; there's only one right answer. I don't care what I look like now as long as you remember that rule. All the pieces have to fit and you don't—can't—have them all. Don't go jumping to conclusions. Good Sudoku players don't guess."

"I have no idea what you're talking about."

Ted grinned. If the roles were reversed, he realized, this woman would be under suspicion. He was a suspect! Of course, he was also innocent, and so was devoid of fear or even concern. "I understand. Just do your job."

"For now, I want you where I can find you."

He told her he had no intention of going anywhere, that his place was here, that Mariah and the others would need him, that he would do what he could to help her in her investigation. Her silence was deafening. She pinioned him with the same gaze intelligent monkeys experience from ignorant zoo patrons, then shook her head in quiet disbelief, spun on her heel, and left.

Ted, who should have been severely concerned about Liberté's attitude and comments, shrugged it off as the idiocy of the unable. His mind was elsewhere. Ted was thinking about Sister Sarah. He would find her and offer to help.

CHAPTER 3

By ten-thirty that night fatigue had overcome fear for all but one of the convent denizens. As the gentle rhythms of exhausted sleep filled the building, she who had risen first prepared last to retire.

Sister Sarah patrolled the inner perimeter of this now besieged fortress of God's brides to check doors and windows, ending in the crime scene room itself. There, in the first silent and alone time of the day, Sister Sarah immersed herself in all that had happened and in the enormity of reality, the finality of it all.

The knife as cross image welled over her. She moaned six words, "Her ark. Her covenant. Savaged. Desecrated."

As if pushed by some great hand from above, Sarah dropped to her knees at the victim's bedside, adopted the pose of a child at prayer, and beseeched her Lord on behalf of the dearly departed. Then she retired to her own room where, with meticulous yet trancelike care, she disrobed from the costume of her servitude. She slipped her nightgown over her head, cast herself upon the bed, buried her head in her pillow, and wept. When she had sobbed long and hard enough to have made her ribs and throat raw, she found her rosary, and once again sank to her knees, where she prayed yet again.

These were not the orderly prim prayers of chapel; sometimes aloud, mostly in silence, laced with rosary but more than anything, visceral. The woman who had given her life to the service of God, desperately pled for divine guidance and strength, for forgiveness, and for mercy.

It began with repeated prayers for the dead, for the repose of Therese's soul and for her easy arrival in the heaven that she must surely have earned.

At some point the focus of the prayers turned from the victim to the detective, Liberté Alvarado. The stately nun prayed to God for strength and wisdom on behalf of the detective. Sarah also prayed on behalf of Liberté for relief from the horror in her soul its scarring that exposure to brutality must cause.

Prayer about violence led Sarah to the issue of hate and her soul; she hated what had been done to Therese and despised whomever had done it. The gentle nun feared now for her own soul as she knew... had been taught... that to hate was a sin. She prayed for guidance.

Then she prayed a prayer of thanks. She thanked God for sending Ted Coulson to be "there" in her hour of need. She told God what a treasure Ted was: strong, knowing, caring. A bastion. A light in a world turned dark and forbidding. She thanked God for sending Ted so that he might guide Liberté through the filth, to guide her to the right answer, to solve the crime for her so that it could be put behind them, and so that they could go back to what they were.

As she prayed around, and for, Ted, Sarah felt her spirits lift and her heart quicken. This man was sent as a savior for them... how odd that he also was a fisherman.

For some reason, a face from long ago crept into Sarah's consciousness. It was Jimmy, the boy from her adolescence, the one to whom she had first given herself. She immediately understood this invasion, and she prayed for forgiveness for unchaste thoughts before she even had them. She prayed for the strength to work with Ted without sinning in thoughts, let alone deeds. She prayed for fortitude. She prayed for her vows. She prayed that she be spared temptation of the flesh, not because she feared betrayal of her vows, but she just could not bear another test.

Finally she began a conversation with her Lord and maker about duty. Why had it been her that had first found the dead woman? Why was it now that the police wanted more of her than of anyone else? Why did the nuns seem now to turn to her for direction? Should she have done anything differently at the moment when this greatest test of her life had first appeared? How was it that they all slept and she could not? Why did Jimmy, an acne-faced testosterone event of her adolescence, show up in her mind now? Was God telling her that Therese's death was a test of her vows, that the battle between the profane and the holy was to be waged now... again... in her? Should she, could she, rely on Ted, or was just allowing the joy of his proximity a sin? If it was a sin to feel joy in the presence of this man, was it a venial or a mortal sin? Was it more or less virtuous to live with temptation and yet abstain from it, than to remain in a safe cocoon of total indifference? Why were the men who had dominion over her not helping now? If her church did not give her succor in this, her hour of need, had she made a terrible mistake in turning her life over to it, to investing herself so completely in it? If this test changed her, could she ever return to the submissive role she relished until the dawn of this dreadful day? If God was looking after her, then why had he permitted this?

Sarah stopped talking to God and began talking to herself. What was she saying? Submission? Vows? Unchaste thoughts? Questioning her church? Weakness of the flesh? What the hell was the matter with her? What the hell was going on?

She realized she was making a deeper confession, on a direct-to-God basis, than she had ever made in any confessional.

It dawned on her that the knife that had torn Therese to pieces had pierced the tranquility of her existence and the world she had avoided was now upon her. She could no longer hide behind a habit, twin underskirts and a wimple.

It was too much to ponder. She pushed it all away with a pre-sleep round of her rosary.

When sleep finally claimed her, the last thing she thought of was that big oaf Ted.

Terrible visions invaded her REM: violent rape, dreams of helpless victimhood. The most hideous was running but not moving, chased by a terrible cloaked monster with a huge knife that became a penis, then turned back to a knife, getting ever closer, her screams going unheard, while a priest stood silently watching but giving no help.

She woke, and bolted upright, dripping in sweat. Alone, so alone in the dark, Sarah tried to rationalize. Since her teen years she had dealt with nightmares by comparing them to the events of the day before the dream, and then willing herself to sleep while thinking "good thoughts," like Santa Claus. Since entering the cloistered life Sarah had not had one single nightmare. Until this night.

She tried her old trick. The knife and the guy chasing her were easy. The bit about the priest was curious because, she thought, the priest in the dream did nothing to help her. So what did that mean? It struck her that the priest wasn't just a priest; in dreamscape, he might be the whole Church!

Was her dream telling her that the Church had abandoned the nuns… her nuns? Not a single priest had made even one appearance during the entire hellish day.

What did the penis-knife transformation mean? Someone had picked on one of the largest sacrifices a nun makes, her sexuality. That person had deliberately violated the womb Therese had given exclusively to God. This cruel invasion made a mockery of that sacrifice. Was questioning the violation in those terms really a way of questioning the sacrifice itself; and if so, what massive sin was that?

Then there was Jimmy! The only thing remarkable about him was the coming of age thing. So, why now? She hadn't given Jimmy a moment's thought in twenty years. Was Jimmy now Ted, or Ted now Jimmy? When she was so desperate was it somehow sinful to rely on, to like, to admire this man, Ted? Was the joy she felt from Ted kindling for a fire that might consume her soul?

The bedside clock forced its way into her reverie; it was half-past three in the morning. She wasn't going to get back to sleep without water—kitchen water—not bathroom water. Up she got, donned her housecoat and slippers, and down the stairs she went.

When she got to the door of the murder room she froze, allowing herself to almost hear imagined noises, finally tearing herself free and continuing on to the kitchen. She took a glass tumbler from the cupboard and turned the tap to cold, waiting for fresh pipe water flow, then stuck the glass under the stream, then turned off the tap, and brought the glass to eye level so she could study it.

She watched the tiny air bubbles rise and disappear, the water becoming clear as they vanished into nothing. It struck her that the water was an analogy. Ultimately, the situation would clear up. She didn't know what the bubbles were... the craziness around her, or... maybe the nuns were going to dissipate, disappear.

She slumped, sipped, and sat staring out at the blackness. Maybe the water was the world and the bubbles were the lives of the people in it: fleeting, brief, unnoticed. The blackness was like the water, and the kitchen light was like the bubbles. Ultimately everything was nothing, just black. She shivered at how small it made her feel to think this way.

Then she had another thought; maybe the water was the Church and the bubbles were the pathetic lives of each member of the flock. The sheep might come and go, but it didn't really matter at all to the church, the water, the blackness.

Then Sarah wondered if considering the Church to be water or blackness was a sin.

The second the thought of sin entered her head, she thought again of Jimmy. "God I wish I hadn't done that," she said to the blackness in the window, but the blackness was indifferent. Then she thought of Ted and smiled, but immediately wondered if she was sinning just thinking about the man. "Maybe this is about original sin," she thought. "No doubt, I'm being tested."

Then she wondered if such an idea was the sin of pride, to think that one so great could take the time or interest to care to test her. It made her tired, so she went off to her bed to try to get enough sleep because she knew the next day would be crazy and that she needed to be strong.

Of course, in order to get to her bed Sarah had to once again pass the door to the murder room. As before, she stopped in front of it and just listened to the silence for about a minute, and then went back to bed. She did sleep, but it was the kind of sleep where she thought she was awake the whole time, thinking about sin, obligation, death, God, and occasionally, Ted.

CHAPTER 4

One day later, an adventuresome camera buff found more wildlife than he bargained for: a body on the sliver of no-man's land where jungle ended and river began. The police faced a corpse with one side of its head shot off, and an ill-fated Burmese python devouring one leg. The primordial beast must have licked the taste of fresh kill from the air. Discerning death, the monster began devouring the body but in the error of haste, began ingestion at the feet of the carcass. Three feet into the act the serpent was trapped by the dead man's crotch. With one leg in and the other out, the slithering death machine settled in to digest what it could and in the process free itself. Stomach acids had not completed this task when the adventurer came on the scene and disrupted the timing.

Mortified humans stood still in shocked revulsion. The reptile didn't twitch. This was not Eden, yet all felt perfect knowledge: natural brutality, fragility of life, the inevitability of death.

A snake wrangler rushed up from Miami. He circled the hunter-turned-prey with the hunter-turned-prey in its maw, then carefully dispatched it with 10 cc's of pentobarbital, injected into the immediate region of the reptile's heart. The wrangler then gave way to the medical examiner, who slit the snake from the corner of its maw, allowing him to pull the carcass free.

The criminology value of the serpent spent on photos, and pentobarbital disallowing recycling to other jungle dwellers, the 450-pound behemoth was butchered, then sent to a Miami for incineration.

Liberté had brought Ted Coulson to the scene. She told him it was his interest and experience, and that she hoped to learn from him. That had pressed his buttons.

From his perspective, she had a decent rack and a nice ass, and now here she was recognizing how useful, how smart, he was. It never crossed his mind that she was playing him in the knowledge that any woman can get pretty much any man to jump through hoops by playing to his ego. Ted was hooked, and couldn't wait to prove his value. Sudoku could wait! He even had two coffees and four donuts waiting for the ride to the scene.

The cruiser was like home, the essence of cop made only grander by the essence of woman. They would get to know each other. He would show her how to get to the bottom of the case. She would be grateful. He would be a hero. He wondered how grateful Liberté might become. He wondered what she would be like in the sack. As they drove out he reminded her of yesterday's prediction that there would be another body, that the knife rape was inconsistent with the theft of the computer. He went further, to share another Sudoku axiom, that, "Unless all the pieces fit, you're not done" and its immediate corollary, "when all the pieces do fit, the puzzle is solved."

At the scene, the paid professionals quickly concluded that the dead man, overcome by remorse, perhaps for the Therese murder, had put the gun to his own head and ended his pathetic existence.

Ted, ever helpful, knew otherwise; the wound was wrong.

The bullet had entered the victim's left temple and exploded out the right side of the head. Using the theory of clue consistency taught by Sudoku, Ted explained the exit should have been more through the top of the man's head than the side, as it in fact was. He had waited, like a seasoned thespian, and then explained the confusion. If this guy had offed himself, as it was made to appear, the silencer, still stuck to the end of the gun, would have forced an acute angle, not a right angle, to the head.

And another thing, Ted wondered aloud, why does a guy in the middle of the jungle, intent on doing away with himself, use a silencer? The lay of the body and the spatter suggested he had been sitting at the time of death. So he had time to sit and think, but didn't dismantle the silencer? Then there was the dead man's watch, still on his left wrist. If he shot himself in the left side of his head, then he was a lefty, but lefties wear their watches on their right wrist. He bet Liberté that trace would find a lot more gunshot residue on the dead man's right hand than on his left.

Yet another thing: the distance of the gun from the target. Doesn't get closer than with a suicide, and in that case they should find a great deal of gunshot residue around, even in, the entry wound. There should have been stippling from the unburned powder. There wasn't.

Liberté nodded silent agreement, eyes fixed only on the partially decapitated, semi-devoured heap of early-stage rotting flesh. Hardened, but not fully, she fought to save her dignity and her breakfast.

Ted, who thought of Liberté as his new student and playmate, was blissfully unaware that she was stalking him for decidedly unromantic ends.

To her way of thinking, he was a babbling idiot who knew what had happened and how and when… probably, she surmised, because he had done it. Ted was officially now a person of interest. If she could glean a motive regarding the computer, find it in his possession, catch him turning it into cash, then the means, opportunity, and motive trifecta would be complete and that would be that.

On the ride home she advised, "Mr. Coulson, I am obliged to tell you that I now find you to be a person of interest in this case. You should conduct yourself accordingly." It was a real conversation stopper. The rest of the ride was silent. When they parted company, Liberté got on the blower to set up a tap on Ted's phone while Ted got on that very phone to find Sarah. He would launch his own investigation.

CHAPTER 5

While Ted and Liberté were fencing with nature and each other, an important meeting transpired at 2200 O'Neill; the convent. A certain Father Brendan Malloy had phoned from the Archbishopric in Venice, Florida to ask Mother Superior Marie to meet him. He had called at nine, and was there by ten thirty.

Father Malloy was a deacon in Venice, meaning he was a recent recruit to priesthood. This was his first visit to the convent, and he had no real relationship with Sister Marie or any of the nuns for that matter.

Marie ushered him into her office and introduced him to Sister Sarah, explaining that so many things were happening so fast that she had decided to involve Sister Sarah to assist and to provide a second opinion, so to speak.

Coffee requested and provided, Sister Marie asked what she could do for her visitor. Father Malloy shifted uneasily in his chair and responded that everyone in Venice was shocked, and sent their condolences, and was praying for the soul of the deceased and the well-being of the living.

Sister Marie thanked him but expressed surprise that Father Malloy was alone, and somewhat tardy in making his appearance. He merely shrugged, saying there was no intended slight.

The nuns nodded, then the messenger began. "I was asked to visit, and to tell you that this matter is, well, it seems that, um, people… high up… have taken an interest in this…"

Sarah interjected, surprising even herself, "And yet they sent a junior…"

Father Malloy didn't bark back. He just slumped a little, and looked at the floor with that hangdog look suggesting he agreed. "Yes," he said, still looking at the floor. "They asked me because of my grief training. I am to make myself available to each of you on your own, or to the convent collectively, to help in any way to make this less difficult."

"Thank you," said Sister Marie, "I suppose there is a good deal of planning to do. We didn't really know Sister Therese all that well, you know. She was just new to us."

"Yes, quite so. I understand that," said the man of God. "I… um, we… um, the Archbishop was very sorry he couldn't come with me today, but he did ask me to convey his regrets, and he insists on helping."

Once again, it was Sarah, "How?"

Father Malloy continued looking at the spot on the floor, "We… um he… suggested that he… um we… will take care of everything from Venice, and you people here can just concentrate on your own grief and recovery."

Sister Sarah could feel the dander characteristic of her pigmentation begin to rise.

Before she could say anything, Sister Marie cut in, "So they want to help in any way but sent a junior who we don't even know? I mean you no disrespect Father, but…"

"None taken my child…"

Both women bridled at the term and its implication of their place in this hierarchy. Marie continued, "What are you not saying? What's got your tongue?"

Malloy continued to inspect that floor the way a doctor does an unknown skin condition. "To be honest, I don't know everything. You're right, I am a junior. They don't tell me everything, but I do know this. The Archbishop is worried. He said that in his forty-something years in the church he has never been contacted by the Holy See ever, except for the traditional stuff everybody gets. Until last night, that is."

"Go on."

"The Archbishop told me to tell you that nobody here is to talk to anyone or make any plans without clearing them with him... er, me."

"What?"

"I am supposed to ask...no, *tell* you... we will take care of everything and you will say nothing."

There was a long moment while all three studied the same spot on the floor.

It was Sarah's turn. "What about the body? We have to arrange a proper funeral..."

"No! We will deal with that."

"Are you going to come up here and sit on our porch and talk to people who come with condolences? Can they use our bathroom? Should we turn away if one of them tries to talk to us? What is this?"

"Of course you can talk to well-wishers. Just tell them that you are in mourning and plans are being made in Venice. It's actually going to make it easier for you, you know..."

Marie snapped back, "That's not how it feels. Are you finished now? Have we got the whole message?"

Father's cup began rattling in the saucer, betraying his nerves. Sarah took them from him without a word passing either way, and after putting them on the desk returned to her seat.

Sister Marie reiterated her question, "Well, is that it?"

Father Malloy buried his head in his hands and mumbled a "No."

Sarah tried kindness, "Father, we know this is difficult for you. Unburden yourself. Just tell us what you came to say. This is not your fault. You didn't kill the woman, and you didn't decide that we had to be muzzled and manacled. Just spit it out. You will feel better."

Father Malloy looked up like a beaten dog that has just been gently patted. "Yes of course. Right. Out with it. I don't know what is going on, I really don't. But I am supposed to warn you all that people in Rome are, any... any disobedience will be badly received."

Mother Superior Marie snorted, "What? What are they going to do, excommunicate us?" She finished with a contemptuously dismissive wave of her hand.

"Have you heard of a woman, a nun, named Margaret McBride?"

Both had, and both started to respond. Sarah shut up and let Marie continue, "Of course. That was a classic case of black versus white versus grey. She agreed to abort a pregnancy for good medical reasons that flew in the face of dogma. They excommunicated her."

"Wrong. She excommunicated herself. It's called "Latae Sententia." That's the point. There aren't a lot of ways to excommunicate yourself: abortion, ordaining a woman as priest or being a woman priest, and being a schismatic... those are the only ways. It doesn't happen often, maybe ten or eleven times in the last hundred years. Castro did it, so did Queen Elizabeth the First."

"So? We're not doing any of those things. We're talking about burying a dead nun and somehow honoring the woman."

"This is so difficult."

Sarah snapped, "Don't whine. This isn't about you!"

Father Malloy looked straight at Sarah, "You're right sister. The Archbishop told me to tell you that someone at the Vatican told him that any disobedience of their rules regarding Sister Therese will be considered to be schismatic behavior. I am quite sure that you have heard enough from me for now... " He pulled himself to his feet and began to move toward the door.

The wind left the room. So did Father Malloy.

The old nun and the young one sat in stunned silence, each trying to make sense of the insane. Sarah felt numb, suddenly exhausted, the way a boxer in over his head must when he answers the bell after a standing eight count. She lifted her gaze from the floor and fixed it on Marie.

Marie sat motionless, white of face, eyes wide open but unseeing. She seemed to have aged ten years, from old to ancient, strong to frail, in the brief duration of Father Malloy's disclosure.

Sarah's first impulse was to rise, go to Sister Marie, and hold the stricken woman's hands in silent commiseration, as if by physical contact she could flow some of her own energy and strength into her stricken superior. It seemed to work. Slowly, Sister Marie raised her blank gaze to Sarah and willed herself to focus. Weakly, she whispered, "What?"

Sister Sarah whispered back, "Maybe this is a good thing."

This seemed to light a spark in Sister Marie. "Hogwash," she spat. "He thinks we're a problem. They won't help us. They'll help themselves. This is about Sister Therese, God bless her soul. We're into something she brought with her. Something very big. This is not normal. We're in big trouble, Sister Sarah."

Sarah thought she should respond. "If we just do what he said this will pass..."

She was stopped by a waving bony finger.

"In all my years I've never seen anything like this. Everyone is afraid, and they'll cover their own… behinds. If everything goes well, we might be allowed to survive. But if anything goes even a little off the rails, someone wants to blow us up. Our whole... everything... it doesn't matter. Someone's setting us up. Someone wants us gone. And we can't do anything to stop it because we don't know why."

"They're just being careful, Sister Marie. I think we should wait and see. No need to overreact."

"Sarah, could you please leave me now. I need to pray. I need to think. We can talk later. For now, why don't we keep this to ourselves?"

Sarah wanted to leave as much as the older woman wanted her to. The obvious fear in the old woman was contagious, and infected Sarah.

She knew she had to keep to herself or be trapped into disclosures she had been ordered not to make. She went to the end of the garden, sat on the bench, and stared into the swamp.

Sarah loved the smothering undercurrent of Everglade primordium, so not Minnesota yet so the same; never tranquil, just cruelly indifferent. She thought about the water and its bubbles last night. Dark. Unknown. Uncaring. Nature with its facade of beauty, but dark struggle; life and death, ugly and clawing for existence, preying on while being preyed upon. Survival, first yours, then for your type, a convent was anathema to nature. Kill or die compared to care and sacrifice? "Serve yourself first" compared to "serve everyone else first"? Propagate versus ignore, sublimate, and waste the most fundamental obligation of natural life?

Under any pressure, civility, like the levees men make, collapse before nature. This swamp, teaming with life and death, was real. The false walls of convent refuge had been breached. The flood, the swamp, the flow of nature didn't care, didn't notice, didn't give a shit, and most assuredly would not obey its ridiculous rules. It was indifferent to life. The water was forever, and life was transitory. The life mattered only to the liver of it, whose innate job it was to fight as hard as it could to live, but in the end, to fail and to die.

Her dark thoughts continued. The Bible starts with a Garden, Eden. Well, thought she, gardens are temporary, and need constant work and a lot of luck. The natural order is "dead." Life is an aberration of death. What then is a life devoted to sacrifice?

She continued her conversation with herself; "Everything in this "garden" looks hunky dory from fifteen thousand feet. But just get closer. There are a million worms in every acre of earth. There are billions of bugs. Most of them you can't even see. And everyone is living in everyone else's poo! The air we breathe is exhaled waste from plants. We build our houses out of the dead remains of little fish and things. Good soil... that's humus... dead stuff, animal and plant's dead stuff. Allergies? Probably a bad reaction to flower semen. But we're special! We're supposed to believe, to have faith…in what?"

She climbed from her reverie hideously aware that survival was clawing at her godliness.

Her phone ringtone crashed the solitude. Ted Coulson was looking for her.

Sarah dialed the number and told him where she was and invited him to join her.

CHAPTER 6

She rose to greet him, and they both sat, the bench just large enough for them and the Holy Ghost. Sarah felt the tiny thrill of close proximity.

"What can I do for you Ted? Your message said it was important."

"Yes Sister. This Therese thing is...well, you were the first person to see her, you know, and the police are treating me like some kind of suspect, so I thought you might be able to help me."

"How? The police think you did it...why?"

"My background. I have a gun. I tested positive for gunshot residue, GSR"

"So Ted. Look at me. Did you kill Therese?"

"No."

She knew he was telling the truth. He didn't get excited, or turn red, or start to sweat, or look away. Her instinct was belief, faith in this man. Inwardly she felt relief that she still had faith. "OK. So?"

"Tell me what you told them. I need to solve this…for them, because they're not that good, and I want them off my…off my case as soon as possible."

She told him as close to verbatim what she had told Liberté. She had seen the light, knocked, seen Therese, taken a moment, gotten dressed, informed Mother Superior, and then awakened the others.

Ted rambled about Sudoku and how few crimes are truly random, and how the violence and the missing computer just did not add up. Sarah bit her lip during this diatribe and began to fidget, but he was so engrossed in his opinion that he didn't notice.

They both went silent for a minute, each reflecting on the moment, each uncomfortable with their ease.

Ted broke the silence, "I thought you were really…good yesterday, Sister."

"Why thank you Ted, but I don't understand."

"Until yesterday you were just any other nun. Younger, prettier, but just like the others. Then yesterday, it was like you were the only person in the room. You just took over."

Sarah blushed, "Come off it. I was just doing what anyone would do. I certainly got a lot of attention because I found her, you know."

"You don't get it. It wasn't about the cops. It was about the nuns."

She actually didn't get it, and found the admiration awkwardly akin to flirting. She deflected; "honestly Ted, I was very impressed with how you handled that woman, that detective. I'm pretty sure you are going to solve this thing for them. She was gathering facts, but you were making sense of them."

Ted basked.

Timidly, Sarah continued, "Ted, what happens if they don't find the computer?"

"Odds are they won't. I mean, if they do, then whoever has it is screwed. If they're not the killer, at least they're holding stolen goods, or maybe suppressing evidence. I wouldn't want to be that guy, especially if I find him. That detective woman has a theory that I did this and it was because of the computer. I could get rich by selling its contents

I guess. Whoever took the thing has me caught in a vice, and I'd like to have five minutes alone with the bastard."

Sarah cringed a bit. Ted realized his choice of words was a bit much, and apologized.

She decided enough was enough and, since she had nothing else to tell him, they should get back.

At the porch they held an elegantly tense silence. Sister Marie came out, shattering the moment. Ted bid each of them "adieu" and left. Sister Sarah climbed the stairs to the porch and was about to enter the building when Sister Marie called her back.

"Sarah," she began. "This is a tough time. Emotions can take us places we regret later."

"I'm sorry, but you lost me there."

"My dear child, be careful. Make wise choices. I am not your judge. You must do that for yourself, and remember that the eyes of God are upon you. Just be careful. You are feeling pressures, and reacting to experiences that may shake your faith. I know that. Faith is a tricky thing. Perhaps you will decide to change the way you live your life. Just please make those choices for yourself, and don't let impulse do it for you."

Marie appeared for an instant to be considering the intimacy of a hug, but that passed, and Sarah slipped through the portal of the fortress convent, back to her own thoughts.

She watched Marie descend the stairs and stroll down the garden to the bench where she sat and communed with the swamp, just as she herself had just done.

From where Sister Sarah stood, it appeared the matriarch was weeping.

CHAPTER 7

Liberté was troubled. She was sitting in what passed for an office, but was really nothing more than a cubicle on the second floor of the town offices building, overlooking Main Street, probably set up so they could keep tabs on who left Sharky's when they were in no state to drive.

She looked, unseeing, at the heap of documents; trace, ballistics, gunshot residue, witness statement substantiation, telephone records, and email histories. The case-hardened cop was also very human, and female. She could focus only on images, real and imagined, of the two dead bodies.

The man's exploded head was, in relative terms, the easier thought. The twenty-five foot reptilian death machine would no doubt become a thing of nightmares.

But it was the knife. Fifteen inches, nine of them blade, slammed again and again into a—the—most private part of a most private woman. What kind of a monster would do such a thing? And if Coulson was right, and someone else commissioned the murder, there were two monsters; the one who said to do that, and the one who accepted the job. They had planned to kill her, for sure, maybe the one with the knife had committed rape first and this was to hide it? Liberté had conquered many crimes and criminals, but this was the first time in her life that she believed she was dealing with the devil incarnate. This was inhuman.

Was Coulson the kind of sick fuck that would cause someone else to do…that? He seemed dumb, and a bit of a "sniffer", but this? If you don't know who would, then you don't know who wouldn't. The perp had literally ripped her guts out. The photos terrified her, but she could not tear her eyes from them.

For the first time in years, Liberté needed her faith; something to believe in greater than the filth of her business, her life. She felt she could, would, talk to Sarah.

Liberté also felt the guilt of imposter syndrome; panicked fear this case was more than she could handle, that she would fail, and be found out.

Thinking about villains had her by the throat. Thinking about her job, her role, herself as a trust for the deceased, brought her back to the present. She gave herself a shake, shifted in her chair, and selected a file.

Still acutely aware of herself, Liberté noticed she had crossed her legs. This was an uncomfortable working position and unnecessary since she was alone, in slacks, and the vanity panel of the desk protected her erstwhile modesty. She intuited a physical reaction to the horror of that knife.

Once again, recognition was victory over the darkness. The detective uncrossed her legs, adjusted her crotch like men do with their "package", and then opened the file of new forensics notes. For an instant she found herself thinking of the file as Sudoku, shook her head, and got on with it.

The deceased nun had met her maker three months short of her seventieth birthday. She had come to Florida to escape the symptoms of some autoimmune disease called Cold Agglutinin, a condition causing the body to attack its own red blood cells when the weather gets a little colder than really warm. Apparently South Florida is a better bet than Rome in winter. The poor woman had suffered; she had fingers that turned blue, was often jaundiced, and lived in a state of constant fatigue.

Therese had been scheduled to retire as soon as she put the finishing touches on her life's work, a detailed inventory of every piece of art and artifact housed at, under, or around the Vatican.

"Now I get it," Liberté said to herself. "That computer held secrets that a thousand years of Pontiffs have guarded. Huge motive!"

So, thought Liberté, that idiot Coulson may have been right. If this was a robbery, plain and simple, then the knife, the violation, the butchery… they were all for show. But to what purpose? No. One job and two crimes… three really. Knife fucking is personal. Involuntarily, Liberté took a moment to re-hitch her crotch. Coulson knew the nun and he knew about the computer. He didn't look like a pervert. But then, what does a pervert look like? He may have been the only man in Florida who knew about it. Well not quite, there was Old Man Tamaros.

A dyed-in-the-wool Catholic and the richest man in the county, Tamaros had hosted the dinner party the deceased nun attended two days before her murder. He had been totally cooperative when Liberté and a Uniform had dropped by for a visit. Tamaros had invited the old nun to a dinner party as she was a bit of a celebrity, seeing as how she came from Rome and had stories, and knew so much about art. Tamaros remembered her as refined but a bit diffident, and suddenly in something of a hurry to get home. He remembered that she had been fascinated by two recent acquisitions of his, a bronze challis thought to date from late Mesopotamia that he had acquired at auction in London, and an Egyptian gold and lapis lazuli scarab from the time of King Tut that he had purchased in a private deal. He remembered her circling the case that housed the scarab for about fifteen minutes, and that she had asked a lot of "who" and "how" questions relating to the purchase, but curiously not to the scarab itself. Really beyond reproach in any way, Mr. Tamaros had nonetheless cheerfully provided an adequate explanation of his whereabouts on the night the nun was killed: he was at the Mayo Clinic in Rochester Minnesota for his annual check-up. That had been confirmed.

The dead nun's eyes were wide open, which indicated a shocking death, and could not be closed, indicating death had occurred somewhere between two and six hours before examination. Not news. The lack of blood pooling in low spots and livor mortis indicated less than eight hours had transpired since the crime. Again, not news. They didn't, they don't, do liver temperature. Algor mortis is determined in some cases by a rectally inserted thermometer, but in the case of this nun at least, perhaps because the knife had ruined that portal, by a thermometer in her ear. It had confirmed the non-news of the other two "mortises."

As she read the algor mortis test detail and outcome, Liberté involuntarily began rubbing her left ear and felt her knees come together. "Get a grip," she thought to the part of her psyche that was not police detective. She continued her review.

The bullet had been a 9 mm dumdum, so it had spread on impact and had literally turned the victim's heart to mush. Anyone can turn any lead bullet into a dumdum if firing at close range. Lead is softer than steel so it's a simple procedure to etch an "x" into the head of the bullet. The irregularity of the crosshatch, at speed, makes for an unclean interaction with the flesh it violates. The lead opens out and flattens into a disk, and in so doing makes a little hole into a big one, and a clean tissue wound to gut slurry. Liberté paused at this. Amateurs and thieves would not be expected to turn normal missiles of death into dumdums; only professionals intent on an instant kill or a real psycho with a perverse agenda would use a dumdum.

The bullet was so deformed that it gave no rifling information, but the spent case had rendered up some fact through a Bunter impression.

The same Glock had killed both Therese and snake man; the Glock 17, 9 mm, muzzled for sound by the silencer that was still stuck on it when snake man was discovered. Each had succumbed to the stopping power of 147 grains, one third of an ounce, of lead traveling at a speed of slightly less than one thousand feet per second. That much lead travelling that fast, configured as a dumdum, had exploded snake man's head and had turned Therese's heart into soup. Both had died instantly.

In order to affix the silencer, it had been necessary first to replace the barrel with an alternate protruding from the gun's maw to accept the required adaptor and then the silencer. "I guess that's why he was shot while the silencer was still on," she thought. "Either he didn't have the tool to remove it or someone else had neither the equipment nor the time."

She knew sixty-five percent of US law enforcement people carry Glocks; many carry the 22 that has the stopping power of the Old West Colt 45, but most carry the 17 because it has enough stopping power and is lighter. Ted's gun was a Glock 22, and importantly, still in his possession after snake man's murder. The great finger of guilt pointing at Ted waivered a little, at least in the mind of the lead detective. He could have had another weapon. Lots of cops and ex-cops do. But, for now, Ted could not be definitively tied to either murder.

The mangled remains of Therese's vagina offered no biological evidence that it had been penetrated by anything other than a post-mortem knifing. In fact, trace found nothing of "the him" on "the her" anywhere. There had been no vaginal semen, nor in any other portal most often used to deposit illicit contributions of unwelcome bodily fluids. The fingernails offered nothing, and her bedding and nightgown were unremarkable as evidence.

Often, multiple stab wounds cause a wet knife hilt, in turn causing a murderous hand to slip, and some perp and victim blood to commingle. Not this time. Nothing, nada, zip. Professional!

There was no overwhelming evidence of property damage to gain entrance to the building in the first place. The killer had just walked in.

CODIS had identified snake man as a regular guest of the justice system, going only by the single name "Leroy", having strayed during his youth in Detroit and never quite got back on the straight and narrow. He had migrated to Florida fifteen or so years earlier and had pretty much fallen off police radar. There were no records of police interaction between Ted and Leroy, but, she reminded herself, that didn't mean it hadn't happened. The report contained a separate entry from years earlier, when Leroy was a kid in Detroit. Apparently some complaint had been lodged against a teacher, a nun, who was never charged with anything because the parents had dropped them before meaningful action could be commenced. The entry probably shouldn't have survived, but sloppy file housekeeping now gave Liberté a possible second motive. How could Leroy even have known about the computer?

A crime that looks like violent passion but isn't? Or one that's violent but not passionate? Even the fact that no one heard the shot... he (it's almost always "he" in these situations) used a silencer. Who brings a silencer to a crime of passion? Sudoku again, "If everything doesn't fit, nothing is as it seems." Ted again. She smiled mirthlessly.

Is an ex-cop with extensive experience in murder investigations considered a pro for the purposes of killing?

"Ted Coulson is an idiot", she actually mouthed aloud, then continued in her head, "He used to be us, a cop, for Christ's sake! He can't keep his mouth shut, and every time he opens it he makes himself more interesting in a bad way. He owns a Glock. He was positive for GSR. The dope even shared theories with me. Mr. Coulson thinks the knife fucking was a ruse. The whole butchery thing was a cover-up to steal the computer. Apparently it's like the damn map in "Treasure Island." Secrets about art at the Vatican. I don't know shit about art, but I know the three keys to murder: motive, means, and opportunity. This idiot's a walk-off trifecta! But it's all circumstantial. I need more on the Vic. That computer is the whole story. Find it, find the killer."

Everyone was looking at everything the beleaguered detective was doing. Everyone was impatient. City council wanted to tell citizens they were safe. To have faith in the system. The chief wanted to tell citizens they were protected. To have faith in the police. The press wanted a story. The District Attorney wanted a conviction. The public wanted answers. The aggrieved nuns wanted privacy. Everyone knew what

Liberté should do. Except her. The evidence pointed to Ted. Liberté's gut told her otherwise.

In clinical medicine and forensics there are test failures yielding false positives and there are also false negatives. Cops often err on the side of false positives but rarely on the side of false negatives. In her core, the detective felt sure that Ted was a victim of time and chance; wrong place at the wrong time.

Like doctors, cops are trained not to ignore the obvious. This case was like a sick patient with many conflicting symptoms. A nun gets murdered, mutilated, and robbed. Maybe there was more to this Sister Therese than met the eye. Perhaps she came to America for reasons other than health. Maybe the whole thing went down because of her past. Good diagnostics required a complete workup on the dead nun. Liberté made a note to talk to her boss. Investigations outside of the town were tricky enough, but this one was going to mean talking to God, well actually, people at the Vatican. Liberté didn't have a clue how to handle that.

The ugly knot returned, bringing her back to where she had started, reminding her that she was in over her head. She had none of the manpower, clout, or financial resources to run an international investigation into the death of this woman. Early indications were that the Church was more interested in closing this case than in solving it. While she thought that a bit weird, she sort of understood it. From her point of view, though, it meant that getting facts, filling in blanks, and looking at all the possibilities would be almost, if not completely, impossible for a small fry from a small town in a country foreign to the best current interests of the Catholic Church. She knew she needed help.

The chief was annoyed. Naples couldn't, Miami wouldn't, and State thought they shouldn't. She was on her own. Her own tentative call to the Pope's pro-nuncio in Washington D.C. met with polite yet firm rejections of requests for meetings or facts.

Worse, since all the requests involved others, those others involved themselves. They weren't bad people, but they were pragmatic. The consensus was to focus on Ted and get a conviction. A clean wrap-up seemed most likely that way, and then everyone, except Ted of course, could return to normal.

Many are convicted on the strength of circumstantial evidence. Besides, Ted was an easy target: a loner living with his sister, a sister, in a convent. The DA was very clear. He could paint Ted so that no jury could do anything other than convict. The DA saw this case as an opportunity. Careers are made of this stuff. Win big cases and move on up. That kind of publicity could make a heretofore invisible man a household name. He might even be Governor one day. Truth can quickly become the first victim of expediency.

The heat was on. Everyone except the lead detective on the case thought Ted was the man, and the lead detective wasn't sure that he wasn't.

The pressure on Liberté was enormous, but she had not achieved her status in life by being a wimp. She was, she reminded herself, the lead detective, which made it her case. Until reassigned she would do her job her way. Ted was safe for now, but God only knew for how long.

CHAPTER 8

The "butterfly effect," theory of chaos and reordering proposes that the beating of a single butterfly's wings on one side of the world can cause thunderstorms on the other. The murder on O'Neill was such a "butterfly". Thunderclouds gathered all about the Globe.

Thunderclouds are inherently both violent and unpredictable. The farmer who prays for rain sometimes gets hurricanes, tornados, hail, lightning strikes, and floods. Typically, thunderclouds become increasingly unstable and unpredictable as they grow larger and darker. Fluffy clouds, innocuous clouds, pretty clouds appear as lovely gentle things, but when they reach their full aliquot of fury, they are dangerous and sudden, causing sometimes dramatic change.

The first fluffy cloud appeared as a speck on the financial horizon of the moribund town trapped between swamp and uncharming beach.

It was noticed first at the Ophrah florist's shop, a place until now a monopoly of dearth. It became what economists call a "leading indicator" as the first beneficiary of the silver lining in the cloud of the butterfly of death at 2200 O'Neill. Well-wishers sent flowers. Call after call, walk-in after walk in, in their droves, ordering floral memorials for pick-up or for delivery to the front gate of the Convent of the Sisters of the Holy Virgin Mother. In equal parts ecstatic and frantic, the proprietor called in his wife, then his kids, finally the part-timers and two summer students that had "helped out" a year earlier. The place became a blur of organized mayhem as two took orders by phone and counter, three filled those orders, and two ran pick-up to purchase more and more "product" for plucking, primping and resale. Two days in, orders from locals were first supplemented, and then overwhelmed by phone-ins from across the region. Then came the referrals from the florist exchange that only months earlier had been considered a wasted relationship. On day one they did a year's worth of business, and it kept growing.

The second wisp cloud appeared at the diner, a third at the gas station, a fourth at the bed and breakfast. Well-wishers became tourists. Ophrah was discovered. The little hamlet just off Desultory Bay was, for the first time in its history, an honest-to-God tourist destination as well-wishers, ghouls, and murder aficionados descended upon it, bringing cash, credit and debit cards.

Each wisp was itself a flapping butterfly, begetting others, together, birthing unknown and unknowable forces of nature.

The Ophrah town council convened an emergency session on day two.

Amusingly their first agenda item was an array of complaints from the staid among the town-folk, about traffic, trash, and lost tranquility.

The second agenda item was the money. And the money talked loudly. Petty concerns of lost haven were given short shrift by the captains of this now-proud ship of state…well, town.

The immediate effect of new money was jubilation. However, it caused changes all of its own, all within days. While some prospered, others struggled. Jealousies flared, neighbors became wary and even hostile to people with whom they had shared their entire existence in peaceful mediocrity.

New faces brought new dynamics. There were economic winners and losers, less community and more personal interest, the crime that comes with transition and transients, a race to capitalism, protectionism, designs and cabals pitting neighbor against neighbor, an increased pace of life as Ophrah denizens were dragged toward a new normal with neither consent nor information, just a pervasive sense of ennui.

The outrageous, the eccentric, the tolerated margin were the first victims of the windfall of, at its essence, the horrific murder. Once considered quaint, they became despicable, were driven farther into the fringe.

The dynamic of economic change is related to the dynamic of the thundercloud; the rain that nurtures many sometimes drowns others; lightening can destroy. With a storm comes the acrid smell of ozone. In Ophrah, everyone could smell money.

One of the leading lights on council had seen "Pillars of the Earth" on TV; they might be living the event. If they were going to keep the good times going, to really commercialize the tragedy, they needed a big show and a bigger shrine.

An emissary was dispatched to the Convent to discuss mutual opportunities. That emissary was politely redirected to the archdiocese in Venice. The archbishop gently but firmly advised the burghers of Ophrah that Saint Peter's Rock remained unmoved

by the sudden economic boom, and that the church's understated but clear moral compass superiority showed a better course. The church would have no part of any shrine.

The coroner had placed Therese's death at somewhere between 2:00 and 4:30 a.m. That meant that everything the deceased had learned and knew, the sum total of her Earthly experience, had vanished completely by, at the latest, approximately 4:33 a.m. When her brain had died from lack of oxygen, the RAM of her entire existence was erased, and hers was an exceptional repository of knowledge. She knew the providence and value of every piece of art and artifact in, under, or around "Citta Del Pelligrino." Fortunately, she had committed this knowledge to the somewhat less ephemeral memory of her Hewlett Packard Model "Compac NC 4000," and the HP was missing. The knowledge stored in the computer was, of course, backed up in duplicate disparate storage locations. But the missing HP itself had now become a massive threat to the security of the Vatican. Secrets, guilty ones with teeth, were stored on that computer. The old saw "knowledge is power" was never truer. In the wrong hands that computer could be a weapon to exact restitution for countless crimes of patronage and providence. The computer could become an unimpeachable reference for claimants alleging previously improvable crimes against them. The contents of the HP, if they got into the right hands, could be used to squeeze blood out of Saint Peter's rock.

Yet another cloud gathered over God's head office in Rome. While the computer was the prime focus of the executive suite, there were flesh-and-blood humans walking those halls. News of the nun's death hit a lot of those Vatican humans hard, as Sister Therese had, in a real sense, been one of them. The woman had spent almost all of her working life in service of the library and then the art and artifact collection. Over the past twenty years, as she had catalogued away, she had made many friends. Everyone who knew her, and who had commiserated with her when health had demanded warmer climes, now watched how her demise was handled. Arrangements would most likely come from her immediate superior, Father Tomas.

Tomas was a power due to an uncanny ability with investments and money, and extraordinary organizational skills, secular but necessary.

When news of Therese's murder arrived at the Vatican, Tomas was the first person called with condolences. A mass was immediately said for the eternal soul of the dearly departed, and then the business of the church, and Therese's farewell, attended to. Tomas had asked for a day to consider how he wanted to handle Therese's launch into eternity. His position was both thoughtful and thorough.

Although a big show funeral might appear to be an opportunity to curry some sympathy and positive emotion toward St. Peter's embattled rock in secular America, the computer that had been in possession of Sister Therese was missing. Until that was found, it would be much more prudent to keep this thing low-key; the less glitz, the fewer the questions. In Father Tomas' opinion, the body should be removed immediately for a respectful burial in an appropriate garden in the Rome Therese had so loved, and that should be the end of it. No special services and absolutely no shrine. For the safety of the surviving Sisters of the Order of Saint Mary the Virgin, he thought it wise to close the Convent and either move the nuns somewhere else, en masse, or send each hither and yon to be absorbed into useful service, in oblivion. The rank and file of the holy halls felt it was a mistake, and more than that, it was cruel and unnatural.

However, they were the rank and file, and Tomas was not. Nobody argued with him and won. As people at the epicenter of Catholicism have been doing for years, each kept his nose clean, his head bowed, and his mouth shut.

More thunderclouds.

Police don't operate in a vacuum. They have the press to dramatize, criticize, and publicize, and a politically motivated prosecutor whose success is based on not just law and order, but speedy law and order.

The murder of a nun is big news in any case, but this one even more so. It had gone viral, and thus there were potentially huge stakes for a political DA; a quick conviction is beautiful on a resume, and a slow one, or a failure to convict can be political death. Pressure began immediately to conclude the case against the obvious miscreant, Ted Coulson. From the DA's point of view, which was political, it was a slam-dunk. If you had enough for a conviction, then you had enough. More was superfluous, and time was precious. He could convince a jury of Mister Coulson's guilt. He'd successfully prosecuted many with less. The chief of police, also an elected official, shared the sentiment. When detective sergeant Liberté Alvarado met with the Chief and DA she was ordered to submit a file for the prosecution to proceed. When she demurred on the basis of doubt in her own mind, she was helped to the understanding of priorities and then asked again. She had bought time by asking for a day to clean up loose ends and close off the niggling doubts.

The DA thundercloud was one known to Liberté. There was another gathering even farther over the horizon. Seven time zones east of Ophrah briefings were delivered, training began, and political blinds were drawn.

CHAPTER 9

Now 43, Sarah hailed originally from a small town thirty highway minutes north of Minneapolis. Hers had been a traditional Anglo-Saxon home with a stay-at-home mom, a professional dad, and a group of "normal" neighborhood and school friends. They even had a white picket fence. She had alternatively loved and despised her older brother Rick. As a child she had dreamt of a career in law like her dad. Strong, affable, athletic, bright, she had been a good student. She even went to State finals on the track team in both junior and senior year. Her family was responsibly Catholic. The child had shown no interest in cloistered life, and had even been a bit of a wild thing. Sarah had done all the experimenting kids do: sex, drugs, rock n' roll. She had enrolled at Loyola College in Liberal Arts, majoring in sociology. In the second semester of her freshman year, she had joined a Bible studies student group at Loyola, and the "Youth for Christ" chapter just off campus.

Sarah had stopped dating any of the herd of young men on her scent, eschewed make up, and increasingly wore neutral colors that served to cover and not to attract. Her flaming red hair, once so bouncy, became a bun. Flamboyant displays of jewelry were replaced with stark nothingness. At the end of the academic year, when others returned home to summer jobs, Sarah joined a holy order in Syracuse and gave herself over to the life of an acolyte. Five years later, at the age of 23, she took her final vows. Her family had been distressed because of their perception of their daughter as "mainstream," but had learned to be proud of her commitment to a life of service, and had become supportive of her decision on how to let her life be run.

None of Sarah's friends had seen it coming, but some remembered how news of a teenage pregnancy had unduly impacted her. She had spoken often about the stress of good marks. She had found the competing needs to comply and conform depressing. Sarah had, on several occasions, confided to friends that the world was too fast and too nuts, and that she wished she could slow it down, focus on doing good as opposed to well and stop trying to be all things to all people. The girl who had been a hub had spun herself to the relative cocoon of Bible classes and Catholic youth group events in lieu of the insanity of college dorm life.

Ten years after taking orders, Sarah asked for and received dispensation to move to the little town of Ophrah in Florida.

The convent was located on thirty acres at number 2200 O'Neill Street, and it was all that was left of the old retreat built in the 1920's by Forest O'Neill. O'Neill was a descendant of the first wave of Catholic Irish immigrants to the young thirteen Colonies. His forbearers had come through New York and then moved south, first into Virginia, then to South Carolina where they had curried their meager grubstake into a fortune from trading and shipping in the burgeoning port of Charleston. With a keen sense of timing and political awareness, the family sold out in 1850 and moved to Kansas City, where the fortune from Charleston was multiplied ten-fold in river, rail and transit stock and transit yards, used alternatively by settlers to push west and by both Union and Confederate armies to fight the Civil War.

Forest's younger sister Sheila had established the Order of Saint Mary the Virgin to bring aid and God to the Seminoles after three wars of attrition had reduced the tribe to 350 souls by 1913. In the 1950s the place required massive renovation and the cost was covered by the Florida Diocese of Venice, with formal title passing at that time. The work with the Seminoles had morphed into teaching and health system support for the neighboring community of Ophrah.

Originally isolated, the convent now abutted the town, which had grown inland from the shores of Desultory Bay, and now included the nuns in its sewer system and census. The convent Sarah had joined was ten minutes on foot from downtown Ophrah, twenty minutes by car from Marco Island, and about ninety minutes from the heart of Miami, traffic permitting. Just east of the property street frontage, some four hundred yards, the terra became less firma as solid gave way to soggy, then to the swampy of that great river of grass, the Everglades.

Sarah loved the wilderness, the people, and the town. Hers was a small, manageable world. Ophrah was a cloister. Her "deal," made at age 23 when she had taken her orders, was working: the cloister for peace in exchange for obedience and a life dedicated to good works. Her deal with God had been an exchange of Earthly ambition and transitory pleasures of the flesh for peace and tranquility of a sort that only heaven can promise. She truly believed in her God and his Church. Her faith had been rewarded.

But that faith was now severely tested. It wasn't the murder. It was abandonment by the men of the cloth.

She didn't leap up to meet the day, but rather, hid from it in bed, and thought her thoughts. Her stomach bore witness to anxiety, and the blur behind her eyes to troubled sleep. Dampness of skin and sheets confirmed both. Images of what had happened and might again assailed her, and were joined by clips of an invasion of her sanctum, her convent.

Police, simply doing their jobs, had defiled it.

She had joined holy orders to hide, she now realized, and she felt shame. She had cocooned herself in the ease of submission for the safety of order.

At the instant of her encounter with Therese's mortal remains, Sarah's deal with God began to transition. A tiny comfort glimmered within her now as she recalled that first instant of sheer horror when she had pushed revulsion and panic into abeyance, and dealt strongly with immediate exigencies. Her normal modus operandi of blind submission had been replaced by initiative and action.

The glimmer left, and Sarah returned to the shame for her years of cocooned submission, for not having been there earlier and thus able to save Therese, for the fact of her secret, and for venial awareness of her hero, Ted.

Sarah, who until yesterday gave the man no never-mind, now viewed him as strong, knowing, reliable, capable; the luster of his charisma perhaps brightened by the expedient of her urgent need. The thought of Ted brought a twinge, a spark of carnal excitement. He was too old, too fat, too not "her". The spark must be something else. But it was a sin. Once around the rosary quelled the fire but did not extinguish it.

After the last "Hail Mary," Ted returned to her thoughts. He alone had stood up to all those people. He alone had tried to defend them. Only Ted had done other than obey and respond. He had made sense, too. They had listened to him. She recalled bits of a dream she had dreamt. All she could remember was mayhem all around, and Ted snatching her from an abyss, sweeping her into his arms and away from an all-consuming fire, sharing the parachute to avoid the death fall from an airplane, and spectacularly taking the bullet that had been fired at close range towards her heart.

Still abed, she pulled the covers up tight and bathed in fantasy, becoming as she did, keenly aware of the pleasuring teasing of her sheets. Increasingly intense and glorious sensations rippled through her as they rubbed their way, ever so gently, across God-given lust centers that were most assuredly not dead, only just sleeping. She cuddled with strategic mounds of sheets and pillows causing pressure for pleasure, and floated in impossible fantasy.

The deeply engrained nun part of her psyche pulled back from the self-pleasuring with a crushing sense of guilt, and a sad awareness of abiding loneliness. Simultaneously she knew it was a sin against God to feel such pubescence and a crime against Nature not to. Was she even meant to be a nun?

Finally Sarah hauled herself out of bed, showered and dressed. As she fixed the wimple and tucked in the last vestige of personality, Liberté came to her mind's eye.

There was a conundrum. The antithesis of what Sarah had become. Liberté was hard, unfeeling. Smart. The woman had guts. She controlled things and people. She talked and they listened, not the other way around. She ordered; people responded. This woman was as at sea as the rest of them on what had happened, but at least she had the helm.

But she really had been a bit of a bitch. Now a little bit of Sarah the nun crept back into her briefly angry consciousness, and she forgave the bitch. After all, it must have been tense for her too. She had to solve the crime, control the situation, deal with all those people, and she suspected, somehow manage her own inner-self reaction to the assault itself. Liberté was a cop, but she was also a human, a woman. Sarah didn't feel affection for Liberté, or even really anything like respect. Just a fascination. Liberté was someone to be explored and analyzed. That she could control, make happen.

Sarah was the last to breakfast. Very strange she thought, that they were all dressed in the traditional garb, as was she. As she entered, the room went silent. All eyes rested mutely on her. They were waiting to hear her speak. "They, we, really do look like penguins," she thought to herself, and smiled. The other ten smiled back.

She took her seat, they prayed together, and then ate in silence. At last Mother Superior drew their attention with a cough, to inform that the archbishop had called from Venice, and had instructed that the nuns should stay inside and talk to no one. He would attend at the

Convent as early as possible; he had thought by mid-morning, maybe ten o'clock.

On the dot, his limo pulled up and he entered. Looking neither right nor left, he went straight to Marie's private office. Marie followed, and as was now her custom, bade Sarah join them. The archbishop noted the addition, but merely shrugged.

Archbishops live like princes. They have been hand-picked and have advanced not because of an excess of Godliness, but because they are proven administrators, and have been observed to share a value system sympathetic to the needs of the head office, not in heaven…in Rome. The Roman Catholic Church is not just a holy center, it's a State. A tightly run, religiously homogenous State that takes care of its friends and in return those friends look after the men at the top. They toe the line. Orders from the top are Gospel.

The gospel of the day was quite a shock to the two ladies dressed in serge communing with the somewhat awkward man in brocaded silk.

The police didn't yet know who was guilty, but according to "His Worship," Rome did. The nuns had brought this on themselves. This attack must have been a reaction, and it was creating problems for Mother Church. He of the brocaded silks lectured on responsibility and devotion and sacrifice. This "incident" could not have happened in a vacuum, and there would be a tribunal established to assess guilt and penance. For the present, Mother Church required the sacrifice of silent obedience, or more appropriately, obedience through silence.

Since uncertainty reigned, and since there was potential for stigma to the institution, the locals were to "zip it" and let the greater brains of downtown Rome man the walls and mend the fences. In all his years, the Archbishop had never heard directly from the papal palace on any basis other than a general proclamation, and he was not amused. He liked Venice, just up the road, and he didn't want a punitive placement.

He did not ask after the women of the Convent. He did not propose even a prayer for the deceased. He offered no comfort or advice. Only lecture and a demand for subjugation. Then he was gone. The Mother Superior was frightened. The redhead was furious. No woman has ever felt more betrayed by the man in her life, than did that redheaded bride of Christ.

Her first "zip it" act was to call Detective Alvarado and accept her invitation to lunch.

CHAPTER 10

Sharky's is that restaurant every small town or hamlet offers: plastic gingham table covers, a daily special, screen door with the ubiquitous Coke ad push-bar, linoleum, booths, huge clock, and an infrared lamp counter partially blocking the not-so-savory kitchen. Like its everywhere cousins, Sharky's is located on Main Street.

Sarah arrived first. It felt good to be out, meeting people, perhaps functioning as a nun. Except she didn't know who was to play what role, and that made her tense. A lunch date with a cop? The woman had said she just wanted to talk, and that it was not official business. But how can someone divorce themselves from who they are and what they do?

The nun took a booth in the farthest corner of the place, believing privacy was in order, ordered a Coke, and waited.

For the first time since entering the cloister, she felt conspicuous and awkward in her habit. She noticed the diners weren't locals; had they been maybe she would have not felt weirded out, but these people stared like she was a sideshow. Their eyes betrayed pity so she knew they knew, but they were from elsewhere, and they made her uncomfortable being who they thought she was.

Minutes later in breezed Liberté, fist pumped Sharkey, then slid into the booth. "Hi. Thanks for joining me. Just to be clear, this is my treat."

"Well thank you, Detective…"

"Please, call me Liberté. Not 'Libby,' I hate that."

"OK Liberté, as I was saying, thank you for the lunch, but why are we here? How can I help?"

"To be honest Sister..."

"Please, just Sarah."

"To be honest Sarah, I don't know. I just feel, well, troubled. You strike me as a good listener. I think you and I are sort of dealing with the same kind of thing. Before that, how are you? This can't be easy for you…for any of you."

"It's a shock, that's for sure. It makes you look at everything differently."

"Like what?"

"For one thing, death. Life and death. You start wondering about your life, what you're doing? Why? Are you wasting your life? Does anything really matter? Does God…?"

"I guess. In my line of work I see a lot of blood, stupidity, violence. You get kind of hardened to it. But not this. This was more than I could handle. I actually woke up last night in a sweat, dreaming about a man and a knife…"

The nun finished it for her, "…turned into a phallus…"

Liberté pointed right at Sarah. "Are you fucking kidding? …oops."

Sarah saved her, "Heard it before. Yes, we seem to have had the same dream. You were telling me you get hardened to death?"

"As an individual, for sure, but hell, half the economy is about death; some people are trying to delay it, others are trying to de-risk it with insurance. Some people make their living burying the dead. Then there are the ones who make the guns, and the ones who arbitrage death by selling stock in all the other ones. Did you know that Wall Street loves gun-maker stocks? Top 10 percent performers..."

Sarah was impressed, "Wow. I was staring into the swamp earlier today, thinking life is just an aberration of death and you are sort of saying…"

"Not exactly the same, but I see your point. It's tough and I understand, but…I was a Catholic once."

"But you lost your faith?"

"I guess. I have faith in the law. I have faith in the innate capacity of people to lie, cheat, and steal… to do

anything they think they won't get caught doing. God is tough when you see what I see. But me, a woman? I couldn't buy the crap they lay on."

Sarah felt herself flush. What this woman was saying was a direct assault on every choice she had made for herself. She collected control, "Ouch on me!"

"I am so sorry. Everybody makes choices. I was just explaining mine. Please, no disrespect intended."

"OK. So?"

"Good. Thanks. It's kind of funny, given what I just said, I really wanted to talk to you. I am so glad you agreed to meet me here."

Sarah cocked her head to one side. If the conversation so far could be called "pleasantries," then the pleasantries appeared to be about to be over. Maybe she was going to be allowed to just be a nun and help this troubled soul. The detective continued, "Can this be like confession?"

Sarah paused, wondering first of all who this woman thought might be confessing to whom, and secondly, how copasetic all this was in any case. She had seen enough TV, and her Dad had talked enough of these things, that she figured the risk lay with the cop. If she garnered evidence under false pretenses it probably wouldn't be allowed in any proceedings. She wondered for a moment if she should just come clean with her little secret. The one bit not in evidence. It might not be such a big thing. She could do it later but couldn't take it back later, so she stayed mum. "Libby, um, Liberté, I'm just a nun, and nuns aren't allowed to hear confession, but I can assure you that what happens at Sharky's stays at Sharky's."

Liberté shifted in the seat, pushed her butt back, elbow forward on the table, leaned in, and drew a breath. The waitress with the pink uniform about two days past its prime arrived and sundered their moment.

The special was grouper sandwich. Both of them ordered it, and the lady of big hair, bosom, and behind was gone, but not unheard. She belted out the order so the kitchen could get started right away and anyone present could know the booth five food proclivities.

As people in crowds tend to do, Liberté began in a whisper, "I told you that I have faith…in the law. But it's kind of under attack. There's some strange stuff going on, things I can't…accept. I want to get the killer but…"

Sarah interjected, "But? What do you mean?"

"Uh-huh. That guy Coulson has "guilty" written all over him, circumstantially. I'm not going to lie to you Sarah; there are a lot of people who think I should just arrest him. But there's something wrong. In fact, Mr. Coulson has said some things that actually make sense to me."

"Does Ted need a lawyer?"

"If he doesn't have one by now then he's an idiot."

"And you're telling me this because?"

"Sorry. It's just that things don't add up, but I'm one person and maybe the only one that's not sure. I'm under a lot of pressure, Sarah."

"I don't know how I can help."

"Sorry. You probably can't, but I need to talk to someone. No one at the station wants to hear anything that flies against the plan to close the file with an arrest…of Mr. Coulson. I believe in due process and facts. They're going too fast. But, there's more."

They pushed back in anticipation of catastrophe as Miss Big banged the cheap china onto the table like a Third World aircraft landing.

After the mandatory first bite, Liberté continued, "Random killings are so rare that we police ignore the possibility. That woman, Therese, was killed for a reason. Everyone wants it to be…Ted, but I keep thinking. One of the last things Sister Therese did was call some dude in Rome. I kind of need to know what they talked about. Don't you think?"

"Uh-huh."

"So I tried. So far, no one has even taken a call, let alone call back."

"Liberté, I don't know what to say. I have less than no power. I can't help, you know…"

"I do know. And I sense you're dealing with the same kind of, you know…"

"Bullshit?"

The distinctly urbane use of such colorful language gave Liberté momentary pause, but she plowed on. "Uh-huh. See, I get it from the Mayor's office that you won't bury the woman here, and there won't be a memorial or even better, a shrine."

"Ophrah wants a shrine?"

"Uh-huh. They smell money. Your dead nun is a real moneymaker!"

Both smiled at the dark irony of the term.

She took a few bites of the special, and then Liberté continued, "There's something else. I get paid to notice things…" The Nun felt her stomach rise. "Everyone over there looks to you." Her stomach returned to normal. "I know that Mother Superior is supposed to be in charge. All I know is leaders are people others follow, and those nuns are following you."

Sarah ignored the comment. "I'm just glad you called. I'm going nuts back there. Half of them want to know why God did this to them and the other half are praying to him for some divine intervention."

"So, you're not so much a believer?"

"Oh ya, I believe. But my Dad watched the fights on TV, when they would cross themselves just before the bell, Daddy used to say that God always seemed to favor the one with the best right hook."

"So, God doesn't call all the shots? So why don't you believe in evolution?"

"Wow, that's a leap! I believe in the immaculate conception and transubstantiation Liberté, so creationism isn't really that big a deal."

Liberté was about to jump in but Sarah showed her the palm-of-hand stop sign, and plowed on, "I know there are fish bones on the top of Mount Everest. Pretty sure God didn't put them there. It took us four hundred years, but we finally forgave Galileo for…being right. I know the Holy Father, the Pope, not God, meets every so often with secular, even non-Catholic, scientists. And he listens. So I think I can too."

Another pause. Another attempt by Liberté. Another palm stop. The nun continued, "To be honest, I'm having a bit of a crisis of faith myself. Not with God. With the church. Your question just helped me to put it in perspective".

"It did? I did?"

"Ya. Let me try this on you. God set everything up so the world would change on its own…so he did that…but then one thing led to another, and man got dominion over the world and everything in it as they like to say. So here's the thing. Some

things get dominion over others even though God started them the same…it's kind of like me, nuns, the church. I'm pretty sure the fish don't believe in God. But nuns are kind of like fish…"

"Little fish" said Liberté.

"Ya. Right. Little fish. So do the little fish stop believing in God, or just the crap that got between them and their creator?"

"Are you a little fish, Sarah? You're good with God, not so much with…"

Sarah looked closely at her drink for a silent minute, then, "I think so. Yes. This is private, right?"

"What happens at Sharky's stays at Sharky's."

"OK. I just feel like…stupid. My whole life is…I don't know. Wrong. Out of synch with the real. Everyone, everything fights to survive, to take, to have. I…us nuns aren't…we just serve, and that's OK, but they're supposed to care, to protect me. They don't. They aren't…"

Liberté had no idea what to say, so just sipped thoughtfully on her coke, shifted a bit on the homey vinyl, studied the stain on her paper napkin, and changed the subject. "How did you grow up to be a nun?"

"Fair question. To be honest, I just fell into it because it answered needs I had, then. I had a normal childhood. Nobody abused me. I was raised as a Catholic but it wasn't shoved down my throat. I have a brother, he's a commodity trader. My dad was a lawyer. My mom was a teacher until I was born. Then we came along, and her career became her kids."

"Where?"

"Minnesota, a bit north of Minneapolis. I went to Blessed Sacrament as a kid and then enrolled at Roncesvalles High in my freshman year. I guess that's when it started. I was a good student, ran hurdles, swam for the Varsity team. Dated. Did all the stuff kids do. The whole thing started to get to me in my sophomore year. You had to get the marks. You had to train harder, swim faster, and just win baby. It was OK, but it was pressure. Then there was the dating. What crowd? Who to sit with at lunch? Who to hang with? Do you know what I mean?"

Liberté nodded, and Sarah continued, "Around Christmas in my sophomore year I joined this club called "Youth for Christ." It sounds weird, I know, but it was, I don't know, safe. They were the same kids who were competing for marks, and racing, and trying drugs, and trying to get laid...oh ya, I was normal Liberté, but the club time was... sane, calm, safe...I just felt like I could breathe. Then I went to Loyola, and the people who taught me and who I got to know, the role models, they were cloistered people. I tried it. They don't want you if you don't want it. But I did. It worked for me. I didn't feel like I was losing anything, I was getting something: purpose, safety, I don't know, *comfort* in life. I had a purpose."

"Do you miss...?"

"Sex? Everybody wants to know about the sex. Everyone tiptoes around it. It's hilarious! Nuns weren't always nuns, and we didn't grow up in a cloister. We can read you know...newspapers, magazines, billboards. We see it. We get it. And besides, we study the Bible. It may be the dirtiest book not banned. Everyone's begetting! Have you ever read "Song of Songs?" She has a navel like a goblet, breasts like grapes. He wants to take her to his mummy's house so they can smell each other and she can drink the juice of his damn pomegranate! John the Baptist gets his head cut off because some dick has hot pants for an exotic dancer!

But to answer your question, no you don't even think about sex, I guess because you're part of something so fulfilling, that it just isn't a big issue for us."

Until just recently with this Jimmy/Ted dream stuff, she thought. "But I have to tell you Libby, er, Liberté, the last week has thrown a lot of stuff up in the air. I'm not as sure of anything as I was before Therese..."

As an accomplished interviewer, Liberté knew to say nothing.

Sarah's whole demeanor altered. Suddenly her voice was clipped and higher in pitch, rising to end sentences, classic anger symptoms.

After a slurp of coke, Sarah continued. "Every one of those nuns has devoted her entire existence to her Church. There are a lot of female martyrs from cloistered life, so no one in 'the life' thinks they bought total safety from this world, but we really did think the boys would cover us when the...shit...hit the fan."

More silence from Liberté. Sarah was leaning forward, right into her subject, hands curled to fists. A red tinge of fury crept from beneath the bandeau, and migrated to her cheeks and forehead. Sarah continued, "But they didn't. Neither did you! It's like we're sheep!"

Penguins actually, thought Liberté, wisely keeping that to herself, "What do you want from us? We're here to stabilize a situation and find a killer. Yes, sometimes people need help, but for God's sake, forgive the pun, you ladies have quite a strong support group! At least that's the way we saw it."

Not yet mollified, Sarah continued, "Questions, no answers. Orders. Stuffed on a bus like felons. Left for hours in a police station. Not even a ride home. Locked out while ghouls sniff through our lives!"

"Oh come on! You can't catch bad guys without evidence. And another thing, everyone in that room was a suspect. Especially you,

Sarah. You were the first to find the body. Not really a suspect, but for sure an important witness."

"Whatever. But you're not the worst. That...that...that man!" Her fist made like it wanted to smash down on the table and every eye turned to them, jolting Sarah back to a steely calm. "He prances on in, doesn't give a damn for any of us, doesn't want to know anything, just tells us how it's going to be, and leaves!"

"Who? What man?"

"Father Malloy, from Venice. His way or the highway!"

"How do you know what he said?"

"I was there. Mother Superior had me join the meeting. It was just the three of us. So they send this junior down to make sure we'll keep our mouths shut. Then the Archbishop comes down in person and gives the same speech, except he told us the whole thing was our fault and he'll get to the bottom of it, our heads are going to roll."

The cop in Liberté was engaged. Why muzzle the sheep? Why was Sarah in the room? She asked her guest. Her guest had no idea on either count.

Lunch over, the bill was wordlessly handled by Liberté. Sarah found that even that kindness riled her; she didn't want to be helpless, beholden any longer.

Outside, Sarah asked, "You wanted to chat? I kind of did all the talking. Did you get what you needed, came for? I can talk more if you want."

"I'm good. Thanks."

They hugged and parted. As Liberté crossed Main Street Sarah watched, thinking idly about how her new friend looked better turned out than she. Recognizing the sin of envy even as she committed it, Sarah loaded up for confession by also noting that as good as Liberté now looked, she was short with huge hips...and that ass would one day be a monster. "Who am I? That is so unkind," she thought.

With Liberté and her hips in the station and out of sight, Sarah turned toward the convent, but walked at a snail's pace, mulling things over. She had learned a great deal from Liberté, one being they both were unhappy with their choice in faith; she with her Church, Liberté with due process. Funny, she thought, blood-and-guts secular and holier-than-holy; same issues, same problems.

Her pace quickened. Someone else needed her help. Ted. She had to find him, tell him. She had to warn the dumb bastard.

CHAPTER 11

The convent was a short drive from Sharky's, but ten minutes on foot. At minute fifteen, close now but not yet home, it struck Sarah how different she had become.

She felt the crush of doubt. Maybe she wasn't really a nun, and had joined for all the wrong reasons. Was she a fraud?

Nuns loved the dark wood walls, long shadows, and silent meditation, all things she merely tolerated. The mustiness of the place, so typical, made her sneeze.

Real nuns had faith in the men of the Church, that they would know and do what was right. Sarah had no such faith, just resentment born of judgment… a sin in and of itself.

Nuns were by nature, subservient; hers a constant act of self-deprecation.

It wasn't a sin to feel lust, once for Jimmy and suddenly and much more recently, for some reason connected to the knife and maybe to Ted. God invented sex! He, she, or it did not invent sex so people couldn't "do it", that was all church.

It dawned on the troubled nun that she needed to be human, perhaps flawed, and the nature of her life was the antithesis of normal. She didn't "want" sex. She didn't covet any part of Ted. She wanted to be part of the world God made, but her vows denied her.

If she acted on these renewed human urges, she knew she would break faith with her church. But with God? Was she rebelling? Was a fundamental living urge a visceral reaction to that vile death? Had that thing jammed up into Therese also jammed itself into the fabric of her life?

She must be cautious, and act thoughtfully. No doubt though, everything in her relationship with God and church was in question.

If using her body as God intended was a violation of faith in the same people that didn't seem to care for the violation of the innocent, such as faithful Therese, then what was she doing with these people anyway?

Was she rebelling?

Was fornication ever really a sin? Even if adulterous. In such a case the betrayal was the sin, and the fornication just the tool. Was God like the law; ten counts of crime? Or was it fairer? Using the tools God gave you might be OK, selection of a counterparty, not so much! At least fornication would be a positive act, and control. Not submission to lust, or to some random man. It was quite the opposite. She would be the predator; do unto others, do the doing!

She needed to pray.

Fully, even lustfully, engaged, her mind ran on. Ted would be easy. Right there, a surprise, not complicated, just in, out, over. No wife, no adultery, except her cuckolding God.

She really needed to pray!

With Sarah thus occupied, Ted sat alone on the porch at 2200 O'Neill thinking about Liberté and delicious possibilities.

Ted had always been attracted to good-looking, powerful women of authority. His very first fantasy involved his second grade teacher, his feelings not understood but enjoyed. More fantasies followed, but always from a distance.

Powerful women unnerved Ted. They made him feel unworthy. They might expose him as a fraud. They cowed him. Fearing the inevitable rejection that unmasking means, he never risked real intimacy.

Now, the clear male alpha, He aspired to conquest. This could work. Liberté could be his.

The separate reveries ended when Sarah climbed the stairs to the porch.

He proposed a stroll to the Everglades and back. She accepted, figuring the twenty minutes it would take afforded the opportunity to alert him to the threat Liberté had explained to her. He broke their initial silence by wondering if the outfit she wore wasn't stifling.

"Yes, but I'm going to wear it until Sister Therese is put to rest."

"Whatever. I guess the others are too?"

"Don't know. I'm not quite sure why they're all dressed in the traditional outfits, but I guess..."

"You don't know? Well, let me tell you. You did it, so they did it. When you stop, they'll stop. I'd say you're the alpha here. I bet that when you showed up, their...er...monthly rhythms shifted." She blushed to a lovely shade of mottled crimson. "Sorry," he said. She nodded.

Awkward silence be damned. She had something to say. "Should you be talking to the police so much Ted? It seems like they think you might be a suspect. I don't have any experience with this sort of thing, but in any novel I've ever read they tell people to shut up. Same on TV."

"Uh-huh" he said. "Here's the thing. I don't have anything to hide. I didn't do anything. They'll figure it out. In the meantime, that woman, that Alvarado woman — she's an idiot. She's in way over her head. They'll never get to the bottom of this till they get their head out of..."

"Their asses? It's OK, Ted. I'm not a doll, or a freak." It was Ted's turn to go red. Sarah was shocked at the little thrill of joy his discomfort brought her.

"Uh-huh. OK, she's a…" realizing that might be a bridge too far, he let it hang. "Here's what I don't get, why the, um, woman, doesn't focus more on the computer. Sudoku is all about patterns. So is solving crime. If you ignore the obvious you'll never get to the end. I'm just trying to help her. She's not stupid, but she sure doesn't belong in the big leagues. I do. I spent almost thirty years working in homicide in Miami… I've seen it all. She'll get it. I figure the guy who killed Therese took the computer, and then the guy who killed that guy took it from him. That fits. That's Sudoku."

"What happens if they don't find the computer?" she ventured.

"The computer is the key. If they don't find it I don't think they're going to catch the bastard that did this…the guy behind it all. Who knew about Therese and what she was doing?"

"I guess we all did. You did, Ted. The people she worked for in Rome knew. The guy who invited her to that party, Mr. Tamaros, he certainly knew she was here, and he knew that she was an art expert. Anyone who read the parish bulletin would have seen the welcome notice; it said what her life work had been. That's why he invited her, I guess. But I can't imagine that he knew about the computer."

"I always like to say the solutions to Sudoku are all there…you just have to find them. If the nuns didn't do it, and I know they didn't, and you didn't do it…" he paused to give her an around-the-arm, from-the-side hug which she was shocked to find herself tolerating, "then, if it was me on the case, I'm looking at Rome, or maybe the Archbishop. He would have known wouldn't he?"

"Uh-huh."

"Not that they killed her. Just that they were into something that got her killed. Sort of guilty knowledge, you know? I'd want to talk to those people and find out a lot more about what that woman did, how she worked, with whom, on what basis. Enemies. Rivals. You know, that kind of stuff."

"How do the cops check out Rome? …the Vatican?"

"Interpol. But I think you need a lot more than a suspicion that they might know something about what someone else might have done. If it were me, I'd call them or go see them. Of course "them" can mean an awful lot of people and right now I don't have a clue where I'd start. Probably with the Archbishop here, he probably didn't know that woman any more than you did, but he could find a lot out and he could open some doors."

"Am I right when I think that my Church isn't exactly helpful when the law comes calling?"

Ted just nodded, "yup. Whoever has that thing is in big trouble. You're right though, with the Church, it's going to be tough.

But here's the thing. That can't be the end of it. They have to have some sort of back up. No, it's not some guy from the church. I mean, why would they? No one goes to all that trouble to kill someone and do what they did to cover their tracks to get something they already have. God, this is "Reality Sudoku"…sometimes you have to go back before you can go forward. I bet I could invent a game like that."

Sarah was edgy. "Well, the police have a lot more resources than you, Ted. Maybe they'll get a hearing. If they don't, they're going to keep looking at you. You better be careful. Shouldn't you get a lawyer?

"Nope. It's all good. She'll figure it out, with my help. The more help I give her the faster this is over. Then Mariah, you, all of you, can move past this…"

Her heart pounded with pride for this man, for his utter lack of fear, even as her head told her he was an idiot. "Ted, why is the computer so important?"

"In the right hands? I figure that thing is a font of knowledge about stuff other people may think is theirs. You know, the art and stuff. I think they call it "providence." You know, who owned it before, how they got it. Stuff like that. It's getting to be a big deal now. I remember seeing something about whole countries suing people and getting stuff back There's been a lot of stuff returned to places in Italy and Greece; people like the Getty museum, Princeton, The Met."

Perhaps naively she asked, "So how does that affect the Church?"

He laughed. Ted enjoyed being the dude. "Sarah, really! That place…the Vatican…doesn't want anyone to know all the stuff they have.

They've been collecting shit for, like a thousand years. From crusades, busted empires, God-fearing explorers. I'll bet half the stuff there, more even, has a shady past."

"They're going to have to give stuff back that they got a thousand years ago?"

"I don't know, Sister. But I do know the world is a very different place now. If I'm right, Therese would have collected all the information anyone would have needed to make a claim, and put it all together in a neat package. If I were the Vatican, I'd be doing everything I possibly could to find that thing. Or maybe it's just nothing…maybe they have some of that fancy "cloud" computer stuff and they can just zap the missing computer and blow it up."

"It's not just nothing," she said grimly. "All this 'do this, don't do that, no funeral, don't play with Ophrah on their memorial thing'… that's coming right from the top. Something's not right. They're up to something." She laughed a bit, "But I don't think they're going to get what they want."

He looked at her. "Funny, why would you say that?"

"Oh nothing. Just, they're not making any friends here. If they ask me for help, it's not going to happen!"

Ted wondered what this bewitching character wasn't telling him. He prodded, but she diverted, "You do know that Mother Superior has told the town council that we will attend a service of remembrance and that we will work with them on some sort of commemorative site…"

"Really? Well good for her, for all of you really."

"Thanks. I can't forget the meeting with that Deacon. He talked about disobedience as a schism, and…"

"Forget it. They're not that dumb. That would make them the laughing stock of the world, and everyone else would feel sorry for you. They'd make you into pathetic heroes."

"I dunno. Daddy always told me to mean what I say and to say what I mean. That guy, Malloy, he wasn't just shooting off his mouth…"

"You'll be fine. You'll see."

When, twenty minutes after setting out, they were back to the foot of the porch, they stood, awkwardly for a minute, then parted; Ted to indulge in self-actualization of unchaste Liberté fantasies; Sarah to pray for forgiveness of her growing weight of guilt.

That night she dreamed she and Ted were falling into a black abyss, both clutching a single computer. Then it was gone. Then he was gone. And she continued falling.

CHAPTER 12

There are rules about books; don't judge one by its cover, autobiographies are self-serving, biographies are slanted, you can't really understand one without understanding the author, they are precious, and so on.

If Sarah were a book, the cover would be elegant, the contents deep, variant, nuanced, with multiple themes, a hint of hidden darkness, and glorious subtexts. The adage "you can't judge a book by its cover" would appear to be happily validated. By contrast, Ted would appear to be a cheap paperback with no spine or real value, and a simple storyline.

By most standards Coulson didn't measure up; he had been a mediocre student, underachieving athlete, failed husband, and notwithstanding his own opinion, a failure as a cop.

His career in Miami homicide was not viewed by the department with the same happy sentiment as it was by Ted. When he retired at age 45, he saved his commanding officer the awkward task of busting him back to uniform. Average case management skills, tardy, poor notes, embarrassment under oath. Way too many sick days.

Ted considered himself a crime Svengali, often inventing revolutionary techniques rather than deigning to tried and true tools of modern forensics. He was an amusing clown, but nobody shared files.

After retirement he had planned on a second career with a private Miami security services firm with operations in terrorism control and high value kidnap avoidance. Ted had called for an appointment. No one had called back. He had found part time night security work.

There were reasons for his idiosyncrasies. During the period in his young life when essence is molded, he suffered child abuse. There was some physical violence directed to him and to his sister Mariah, but mostly it was indirect, watching their father yell at, hit, and humiliate their mother. Whatever he did or said, it was deemed inadequate, and he useless. Young Ted built a defensive shell and withdrew; he became an introvert. His weapons became invisibility and silence.

For him, every relationship was a threat. He craved friendship and respect but was petrified of judgment, so he built a mask and never revealed his true self. That didn't foster friendship and he was left out, in the process becoming increasingly withdrawn, chronically depressed. He was fringe; known but excluded, part of, but not really.

He found a way. By being amusing he could hide his reality and even get positive attention. Tomorrows got sacrificed for vibes today; energy thus frittered cost real momentum.

No one was more deluded by all this than he himself. Despite repeated failures in career, love, money and self-actualization, Ted believed in his masked existence, seeing constant reversals of fortune as despite, not because, of him. He kept his big unaware chin stuck right out there.

Ted types lack perspective of the big picture. He could analyze the hell out of a file, but inevitably got bushwhacked by the thing from out of nowhere. The Miami police gave up. They just didn't care, because they needed results, not reasons.

The police now investigating Ted saw something else, and it was troubling. Only in extreme circumstances does exclusive devotion to a guy's sister merit respect. Pretty much everywhere else, it gets treated as weird, even suspect. The mere fact of Ted's annual pilgrimage to the convent was troubling to the Ophrah minions of justice, including police, DA, and the judge. Circumstantial evidence fits better if the suspect is weird. They thought Ted was weird. For the most part they figured the circumstantial evidence fit well enough.

Ted should have known. The fact is, he did. He didn't damn the torpedoes as a hero, but as a coward. His only concern was facade.

To judge Sarah by her cover, one would see a beautiful woman who had chosen the life of the cloister because of a deep faith in her Lord and a desire to help her fellow man and womankind. Yet both Sarah and Ted were hiding, he by facade, she by habit, both masks.

But she was deeper than Ted. The ghastly sight of Therese with that thing jammed up her broken body smashed the myth of her own sacrifice for security. The same event that caused Ted to tighten down his mask caused Sarah to begin to renounce hers.

The real woman was waking while the man-child cocooned.

As nature, and its dark ways, welled up inside her, Sarah began to take the measure of all around her, and to begin to understand her ability to command rather than to serve. Innately she understood Ted; a pawn with technical knowledge - a disposable pawn that she could use to many ends. He was of important but limited use. She intuited his neediness, watched as he ogled Liberté, and instinctively knew he could be compromised and suborned. Ultimately consumed.

For the second time in two days, Sarah and Ted walked to the fringe of civilized, to the very edge of the garden, and sat staring into the unknown of the primordial swamp. She sucked in the power of the wild as he became increasingly tense with the silence.

"So, you wanted to tell me something?" he finally asked.

"I do, but I need you to promise first..."

"OK, what?"

"I did something. It was right at the time. But now it's...not good. It was right. Now I don't know what to do."

Ted sensed the fear she wanted him to, and shifted toward avuncular proximity. It was as she expected. "Out with it. I won't tell. I won't judge."

Tears were forced. "I didn't know Ted. Everybody thinks that damned computer is the key, that it's what the murder...-they're wrong Ted…"

His look meant he had not a clue what she was trying to say, and his silence insisted she continue.

"Ted, that morning when I went to her room, I had to do something. I couldn't just…"

"What? Just tell me! What the fuck did you do?"

"The computer. I hid it."

The wind left the ex-cop. "You hid it. Where? How?"

"I thought it was so important and if it became evidence then it might get opened and…"

"Holy shit, Sarah! You suppressed evidence. We can't tell anyone right now, or you're dead meat."

She felt the hormonal rush of a teenager. Not pubescent. The thrill of the hunt. The moment when one dominates the other. The instant when one dies so that another might live. It had been so easy; he was in her thrall because he had to be. It was his nature, and she had known it, used it, stalked him, and brought him down.

He asked not even one intelligent question, like, "Where is it now?" He was so into being supportive, milking every vestige of transitory good will that he accepted her guilty knowledge and agreed to keep her guilty secret. Ted thought "chivalry", like the romantic Round Table set, in this case, truly a knight errant. Had he been otherwise, Ted might have been off any hook with cops and DAs. As a simple book, he was an easy read for her.

The more interesting, and much more complex read was the nun. As a gator stalks, plans, assails, so had she. Acting instinctually, she had read his weakness. Nuns do that. She had used his weakness for her benefit. Nuns don't do that. She would consume him. Not nun-like.

The disclosure and separate, private afterglows were abbreviated. She was summoned back to the dark wooden mustiness of her current status to continue toward her new one.

CHAPTER 13

Once alone, Sarah struggled with what she had done to Ted, and to understand the enormity of her conquest. Disclosure concerning the computer had been brilliant strategy but bloody minded. Ted was compromised and she not even remotely so. It now dawned on her that she was linked to that computer by far more than innocent stewardship. She had lifted it with pure purpose, to be sure, but now began to appreciate its potential. She had no plan except that she wasn't giving it back. If Ted ratted her out, she would deny and he would paint himself as a craven liar, digging himself an even bigger hole than he already had.

By sharing her guilty knowledge she had obtained complete control over Ted, and she already had complete control over the computer. Her challenge now was how best to use her control over both

Years of subservient moral behavior weighed in. She prayed. But her rosary no longer mattered the way it had, even yesterday. Half way in she lost concentration in favor of a Jimmy appearance. He brought clarity.

That night years ago, in that car, young Sarah had crossed a line, had rebelled, risked, pushed parents back, stepped out of blind obedience. Now he was back. Then the fear of the event had dueled with carnal awaking and teen neediness. This was different. Not remotely hormonal nor carnal. Just rebellion and the end of blind obedience. And crossing a huge line.

So far, she had not done anything that could not be undone. Surrender of the computer with a confession of fear and concern could, if needed, resolve things to where normal penance would be all she would pay. But if she...cuckolded God?

The immediacy of the rosary not enough, Sarah made her way to the tiny den-turned-chapel on the first floor. On her knees, she wanted to pray but was afraid to start. Communing with God seemed to stimulate a Jimmy incursion, in turn to troubling thoughts, then to guilt, and back to prayer. Had she already broken her vows? Why was communication with her Lord now broken? She needed a priest! No! It wasn't really God she was struggling with, it was them. She had not lost faith in her Lord and Savior, just his agents here on Earth. Their abandonment at her hour of need made her angry. Anger brought on Jimmy. Sarah was alarmed by a growing warm tumescence that she reveled in even while despising the complication of it all.

It came to her in pieces; it all sprang from the barbarism to Therese.

First, the obscenity, the assault on the dead woman's most private, most uniquely guarded privacy, thrust itself into her psyche. In all creation, God's creation, the rarity of willing asexuality as a gift to the creator of that carnal need? How completely unnatural. And bleakly farcical. That same sacrifice so often the target of violence, a history full of nuns raped and then murdered. Celibacy, an un-respected, unacknowledged, wasted sacrifice.

Then, the men of the church, they abandoned her...them... in their hour of need. What was faith, really? About God? Or his rock on Earth? Could you have one without the other? Who would, could, intercede for her? Surely not them! But, they weren't evil. She knew them, and had for years. Then what, and why? More faith, trust us but ask no questions, expect no answers. Blind faith. And obedience. It didn't make sense.

They no longer owned her. But where, then, did she belong? And if celibacy was their yoke, then sex was her rebellion. Not

carnal. Not sinful. God couldn't care less. Just no going back.

Caesar crossed the Rubicon. George Bush had his line in the sand. Her line was simpler, private. Ted.

This time Sarah didn't pray. She preyed. She waited. The door to the guesthouse creaked open, then shut.

Unemotionally, Sarah lifted her skirts and removed the safety net of panties, then strode meaningfully, and otherwise clad as she had been, to the guesthouse and knocked. Caught mid change, shirtless Ted peaked out the door. She pushed by him, locked the door, and then shoved him to the bed. He didn't resist.

It wasn't sex. It was rape. Whatever he was thinking, or reservations he might have had, his penis was unfazed and immediately rose to the occasion.

Sarah forced him onto his back, undid him enough for her purposes, and mounted him. She leaned forward using his throat for support, and rode him in fury. It was brief, then she rolled off and straightened her skirts as he gulped air wordlessly. They lay side by side for a silent minute. He thought picket fences. She wept. He thought love. She despised him. He glowed; she sweated. He was in heaven, she in hell. He remained motionless as she rose and left.

The enormity!

Her vows! She was a fallen woman. Would God forgive her? People would know. How could she face her family? Shame enveloped her.

What if she conceived? Sarah drove directly to a Marco Island Walgreens and used every cent of her allowance to purchase the Plan B "morning after" concoction. She downed it, then dumped the container and invoice in a trash bin, and took herself home. She drove aimlessly, stopping intermittently to weep for what was, and what was to be. It was late when she got back, so she got in without the need for additional sin. Her final thought before sleep was that maybe no-one would ever know, maybe it could remain between her, God, and Ted. She was sure Ted wouldn't be a problem.

Next morning she neither attended prayers nor joined her sisters in Christ for the morning repast. She had risen at 4 a.m. from sleepless torment. The throbbing in her temples and the knot in her stomach were intense and inescapable. Two hours of prayer went unheeded, but a shower brought relief. As the hot water pounded her, the prodigal nun felt her head clear; the heat relaxed tense neck muscles, cleared sinuses, freshened her spoiled body and roiled soul.

Emerging from the shower, Sarah stood naked before the mirror, peering deeply into her soul. Rebel yesterday, repentant recondite today. Hers was a double treachery: the sex, and then the pill. One venial, the other mortal sin. Life in cloisters is about vows. In one day she had destroyed her faith in herself to be one of them. There had to be consequences. Prayer was not enough. "He" might forgive her. God knew, or ought to have known, of her repentance, thus forgiveness, and entitlement to unqualified membership in the congregation of Christ.

The congregation of the Order of Saint Mary the Virgin might be another matter. Ditto for the men of the Church. She wondered if she were them how she would judge herself. Not well. Their faith in her might be beyond redemption. They, the convent, were already under a cloud and at risk of serious repercussions for blamelessness, so how could she hope for the kindness so ingrained in Christ but so missing in his church. They were hateful…that's why she did this…whatever happened was their fault, not hers. But how would their rush to unreasonable judgment affect the women of the Convent? She had rashly done them harm. She must not do more, and undo what she had. Perhaps a formal confession and forgiveness by a priest would finish it. That might be best. But only temporarily. She had crossed a line because she had to leave…move on, divorce. Like an unhappy wife with small children and economic dependence issues, she would wait.

Then there was Ted. She had raped him, but who would believe that? Of course he was entitled to weakness of the flesh as he had given no vows. But a nun? A guest in the home of a blessed order of cloistered women? He would be the fox in the hen house. The woman in the mirror flushed. She was Eve, cast from Eden for her sin that tainted all, forever! Ted would be a laughing stock and pariah. He would have to be an idiot to tell anything, ever. Perhaps there were options, at least in the interim.

Sarah of the mirror moved back into her own skin. Her plan was well enough thought through for the present. She would say nothing and count on Ted to do the same. When Caesar crossed the Rubicon the men of Rome knew it, and the fat was in the fire. But no one, except herself and God, knew about her Rubicon and with luck Rome never would. As long as her secret remained safe, she had choices. The best route was to keep all options open.

Ted had a different take. He of the simple male persuasion saw not rape but an act of love. He took Sarah's sudden departure as mere complications of her profession and life choices, and was euphoric. And committed. If she could do that for him, then surely he must help her forward. He would take the reins. Finally he had found a woman who could love him and with whom he could be happy. It would be awkward, but she would leave the order and they would live happily ever after. He could not wait to share this wonderful turn of events, and sought out his sister, Sister Mariah.

Mariah was not amused.

First, she ordered Ted to pack and leave. Then she informed Mother Superior. By the time Sarah descended the stairs, the whole convent knew. By the time Sarah met with the Mother Superior for a debriefing concerning the debriefing, Detective Sergeant Liberté Alvarado had heard the rumor and was on the phone for details and implications. When asked why, Liberté had said something about possible motive.

So Ted was now in big trouble with the police. Sarah was in big trouble with God. They both had issues with the convent. Ted was in even bigger trouble with Sarah. Liberté wanted to know what her newfound friend was thinking.

And one over-the-hill Mother Superior, expected to be somewhere between devastated and furious, was in a state of glorious rapture.

While Sarah had been committing and regretting, Mother Superior had received a call from Deacon Malloy that changed everything.

CHAPTER 14

The gathering clouds grew darker.

Rome focused on damage control and property recovery. Secrecy became integral to the plan. Their premise held that as long as the computer was missing, the fewer who knew its opportunistic potential, the smaller the number of fortune hunters, the lower the odds of untoward ownership.

It was Father Tomas' strategy. His strength was pragmatism. A latecomer to holy orders, he was previously a military veteran having served two tours of duty in the Italian army and holding graduate degrees in business and investment management. His recruitment to holy orders had begun with a chance encounter he had with the Cardinal Vicar of St. John Lateran's Arch basilica. That is the technical seat of the Diocese of Rome, and its boss, the bishop of Rome, is Pope. While the Pope ran the Church, the Cardinal Vicar ran the Arch basilica. It so happened that Tomas attended confession and ended up in discussion with the Cardinal Vicar. The Cardinal Vicar saw a great mind and a tortured soul. The church and the penitent could be good for each other. The penitent had given it a go, and the church had been rewarded.

Tomas evolved into a financial genius controlling some $10 billion in assets, all accumulated through programs he himself imagined, designed, implemented, and now safeguarded. It was held in special reserves, garnered through a variety of marketing endeavors to the faithful. The reserves were to settle an assortment of real and contingent claims against the Church for offenses ranging from child sodomy to fraud, misappropriation, money laundering, child abuse and unlawful death. He alone had seen and acted upon the potentially devastating exposures emerging from creeping secularism that spawned legal claims and problematic public relations.

Father Tomas reported directly to the Carmerlengo, the most powerful bureaucrat in the Curia. The Curia is like the "C-suite" of business, so Father Tomas reported to the head of the business of the Church on Earth, and that man reported solely to the soul of the Church, the Pope himself.

A quiet man, Father Tomas lived alone in rented accommodations just outside Santa Anna's gate, so he could come and go easily and efficiently.

He remained a troubled soul; two of the people closest to him had died tragically.

The first was his army buddy Luigi de Parma, who committed suicide, and for whom Father Tomas had obtained special dispensation for burial in holy ground, a tomb which he visited once a week when in town. The other was Sister Therese.

When Luigi had passed away, Father Tomas had been inconsolable, and five years later was still distant.

Now that Therese had died violently, people who knew Tomas were fearful for his health, physical, emotional, even spiritual. The fact that issues derivative of Therese's murder were within his ambit did not make things easier, and people worried for him. But Father Tomas did not become the force that he was without fortitude, and he dealt with it, apparently seamlessly.

When first confronted with news of the murder, Father Tomas had swallowed his pain, pushed personal issues to the side, and cut instantly to the chase, to the real problem: an orgy of reporting.

This was everything modern America liked in a story. It would sell copy. There would be no end of special reports and updates, interviews, and speculation. Americans would be sympathetic to the woman herself and ruthless to the institution of which she had been a part.

As a cause célèbre the dead woman would be dangerous. Sooner or later there would be innuendo about her work. Questions would be asked about the contents of the computer and their worth. In no time at all, ruthless reporters would invent possible scenarios that would implicate Mother Church in all kinds of vulgar activity. He could imagine it all, the lower echelons of journalism featuring the gore with the weeklies and the monthlies into the greater questions of whom and why. These people sold intrigue and conspiracy. None of which would sell membership to new Catholics, but chatter about money and cabal would breed more and more reports, never casting Mother Church in any kind of a good light.

Tomas ruefully referred to the press as vermin. As they picked over the story, like bugs in a slag heap, some would inevitably begin to shit out some gold. What if they started to hone in on the whereabouts of the damn computer? Hundreds, maybe thousands, of gold diggers would join the hunt. After all, in such a corrupt world, a lucky find would turn into an auction to whoever would pay the most for information they could use in some existing or future claim against his settlement trusts…his money.

And what about lifestyle questions? He could see the litany of "what and why" concerning women living alone, and not needing men, and on and on. It would end up as some indictment of Mother Church as promoter of unhealthy lifestyles, or unwilling to protect its people, or even worse, why were nuns, all women in fact, not treated as equals?

He concluded that while nothing good could come of Therese's death, much evil might. It needed to go away as quickly as possible.

The best way to kill the stories was to starve the writers.

There were to be no interviews given by any nun. There would be no drama, so no formal or informal tributes, monuments, gardens, or displays. That included the funeral. The remains would be removed from the public domain, no photo-ops of coffins and grieving nuns. There would be no speeches discussing the woman, her life, her work, or her family. God no. No family. That could go viral, with a life of its own. No, she was dead and as such she must be buried, along with the story.

He couldn't control the press but he could control the nuns. He couldn't control the police, but he could limit their effectiveness. He couldn't stop the show, but he could rob it of content.

Father Tomas used thoroughly modern logic to conclude that thoroughly antiquated solutions were best. He issued a memo on the subject for the eyes only of the Carmerlengo. In it, he argued that while he couldn't guarantee success in silencing the secular world, he could limit resultant exposures of God's head office to ridicule and ruin if he could render the gossip cancer benign.

Dictum passed to Venice, and thence to Ophrah. The ladies in the swamp were to talk to no one about anything in any way related to the case. Therese, who might otherwise draw too much attention to herself, was to be returned forthwith to her home in Italy for private interment. The Church was not to participate in any displays around or about the nuns of the Order of Saint Mary the Virgin.

It wasn't a bad plan, just unworkable. The genie was already out of the bottle and wasn't going to be stuffed back in!

The first problem was the nuns of the Order of Saint Mary the Virgin. They just could not understand the merit in such an approach. They were deeply devout, with beautiful souls and they just couldn't turn their back on the incident or its victim. And as humans, they craved closure.

The second problem was the good burghers of Ophrah who had come to see the light...of capitalist gain. Murder most foul wasn't just silver lining in the proverbial cloud. The tragedy at the Convent was pure gold.

Ophrah, and its powers as it were, staked claims. Pilgrims needed goods and services. The place was discovered and becoming a tourist destination. Commercial property was moving up in value. Money was being made. PR would be good. A funeral would be awesome. A shrine could be a long-term draw. The inner sanctum of municipal affairs, the boys of Sharky's, were alternatively conniving together and against each other on what and who and how the big money could be made. By the time the big money arrived from elsewhere, every piece of useful property would have been owned by one or more of those boys. Special attention was given to prescriptive and proscriptive ordinances to advance the cause of select well-being.

In a sense, the big money interests of God were colliding with the big money interests of local Gods, with the truly godly caught in the middle.

Almost before Therese's blood had fully congealed a posse of the Sharky's boys had dropped by to pay respects, offer assistance, and ask about a send-off. The nuns had been warmed by this show of concern and had readily endorsed the concept of an open farewell that could accommodate all and sundry. After all, these people of Ophrah and environs were the Convent's flock and it was important for the ladies to feel their warmth. When the very next day the Archbishop had sent his emissary, Deacon Brendan Malloy, to set the ground rules excluding such rites of passage, the nuns were not just dismayed, they were angry.

Mother Superior Marie had convened a prayer session in which she hectored the nuns on obligation and station in life, but even she didn't believe it. In this very first instance in years where one might reasonably expect the boys on top to look after the immediate needs of the girls on the bottom, the boys proved themselves inconsiderate, selfish, unfeeling, and wholly inadequate.

Sister Marie had handled the reneging of the kind offer of a public funeral by phone. It didn't stop anything. It just changed it.

The funeral would be a service of remembrance. If Pooh-Bahs of the cloth wouldn't, then the politicos could. The vacuum created by church recalcitrance was filled with ungraceful haste. The Governor of the State of Florida would attend. One can't survive in a job like his without a well-honed scent for good press.

Here was a podium from which he could preach law, order, and good government. He couldn't look bad; no debate, not an issue of his making, just a good old local tragedy where he could glad-hand, appear sensitive, and get his message across without all the sniping typical of life in Tallahassee. This would be a great forum for a sermon on the religion of the millennium; security of person and property. His team of writers included references to more police and a very real need for courts to deal quickly and decisively with the guilty. Of course, it would be nice if the aggrieved ladies could play a role. They were clear on that. They would not be part of any platform party. Would they attend, fill the front row, maybe wear those traditional blacks?

Papal permission denied, the invitation was accepted anyway, and Sister Marie agreed that she would say a few words to the assembled host. She told the Archbishop of her decision, who in turn notified Rome. Through this conduit, positions hardened; Rome insistent on conformance to its edict, Mother Superior Marie to her conscience. She agreed that not only would the nuns attend the service, but they would also work with the town to establish a bit of an on-site shrine to the memory of Therese.

When it comes to its own flock, the Rock has tools, the most delicious being excommunication. In the old days it was employed largely to keep Kings in line, because an excommunicated person could be killed by anyone who had a shot, and the excommunicate would go to hell for eternity and no one on this side of the River Styx had to obey him or do his bidding.

Now it's clubbier. You don't lose your eternal soul, they just kick you to the curb. And the organization that fashioned such novel approaches to loving your neighbor and turning the other cheek as Crusades and inquisitions, came up with a fabulous new trick:

automatic excommunication. In Latin it's Latae Sententiae. The theory behind it is brilliant. If you do certain things you have actually excommunicated yourself!

That's how a Phoenix nun named Margaret McBride did it. As an administrator of a hospital she sat on a committee that decided a classic "gray area" issue, and chose the life of the mother over that of the eleven-week-old fetus. Bang. Gone. A woman dedicated to her church and her people, close to the end of her working life, was kicked to the curb because she met her conscience in good faith and broke their rule.

So abortion is one of the three reasons that gets one automatically kicked to the curb. The second is being ordained a priest if you're a woman or being a guy and doing the ordaining.

The third is running a schism.

In technical terms, if you are apostate, heretic, or schismatic, then you have separated yourself from the communion of the faithful and are banned from all ecclesiastic offices, the Eucharist, and other sacraments. Some examples: Luther, Henry VIII of England, his daughter Queen Elizabeth I, the antipopes, Fidel Castro, anyone who was communist, and Napoleon.

More recently there was the Brazilian mother who had her nine-year-old remediated after rape, and Margaret, as mentioned. Now, a whole colony of Brides of Christ. The root of their Latae Sententiae? Their desire to honor their recently fallen member, the late Sister Therese. Their lack of obedience in not immediately accepting the dictates of the old men in dresses got them kicked to the curb.

It was Father Tomas who established their status as excommunicates by their own actions. From his perspective, there was no choice.

Of a sudden, these women who had sworn themselves to a life of penury had the rug swept out from under them, and to complete the analogy, were left hanging. Their "deal" had been to do God's work on Earth, and God would house, clothe, and feed them during their Earthly sojourn. Now all bets were off and they were cast asunder.

It got worse. In the same telephone message that advised the Mother Superior of the ouster of her and her flock came a second shock. The property at 2200 O'Neill was to be sold. The ladies had a week to vacate.

The Mother Superior had been alone in the office she now shared with Sarah when the call had come. The call had come from the Deacon, that Malloy fellow. He had obvious sympathy for Marie and her flock, but was barred from further communication with them unless and until they made peace with the Church. He had been unsure how they might do that, given as how no member in good standing was technically allowed to talk to an excommunicate. He was pretty sure that a public recantation of their schism could get the ball rolling, but only after a decent period of time. He thought maybe a year.

It stood to reason that, as schismatics, the nuns could no longer reside in Church property. He was sure there would be no bailiff, but, short of buying the place back from the Church, he didn't see how the nuns could stay at 2200 O'Neill and also make peace with the Church. Malloy had closed by saying that excommunication in the modern world did not consign anyone to hell; only God could do that. Their souls were safe, just not Catholic anymore.

When the call ended, Mother Superior Marie called out urgently for Sister Sarah, but was told that Sister Sarah had been out earlier, had returned just long enough to get the car, and was now gone again. Marie got Sarah's cell phone number and dialed it, breathing a huge sigh of relief when she heard it ringing. Then Sister Mariah came thumping down the stairs with the targeted phone, still ringing, and announced that she had heard it on Sarah's bureau.

Mariah handed the device to Marie and left in a hurry, oblivious to the panic in Marie's voice, as her brother Ted had called and asked to speak to her as soon as possible.

CHAPTER 15

Sister Marie had been Mother Superior for forty years. Now seventy-eight, and coming within sight of the end of her Earthly travails, she no longer bustled. Until recently, her single most pressing problem had been succession; all potentials had failed.

At various times over the past decade every one of her minions had been considered but found wanting. The process, repeated so often, had become a sort of self-incrimination as each nun, in turn and under increasingly difficult scrutiny, had come up short. The venerable Grand Dame had often wondered if fault lay with the test, and not the candidate. Such thoughts had been dead-of-night considerations; light of day brought new evidence of ineptitude every time, and so Marie struggled on with this last cross of her service.

Sarah, the youngest minion and current unknowing candidate, was now held by the Matriarch as steeped adequately in the mysteries of the

Convent, capable, and a clear leader. Yet status of "potential leader" had not been conveyed to the candidate. Had she known, the Sister Sarah of a few days earlier might have begged to be excused from consideration on the grounds that she was neither capable nor deserving of the exalted status. Ironically, this blithe submission to rule and order from above was the attribute Sister Marie saw, to date, as most meritorious in the candidate.

Marie knew from her many years of service how important modest aspirations were in a candidate for leadership in an order such as this. In practical terms she was a den mother whose prime responsibility was to foster obedience and acquiescence among her little flock. Real decisions were made in Venice, the one in Florida, at the archbishopric for South Florida.

Like a shard or stone in surf or a gem tumbler, Sister Marie had been worn to smoothly decorative. By dint of constant experience she had learned the place of her Order, indeed herself. She may have been a bride of Christ but she was a lowly servant in his house on Earth. Devotion and sacrifice were not only her onus, but also her only reward. She and her girls lived in quiet penury, with basic needs provided as some sort of largesse by those for whom they toiled for free. The ladies gave everything they had or received, and in return were allowed the quiet sanctity of minimal security and the comfort that their immortal souls were safe. Mother Superior Marie had faith, a faith often tested, but hers was up to the challenge.

It wasn't her faith in some great redeemer that saw the Old Girl through. It was her blind faith in her faith. If she did as required, all would be well. Sadly, faith in a faith is submission, not to one's Maker, but to the people controlling that relationship. So, the great love of God had become a great love of God's franchise on Earth, his Church. The quality of her sacrifice and the surety of her soul were assessed by God's men, or more particularly in this case, his man—the Archbishop. The Archbishop had over the years, actually been three different men, but her role had always been the same: willing, trusting, loyal—an unquestioning servant.

Truth be told, Marie was more than a little passive-aggressive. The fires of her faith in her faith were, in fact, a form of misdirected fury. The apparent elegance with which she took direction from above was the "passive." The iron rule of those below was the "aggressive." And it was all called "faith." Her frustration made her a harridan. The harsher her rule, the greater the isolation; the greater the isolation, the greater the fury. She had given her entire life to Mother Church, and return got trial and torment. Abuse from without; fear from within. But always blessed and venerable, she had soldiered on. Now, nearly eighty, and ready for her heavenly reward, Marie wanted only to finish her time on Earth in the tranquil peace of nurtured retirement. If only she could just find a decent replacement.

Sarah was proving a good candidate. A bit of an Eeyore, Mother Superior had wondered if acceptance of her for the big chair was more desperation in the tester than proven mettle in the candidate.

Then came Therese, the murder, and all holy hell.

For the first time in her professional life Sister Marie was caught in the middle, between her faith in her faith and her obligation to her flock.

The little rock worn to that fine patina by the tumbler of her faith in her faith was now to face the grinder of real world ambiguity.

It started with those damn flowers!

The town of Ophrah was as faithful to its interests on Earth as Sister Marie was to her faith in her faith. People in Ophrah were coining money because the world had discovered them. There were visitors who needed gas, victuals, and rest. The first official act of council, post Therese, was to approach the Holy Order of Saint Mary the Virgin and propose some sort of shrine. The ladies of the convent, being human, had thought that a great idea; the archbishop, apparently less so, had nixed it. Emotionally, Sister Marie had found herself wedged awkwardly onto a sharp picket fence; she agreed with the ladies but was duty-bound to obey the archbishop. She had taken matters into her own hands and had gone alone to see him. He had told her his hands were tied. He was not the problem. As far as he was concerned a shrine could be a good thing. However, he had intoned, Rome had insisted. There would be no shrine. She had reported this to the Sharky's team. But something clicked in Marie.

She, they, had a right to receive closure on the trauma and on the loss of what really amounted to their visitors. An outright denial of such basic decency, without so much as a reason, was such a slap. It slapped it into the head of the seventy-eight year old Mother Superior that she and hers were of no consequence and that they had been abandoned in their own grief.

The woman known for her steely countenance gave herself to weeping, not for the deceased, but for herself. She wept in fear, anger, frustration, and hopelessness. Deeply, in her core, she knew her faith in her faith had been a waste. More than anything she had wept for the waste of it all. She just wanted peace. No longer could she soldier on alone. The burden of what was and what was to be must be passed on to younger, stronger, and yes, more capable hands.

When Marie had agreed to attend, and perhaps to talk at, the memorial service for Sister Therese, she had performed the first act of open disagreement with the boys in charge, and that, in and of itself, convinced her it was time for her to move on.

God had, she now realized, sent her a sign. The newbie Sarah did not herself know it, but she was the one the others would follow. Sister Marie was old but not blind, and she knew that Sarah had been sent as her replacement. That business with the reversion to the penguin look had been the insistent rapping at the door.

Sister Marie was now not just tolerant of the idea, but welcoming. The weight of responsibility now crushed the Old Girl. She was ready to stand aside, even as she recognized the sea of change that would bring. This girl Sarah was showing every sign of inner struggle, of crisis of faith that she herself was feeling. Well, so be it. Maybe it was time for that too. Maybe the output of her entire life, this Order, was as antiquated as she. Maybe it was to be swallowed up into the sands of time, molded into something more...dare she even think it...relevant, to the world of here and now.

She delayed pulling the trigger on what Marie saw as a mortality issue.

Then came the call from Venice.

After hanging up, the embattled Matriarch had sat silent as tears flowed freely down her cheeks and onto her lap. It was about half an hour before she wiped, honked, and went looking for Sarah. When she learned that Sister Sarah had been out of sorts that morning, and was not in her room or anywhere on the property, Marie had closeted herself to think through her investiture approach. It was during that deliberation that Mariah had arrived.

Marie responded to Mariah's news of Ted and Sarah's assignation in a magnificently unexpected manner.

The old girl laughed madly like one on a sinking boat about to be saved.

Mariah stood incredulous, then Marie ordered that she must immediately tell Ted that to err is human but that to forgive is divine, that he was both welcome and needed at the convent, and that she devoutly hoped that he would stay.

Stunned, Mariah left to do as ordered, so did not see Marie drop to her knees at her prie-dieu, to thank her Lord and savior for his intervention and this holy sign. Sarah may have broken their rules, but their rules didn't count here anymore. Sarah was sent as a savior.

CHAPTER 16

Liberté laughed so hard the water leaked a little from the corner of her mouth, "You're incredible Sarah. You're a nun and you want to kill the bastard. I play with guns but I think he just needs a good spanking!"

The two were back in the booth at Sharky's. It hadn't started well, what with Liberté's questions about Sarah's naughty tryst. It had been a lot of confrontation, and big confession, but there was an absence of contrition. Liberté had come right out and asked if Sarah wanted to be considered a suspect, or just an "aider and abettor." The sex had redefined the relationship between the nun and the number one suspect. It had also brought Sarah down off the pedestal generally awarded to self-deniers of pleasures of the flesh. In fact, a fallen nun drops below the floor of standard disregard into a hellish new brand of disrespect.

Liberté believed Sarah when she had said it was angry rebellion, that Ted meant nothing, and how she would happily strangle him for allowing her to use him. Then the cop wondered if she really believed her friend, or it was just that she wanted to believe.

It was the anguish over the "Plan B" pill that made a full believer of the policewoman. She listened to Sarah's halting voice and tearful emotional restraint telling of the drive to Marco Island Walgreens at Sea Grape and Pomegranate where no one would know her, the bathroom stall, the furtive disposal of the wrapper, the shame of her betrayal, the fear, the regret. It had been the euphoric declaration of severe side effects, like a sinner's painful orgasm from the welcome scourge of corporal punishment. She related the dizziness, cramps, and near-mortal exhaustion. Now, two days later, she still had the headache, but prayers for her period had been answered.

Liberté noted how Ted's name never came up. He really was irrelevant. Not the bleating of an "outed" lover.

"So," ventured Liberté, "What happens now?"

Sarah appeared not to hear, but her mind raced. Enough of this line of questioning. It would be too easy to make a mistake, too disastrous to slip now. Liberté reiterated.

"Now?" responded the increasingly complex redhead. She appeared to will herself from her plight, straightened her posture, brushed back the hair, touched the paper napkin to her eyes, lifted the menu and declared, "We've just done confession, so now I think I'll do communion." Then in a loud voice, while waving a little outrageously, "Waiter, a bottle of your best red wine, please." Then to Liberté, "I'm still very poor. You will have to pay."

After the first soulful slugs of third-rate ambrosia substitute, Sarah sighed and replaced her glass to the table. "Well, at least that communion had blood. And I could serve it myself. Here's the thing, Liberté, everyone knows about the bonga-bonga with…Ted…but no one knows the real crime!"

Somehow fearful for the next disclosure, Liberté leaned forward, shut her mouth and listened. The God cuckler continued, "Those assholes threw us out, Liberté."

"What? Who?"

Sarah poured another glass. "Uh-huh. Out! They excommunicated the whole damn lot of us. We're supposed to get off the property by the end of the week. Every one of us. Me? Maybe they should have, I don't know. I mean, their own Lord and savior was a lot easier on sinners but who knows. But Marie? She's almost eighty for the love of...oops. Sorry." More libations, then, "apparently they think we're some kind of schismatic sect down here because we thought it might be nice to throw a funeral for Therese!"

"What the hell are you talking about?"

"Ever since the old...you know, got...you know, it's been "do this" and "don't do that." They're vile. Why can't we have a memorial? Why shouldn't we have a funeral? Who does that hurt? I mean, we saw her dead body with that thing stuck in her...you know! We saw the blood!"

Up came the hands, out came the tears. The sobbing stopped as quickly as it had started. Sarah became very calm, but also very white. "Everybody here has been so nice. Everybody there has been so... unchristian. I don't know what it is, but I know what it isn't."

Ever the cop, Liberté thought she knew what it might be...some sort of cover up, after the fact. She didn't tell her friend. "Sarah, how did you find out you were evicted? Excommunicated?"

"I'll tell you, but there's something else you don't know. You know the old nun, the Mother Superior, Marie?"

"Uh-huh."

"She told me she was going to step down and that I was to take over as Mother Superior. I knew something was up...hadn't been away from her for days, except for the, you know...with Ted. So after I got back, Marie, Mother Superior, comes to my room. She told me she found out about the...sex. It was amazing! She didn't condemn me, or get angry, or anything. She just sat down on the bed and hugged me. Then she told me she was proud of me, and that God was clearly sending both of us a message. I didn't have any idea what she was talking about. Then she told me the archbishop's guy, the deacon, had phoned and that he just told us that a decision had come directly from Rome that our whole order was schismatic and we were out. She said it was a Latin term but it meant we had been excommunicated…thrown out of the church. He told her he couldn't elaborate, because if he did, he could get himself excommunicated too. He told us that the archbishop had tried to get us some sort of hearing, but they, Rome, had said it didn't matter; they hadn't excommunicated us, we had excommunicated ourselves. As some sort of concession they gave us a couple of days to get off the property. I have no idea what I'm going to do."

Liberté was in shock. She had brought her erstwhile friend and witness down here to corner her about the sex thing, to find out what was between Ted and Sarah. This new disclosure pushed that way to the back of her mind. Was what she was hearing something from a bad novel, or was this evidence? How should she treat this woman, as a friend in need or as a material witness now vulnerable enough to talk? Liberté knew that she was way over the line, that she had breached protocol, and might be compromising the whole case. She opted for human. "We…you…will get through this. Just have faith"

Sarah looked at her like she was nuts, "In what?"

"Yourself. Me. The law. The people here will help you. What are you going to do? What about the nuns?"

Sarah began to weep. The nuns were on the street because of her… if Rome had the computer, no one gets ex-anything. She alone had turned one woman's murder into a possible death sentence for Ted, destitution for the women of the convent, possibly the death of Marie. There was no turning back now. If only that dough-head hadn't told his stupid sister about the fuck. So, it wasn't just her fault. "Get under control," she thought. She brought the tears to an abrupt halt. "I don't know. I have to try. I used to believe in miracles…"

"Not I," countered the cop. "My only true act of faith is driving on a two-lane highway. But you can count on my help, for whatever that is worth."

Sarah took another sip of her wine, and then continued, "So, we're sitting there on my bed, and Marie tells me I haven't broken any vows because they were no longer valid because I wasn't a Catholic anymore. I told her my vows were to God, but she said this was all a sign from

God, that he had wakened something in me because I had more work—a special assignment."

"Are you kidding? Do you actually believe that?"

"I don't know what else to believe. Mother...I mean Sister Marie, see, she thinks I'm the Mother Superior now...she begged me for help. She told me she was too old and this was all too much. That I was the person sent from God to save the Order, and the sex...He wanted me to rebel...He made me do it, so I would be unbound from the Church and ready to do his bidding...not theirs."

"So...are you...?"

"Going to stay? Right now I have no idea. It's not like I have anyplace else to go, and we don't have to leave the place until the end of the week. I guess this little town, Ophrah, is going to be about as sympathetic to me...us...as any other place on God's Green Earth. Maybe I can get help."

The cop looked her up and down. In her opinion, her friend needed support, not a reasoned argument on signs from heaven. She said, "I hope you stay Sarah. I think you will make this work. Shit, I don't know, maybe it *was* a sign from God. They keep saying he works in mysterious ways. He asked his own son to die for us, so how bad is it for him to ask you to put out for some old fat guy?"

They both laughed.

"You know," started Sarah, "I'm really not that stupid. I know the world has been around for more than twenty minutes! All those bones and things...human spines looking a lot like fish spines..."

Then it was Liberté's turn. "Evolution for sure, but the rest of that crap...I tell you...science this and science that. So what do they know?"

"A lot?"

"They. Who are "they," anyway? Some article in the Herald the other day was talking about the "God particle," if you can believe it."

"Believe in what?"

Liberté drained her glass, ordered another bottle, and continued, "Good question! Those assholes spend billions, enough money to feed all of Africa for about a century...how does money feed everyone anyway? They use all this money to build some kind of accelerator so they can smash little...I mean *really little*...particles, smaller than atoms, so they can find something that...I don't know...gives weight or mass or whatever to everything in the fucking universe."

Sarah helped herself to another slurp from her glass, replenished it from the newly arrived replacement bottle, and quipped, "Is there a point in there somewhere?"

"Damn right there is. Your people...well, your old people... tell you to trust them, have faith, they know there's heaven and hell and God but they can't prove it."

"That's your point? How drunk are we?"

"Quiet. I'm not finished. See, the science guys tell you to trust them, and have faith, they know there isn't a heaven or hell or God...but now they say they actually only know about, like, five percent of whatever the universe is. The rest is all..." At this point Liberté got all conspiratorial and, leaning across the table, whispered, "Dark. Dark matter and dark energy...I love it...they don't know what it is so it's dark."

"Wow. Get you drunk and you go all professorial..."

"Listen to me my naughty little nun. Your people are just like my people. Its trust the system, trust the cops, trust the government...we know what's right. Secrets of God, my ass. How about all the secrets our own, let me remind you, our open government, has and won't tell us because it would be bad for us to know. Science doesn't know. Priests don't know. But we're all supposed to have faith. I say fuck 'em."

The redhead raised her glass to toast, and the two glasses met with a clink. The cop continued, "That reminds me. I'm sitting here with a chaste young bride of Christ who just did the nasty, and I haven't been laid in months! I'm starting to lose faith in men, too!"

They went quiet then. Liberté paid the bill, and the two staggered back to their own corners.

CHAPTER 17

Fortunately Sarah had been tipsy as opposed to drunk when she and Liberté had left Sharky's. When she got to the doomed convent Marie was waiting to inform her that at dinner that night, Marie would bestow the mantle of power upon Sarah, and would, at the same time, explain the current reality of "things". Sarah remonstrated for time to think, but the old gal intoned, "God built the world in seven days, Sarah. Time is not our ally. You'll know soon enough if you're going to fail. You won't fail. You…we…are in God's hands."

Dinner was awkward; there were many questions, and no answers.

Crises alter people. The ladies of the convent had all had their lives turned upside down and were facing the perils of unemployment and homelessness as well as divorce from the institution that was life for each, but remained surreally calm. Maybe it was shock. Maybe it was the change from Marie at the helm to Sarah. Maybe they agreed with

Marie's theory that Sarah's tryst was preordained, a sign and not a violation. Whatever, they agreed to play out the string at least until eviction day. Then they prayed and went straight to their beds to sleep deeply in the knowledge they were being watched out for.

While they slept, their new leader fretted.

By morning she had framed the bits of thoughts that had invaded her sleep piece-meal into, if not a plan, then at least an immediate course of action.

Her first call was to the office of the mayor of Ophrah, asking for a meeting as soon as possible. She planned to sell him on the merits of the order as part of the town infrastructure of care and education, and would throw a caretaker role for an on-site shrine into the deal. All that the town had to do was buy the property. It was a long shot, but it was worth a try, and a hell of a lot better than hanging around and doing nothing.

She then placed calls to the diocese offices of Baptists and Presbyterians in Miami, Naples, and Tampa.

She made all her calls before 8 a.m. Now it was 10 a.m. The phone rang. Sarah felt her heart pound with hope, took a deep breath, crossed her fingers, and picked it up.

"Hello, this is Sister Sarah,"

Clearly, it wasn't the mayor. The voice at the other end was husky and accented, definitely not American. Maybe German or Swiss. It identified itself only as "Floyd, a real estate person who was acting for a group interested in the property at 2200 O'Neill." The voice asked if they might meet, and if it was talking to the person who could speak for the convent. She told the voice that the Archdiocese owned the property, but the voice insisted on a meeting.

The knot in her stomach and the sudden flash of heat in her neck spoke to the stakes here. Was this voice a threat or an opportunity? Who was this and why? "Who are you acting for Floyd? It is Floyd, right?"

The voice confirmed its name, denied further information, and proposed the expedient of a coffee and thirty-minute chat. It was not necessary to meet at O'Neill Street, in fact, it was preferable not to. The knot grew tighter. Why would someone calling about property not want to see it? And why then not at Sharky's right here in Ophrah? She sensed risk, but knew she must take it. He could be a good thing for the Sisters, and how bad could it be anyway? She agreed to meet him for coffee the next morning at Mario's on Key Street on Marco Island. It was only twenty minutes away and it was public enough that she could feel safe.

The mayor never did call, and Sarah spent the day dreaming up scenarios of how to raise capital. She had no idea about finance, but kept playing with assumptions and numbers anyway, trying to make the 30 acres worth much more if she could plot some sort of development around a shrine to Therese.

She was dealing with the crushing stress of impending doom, too. In a matter of days, the Diaspora would be on; the sisters scattered to the wind like chafe from the grinding mill of the men's club in Rome. Forget the dramatic or wonderful literary references, she had told herself a dozen times. Find a way to keep them fed and sheltered, then find a raison d'être for them to continue to exist, and sell whoever on both. She would deal with the future later; for right now, she would keep the bread and the roof.

She couldn't call Catholics, because while they might be sympathetic, they could risk their own excommunication, and many who might help would turn their backs when facing personal risk. She spent the day contacting schools and hospitals, to discuss working relationships. Every call ended with, "Sounds interesting, this will take time, let me get back to you." Death by a thousand cuts, she thought.

Marie had finally showed up at 2:30, whereupon Sarah updated her and asked if she could make the meeting with this Floyd fellow. The car would be available but the ex-Mother Superior would not. Sarah would be flying solo.

Next morning, Sarah rose earlier than usual, shoved back some cereal with fruit, washed it down with a cup of tea, and sallied forth.

She arrived at Mario's just before nine, circled the place twice, then parked across Key Street from the front door and waited. She wanted to scope Floyd out before introducing herself, not something her head had told her to do. It was her stomach that so commanded. There was this "it's too good to be true" thing of her childhood that made her doubtful. There was the graphic specter of Therese's ravaged and slaughtered carcass. There was the desperation of this situation. There was the practical brain of an intelligent person in unknown territory. She would get there early and take a look at Floyd, make some final decisions when choice still played a role. So she waited for him to appear, absently wondering how she would know that it was him.

She soon realized the flaw in her plan. She had chosen Mario's because she knew it was a hot spot. Lots of people were to have been her protection. But lots of people have to arrive, and in so doing, they destroyed her plan of a pre-sighting. It would be hopeless to pick him out of the crowd. The next best option, she thought, would be to get seated early, pick the seat with all the best options. At a quarter of ten she made her move. As she locked the door and turned toward the restaurant, she came face to face with a gentleman who extended his hand and said, "Good morning Sister. I'm Floyd. Let's get some coffee and chat."

Both shaken and stirred, she made a quick assessment. The most remarkable thing about Floyd was how unremarkable he was. Average height and weight. Dressed like every other mid 40s businessman in dress slacks and loafers, with dress shirt open at the neck. He was neither too gaudy nor too staid. His brown hair combed, but not plastered. Wristwatch and wedding band. No neck bauble. No other jewels. But his eyes were dark, intelligent, knowing, and piercing. He had an accent, but not English, something European, but not French. Maybe Italian. This flashed through her mind in the instant of the handshake, and she thought to herself, "What am I? Some kind of spy?" She was immediately comfortable with the fact that she was in no personal danger with this man, but the knot continued. She realized she was tense from the anticipation of something good now, and not for fear of something bad. She began to enjoy this little adventure.

His golf hat lay upside down on the table cradling car keys and sunglasses. The hat covered but did not conceal the legal-sized bulky envelope that lay beneath it.

It struck her that Floyd had usurped her plan; he had come early, picked a table, then cut her out of the herd. Her subconscious also noted it was easier for him to hunt her down than the reverse, as she still wore the habit.

Floyd gestured, and they sat. Before anything was said the waitress showed up with two iced teas. After the standard "Y'all call me if you need anything," she took her leave and the dance began.

He was very direct. "Sister Sarah, thank you for coming. I can assure you it was a good decision. Fate has it that our paths have crossed."

Her silence screamed to get on with it, and he did. "My task here today, Sister Sarah, is first of all to make you my friend. I bear gifts." With that he pushed the envelope across the table and proposed that she open it.

There were two documents, and as she realized what she was looking at, her spine tingled while her eyes grew wide. One document was the deed of ownership to 2200 O'Neill Street and the other a mortgage in the amount of $280,000. She did not recognize the new owner's name. She looked up questioningly, and the man who was beginning to look more remarkable continued. "Sister Sarah, you are safe in your home. This deed means you can stay where you are for as long as you wish. The mortgage means you have to pay us...me...for it one day, whenever."

No fool, Sarah asked, "Why? What do I...we...have to do? Who are you?"

"I will explain. Sandwich?"

The sandwich could wait. "Please, explain."

"Of course. Nobody gives things like this away to strangers. I just want you to listen. For listening to me, you have the property. You will pay us when you can. It is of no account. Please, will you listen?"

In her mind she said, "Duh?" but that translated to, "Yes, of course."

"Good. Thank you. Do you know the story of Gideon? Ruth?"

"The ones in the Bible?"

"Those ones."

"Sort of. I mean, we do Bible studies, but it's more New Testament." He gestured to cut her off.

"Sister, Ruth was a poor woman, apparently abandoned by pretty much everyone. She was a widow at a time when widows had bleak prospects. She was told to go her own way, but decided to be loyal, in her case to her mother-in-law. She was not Jewish, but her husband had been and so was the mother-in-law. Ruth stuck with the mother-in-law, and she went on to become the progenitor of our David and your Jesus. She became known as a "Jew-by-choice." She is a heroine in the Lutheran Christian Church. I think you can become a modern Ruth."

Sarah had no idea what this sort of good-looking man was talking about, and she felt the nervousness that people feel when in close proximity to insane strangers, but there was the reality of the deed. "What are you talking about?"

"I guess I sound sort of nuts," he chuckled. She waited. He continued, "Right now all you need to know is that I am your friend." He pointed to the documents. She nodded. "Good. We want to be your friend because we think you can help us."

"Who is 'us'?"

"This is all about Gideon, Sarah. God wanted Gideon to help him and had to convince him that he could do it..."

"So now I'm Gideon? I thought I was Ruth. Are you God?"

"No and no. You're Ruth."

"And the deed is...?"

He laughed gently. "OK, so I tell you the story, right?" She nodded. "So, this Gideon is minding his own business and God shows up. Wants him to smite the Midianites. Gideon is unwilling, but God shows him a sign...once he makes the dew fall everywhere but on the fleece, once the other way round.

"I don't smite people. I'm not ever, ever going to be Gideon."

"Understood. That is not your job. You're Ruth, but you're being asked to help Gideon. Please, just listen. After I finish, you ask, I answer. OK?" She nodded. "There has been stuff going on for a long time now. When your Sister Therese was murdered, things accelerated. I don't think she was in anybody's plan like this, but things got out of hand. There's a lot of money at stake, and Therese had a computer that may be the key to it. We know you were the first to find the poor woman, and we know you are now in charge over there."

"How do you know?"

"Later. For now, we know. This is a very big opportunity for you Sarah. Tell me whatever you want, and I will help you to get it. I just need that computer, and you either know where it is, or you can help us to find it. No way the murderer took it."

Now quite unsure of herself, Sarah ventured, "I don't even know you. That computer is so important? I have to betray my own church…"

"But Sarah, it is not your church. They have betrayed you!"

"So I help you and you pay me? Does that make me some kind of whore? What are you going to do with the computer? How much will you pay? How far will you go? What if I don't help?"

"If you don't help, too bad. Keep the place. No hard feelings. We will find that thing, but this would have been cleaner. If you don't help, you will miss one of the greatest opportunities in your life."

She shrugged, but she didn't leave. It was he who rose to leave. "So think about it. I will call you tomorrow at nine in the morning to make a second meeting. You will say yes or no." With this he reached into his pocket and produced an envelope, which he handed to her, saying, "If tomorrow is a yes, then you will need some getting-around money, and even for food for your new home. This is a debit card. The chip code is 007007. It is already activated. I want you to use it now to pay for this, while I am here, so if there is a problem, you don't get stiffed. OK?"

Sarah learned the intricacies of electronic money and they parted. All she could think of was Marie's comment about signs from God.

For her entire life she had been a perfect little Catholic, but there were no signs. In the last couple of days, bang! Signs everywhere. This handsome devil had just solved the immediate problem...number one on her list...food and shelter for her little flock. And he had intimated there could be more. He thought she might know where the computer was? Ha! She knew exactly where it was. But she was damned if she was going to tell him before she knew the price he was willing to pay. She began to think she was pretty good at all this stuff.

After the nun drove away, Floyd typed a brief report into his secure blackberry and pinned, "Got her. She took the card."

CHAPTER 18

Floyd had been correct. Had she been a fish, then the hook was in but not irretrievably so.

The night of her meeting with Floyd, Sarah dreamt the same fish dream several times, each with a different ending. Once she broke free of the hook and swam in circles around the boat while the fisherman, played by Floyd, hollered that he meant her no harm. Once she conceded and entered the boat, only to realize she was to be gaffed. Once she came close enough to see him eyeing her with an evil grin and a threatening net. Another version had her flopping around in the bottom of the boat, gasping for oxygen, while he meditated on what to do next. In one dream, Floyd was giving a speech to a large number of people from up on a mountain, as audience members feasted on fish he parsed out. In the only dream with a happy ending, she was a large fat fish lazily swimming in a beautiful aquarium, watching Floyd prepare and spread her food on to the water.

In the morning the poor fish went for a swim in her not-so-private shower, wondering if she were in heaven or on her way to hell. As she prepared to meet the day, she felt the need to put on the best presentation of herself as possible. Absently, while reflecting on her youthful face, she reminded herself that vanity was a sin. Just a little one, not even requiring of confession, but one step away from the grace she used to strive to achieve as recently as a few days ago. Her eyes welled at the enormity of what she had wrought on the convent. Those eyes cleared immediately as she intuited risk in going further with Floyd. With that, came a new, warm sensation; earthy, visceral tumescence. The woman in the mirror smiled a tiny acknowledgement with lips and eyes. The nun felt no guilt, and found pleasure in that fact alone.

By 8:15 a.m., Sarah was at her desk, trying to read her USA Today, but more than anything else, she was staring at the telephone. She noted absently how anticipation might be the answer to immortality; time moves so slowly when one waits so anxiously for it to pass.

At 9 on the nose, the thing jangled. About to yank it to her ear, an inner devil made her stop. He could wait…but not for too long. For this brief instant he was the fish and she the fisherman. She wanted that fish badly. Three rings were enough! "Hello."

"Hello Sister Sarah, or Ruth, or Gideon's girl." He laughed a bit and she joined. Ice broken, he continued, "So, we meet again?"

"We do."

"I think you would very much like the La Cote restaurant at the Fontainebleau Miami Beach Hotel. I have booked a table for us for one o'clock this afternoon. For now it is better that we not be seen together in Ophrah. If you can take a car from the Convent, then please, fill it with the card. If not, then go to National on Marco and pick one up. Just mention my name to Jerry, and he will give you one."

Such intrigue! On the spot she decided that this fish wanted the comfort of her own boat. "That's fine. I'll meet you at one o'clock, but it's OK, I have my own car."

It would take ninety minutes, at the outside, to Miami which meant departure at 11 a.m. just to be sure. With the better part of two hours to kill, Sarah decided on a walk to the swamp. Upon arrival she plunked herself on the bench, twisted to de-kink her neck, and slipped into thought.

Her thoughts were random, and they careened and crowded each other. There was Ted, then Floyd, Sister Marie, then Liberté. She thought about blood-soaked Therese and that knife, about Loyola and herself now as pariah to her church, then how her only sin before the Ted rape was protection of Mother Church property. She wondered what her Dad would have said had he still been alive. She thought about how Sister Marie had just dumped survival on her, then those first seconds with Therese, doubting that first decision. She had a vision of the laptop rent by multitudinous hands, torn as on a torture rack, gushing blood, then transubstantiated to a grand, nutritious fish. Her throat closed, sweat became profuse, tears came, vertigo struck.

She couldn't do this. Maybe it wasn't too late. She must stop this. There would be no Miami. The little theft, the Rubicon...not irrevocable...this man...this Floyd...he would own her...

Sarah rose and began her walk away from the abyss, toward the civilization of the convent, first gingerly because of the slippery slope, then decidedly rapid, finally in a panicked trot. Upon arrival she called Ted, instructing him to meet her at Sharky's at noon. She would explain, release, enlist, rely.

As always, an ambivalently placed call is always answered. Ted was keen, solicitous, excited. The confused and compromised fish felt out of water, but agreed to meet her tool-from-God, subconsciously aware she was using him again, yet was unsure to what purpose.

Alone now, and in no great rush, Sarah engulfed herself in psychoses of guilt, fear, and self-loathing. She despised her computer secret, her act of rebellion, her scheming self. Was Marie correct that she was an instrument of God? Is this how God's favored, Moses, Jonah, and Gideon felt? Blessed to be his servant was horrid. She remembered Floyd's reference to a great opportunity. The dark spell lightened.

How much might that thing be worth? Who else might show up in search of it, how much less graceful might they be? Why should she protect Church assets? Could she ever go back? Did she want to? Why was Ted so stupid? Did his stupidity make her responsible for him? How could she just take the deed to 2200 O'Neill and not even hear Floyd out? What had he meant when he said that if she wouldn't help then he would find another way? Was he threatening her when he suggested that playing ball would keep it all cleaner? Notwithstanding anything Marie had said, was her unconfessed sex now a mortal sin? How could she be sure she was acting for God? Was she already damned for all of eternity?

While thus engaged, and having decided to eschew the Floyd meeting, Sarah began preparing anyway.

Faced with what to wear, she despised her choices, feeling like an isolated frump. She didn't belong here anymore and was ill prepared for anywhere else, most assuredly not at the Fontainebleau.

Standing before the mirror, working her once-legendary tresses to moderately civilized, Sarah fantasized about how she didn't need the debit card and would never use it.

At 11, long before her Ted assignation, frumpy Sarah slid behind the wheel of her equally frumpy nun-mobile, headed north toward Tamiami Trail, then turned east toward her only future. At the first gas station outside Ophrah, she filled up, using the debit card.

At the instant of payment, an electronic signal of "account balance change" was initiated in the bowels of an Interac center, causing a red light to blink unrelentingly on the blackberry on Floyd's belt. Within seconds of Sarah's purchase, Floyd was aware of the event, the location, and amount.

Sarah found her way through the morass of Miami traffic, searching while driving for her turn onto Arthur Godfrey, thence left at Indian Creek to Collins Avenue and onto the grounds of the Fontainebleau.

During the entire trip, Sarah thought not once of Ted, who now waited patiently, excitedly, for her in a booth at Sharky's.

As she shut the frump-mobile down, Ted crossed her mind. She shrugged, and continued on her new adventure.

Feet now on the ground, she took a good look around. Four towers, 1,500 rooms, 22-acres, a $1 billion makeover; this was the epitome of wealth and hedonism. There was security everywhere. She knew she was out of place, and thought of leaving, then realized she was here for the money, not for the good times.

Daddy's maxim "Head up, tummy in, chest out, shoulders back" came to her. She squared herself, and felt the confidence of purpose infuse her every fiber. She might not quite fit in, but she sure as hell belonged!

The trip from car to building involved the usual rubberneckers. They looked her up and down with the thoroughly modern disrespect for privacy that women, foreigners, and religious cultists constantly endure. For the first time since her early days as an acolyte it bothered her.

She entered the lobby and was lost. She almost asked directions from three different people, but two were of the unapproachable business category and the third looked like a drug lord just up from South or Central America.

While contemplating the relative merits of using the cell phone versus asking in person, she felt a tap on her shoulder. She knew without turning. Floyd. They had a moment of marvelous awkwardness as he went to shake her hand and she to give him the traditional peck on both cheeks.

The maître d' took them to a lovely table by the window, and after the fuzz of bread, water, and drink order they sat face to face in a gulf of silence. She went first, "This is very exciting. I mean, this place is so… gorgeous! Not what I'm used to."

Floyd smiled, "I have a feeling you will get quite used to this way of life. Wine?"

"Hmmm. My Lord and savior certainly believed in wine. It's there in just about every story in the New Testament, and he never made a major statement without wine in the deal. Yes please. Please, you choose."

He got a bottle of Mouton Cadet...elegant, but not crass. After the de rigueur testing, they touched glasses in a silent salute, and each savored the delicious burn of the blood of the grape. Then he began, "So Sarah, I am glad that we may work together. Today I will tell you some more about what's what."

She ventured, "Will this be dangerous?"

He laughed, "No."

"Illegal?"

This time he laughed, but instead of a direct answer, came back with, "Please, I will explain. You see, your Sister Therese was killed because something went wrong in a plan that has been hatching for many years now."

Just as he drew breath to really get into it, their cone of isolated concentration was shattered. Waiters don't wait; they break in, and almost always at an inopportune moment. With good grace, Floyd led Sarah through the intricacies of the menu, and they agreed on two orders of sautéed snapper with warm lentil salad and salsa Genoese, watched the waiter disappear into the kitchen, and then turned back towards each other. Floyd continued, "There is a plan to steal a great deal of money from the Catholic Church..."

"You want me to steal money from the Church?"

"No sister. We are going to steal it from the man who steals it from the Church."

"But you're not giving it back to them are you? If you were we wouldn't be talking, would we? You'd just call the church, whoever that is, and tell them about the robbery before it happens. Right?"

"True." He didn't flinch, and she didn't leave.

"So?" she asked.

"So, we think maybe about $8 billion, perhaps 10, Sarah."

"Jeezus, Mary and Joseph! Oops. Sorry."

Floyd laughed, "For that much money I expected more!"

Her brief flush of embarrassment faded quickly and she asked him to continue. Just as he did, the waiter arrived again and with grand flourish, presented the food and left. She ate while he talked.

"OK...so there are a lot of people who think they have legal claims against your, er, ex-church. These people can't get anywhere in any kind of court...they can't sue because they aren't sovereign states, but the Holy See is; so we thought we would take the money from the thief and use it to settle those claims.

"Who is 'we'? What claims? The sex stuff?"

"No Sarah. We are going to settle old claims against the Church that arose out of World War II and Nazi atrocities. You know your old friends were implicated, don't you?"

"I've heard, read, don't really know...of course, I got a lot of one side and not so much of the other you know."

"Fair enough."

"So where do I fit in? Who are you?"

"I cannot give you details, Sarah, but I can tell you that I am not working alone."

She sat transfixed. Every instinct told her to run, but her brain told her to stay. If "they" could sue when the others couldn't, "they" were a sovereign state. A state that knows what everyone is doing. So, if this guy is working for that state and is planning to steal something, then he had to be a Goddamn spy. All his "Ruth" and "Gideon" stuff!

Now comfortable with her expanded lexicon, Sarah cut him off. "Holy shit! You're Gideon...you're a spy...you're those people that kill terrorists, what do they call them? The Mossad?"

Floyd sat impassively during this predictable epiphany. "I can neither confirm nor deny that. What I can tell you is that we know all about the plan to rob the Church, where the money is and how to get it. But we don't know all the details about how to use it to properly compensate our people who got screwed by your people...to settle those claims, you know. That info is in the computer. Your Sister Therese recorded every detail of the provenance of all the art and all the artifacts at the Vatican, and a chunk of it was stolen from Jews during the Holocaust."

"So you steal the money from some guy, and the computer? So you use their money to buy claims so you can sue them for more money? And you use their info in their computer to make the case when you do sue them?"

"Sarah, just please listen. We will give you all the details you need, but for now, here is what you need to know right this minute."

His tone had changed. It wasn't threatening, but it was steely. She suddenly felt small. She sat back in her chair silently, and waited for him to continue.

He did, "See, Sister Therese is the key. We think that she found out what we had known for years. The thief was stealing here and there, but hadn't done the big job. That was his mistake, making the little thefts. We know he was pilfering odds and sods of stuff, fencing it through Switzerland. We think he just got unlucky...that Therese figured it out, maybe came across something that she knew was supposed to be in storage or control...out on that loan program of the Vatican. He had no choice. Just a tiny thread can unravel the whole thing. He kills her and makes it look like a weirdo...then he kills the weirdo."

"You knew he was going to kill Sister Therese?"

"We...no."

"So you know everything about everything, but not that? Could you have stopped the murder?"

Floyd looked straight into her eyes. "No, and this is not productive. Her murder was a sudden change. We were going to take the computer, but only when she had done all the work. We didn't keep a 24-hour watch because we knew she wasn't going anywhere. We weren't there and we didn't know. We could not have saved that woman. Got it?"

Sarah sensed the truth but not the whole truth, so decided to change her tack. She now knew that she was dealing with very tough people on all sides; survival and prosperity meant caution. "Who in the name of God can just scarf stuff from the Vatican vaults? Who has the ability to steal the kind of money you're talking about?"

"Just one man, Sarah."

"Who?"

"I cannot tell you that. That would put you in harm's way."

A cold chill passed through the ex-nun. "So I name my price and help you sue my ex-employer, and to rob a guy that you say is thieving murderous scum?"

"No to the last part. Yes to the rest. Can you help us find that computer?"

Another transfixed moment. Sarah realized her next words would chart an irrevocable path. The thrill of fear mixed with the excitement of the game and made her feel more alive than she had ever felt before. "Maybe."

"OK. That's it for now. I tell you what I think, you are very smart, and really very badly dressed. I want you to finish up and then go get some decent clothes. Use the card. I will call you tomorrow at 9 a.m. and you can tell me if you want to go further. Right?"

And then he left.

Sarah sat for some time staring out the window, her mind a whir, her stomach in riot. She knew she was being managed. Was she the mouse and he the cat? Or were they just equals and she at an initial disadvantage? He was lavishing money on her. She must have cards. All she had to do was betray the sacred trust of her...what were they? It's all well and good to intellectualize the break that excommunication means, but it's quite another to live it. Sarah had an entire life wrapped up in the church, and deep down inside, was beginning to understand that her problems with her church were somehow part of what this spy was flirting with her about. She was being tested. Did God send her a sign that she should rebel, as Marie had said, or was all this to find out how moral she was, and if she was a truly good person? Was this temptation or duty?

One thing Sarah did know was that the past few days had been the most exciting of her life, and she had loved that. The way forward, with this spy Floyd, would bring more excitement. If she turned her back on him, and she didn't end up dead or in jail, then what waited was the humdrum of normal spiced up with the potential of starvation and loss.

Sarah came to a very self-serving conclusion: to keep playing, learn more, make a decision later. The slippery slope of indecision is itself a decision. Sarah was more excited about prospects going forward than she was fearful.

The habit had to go. She shouldn't look like a nun if she wasn't one and wasn't acting like one. If she was into devious dealings she probably should dress differently so she wouldn't stand out like a sore thumb.

Sarah placed the card on the table in the standard signal that she wanted to settle up. When she was advised that the bill had already been taken care of, she left.

On her way through the lobby she stopped, and on a whim, asked the concierge for directions to the nearest Niemen Marcus. She repeated the directions twice, and when he confirmed that she had them straight, drove directly to that local chapel of the modern religion of consumer excess, where she employed the

card in pursuit of bare necessities including two blouses, a skirt, jeans, a pair of flats and a pair of modest pumps. Then, getting into the spirit of this adventure, she filled out the mini-wardrobe with some very modest stockings and some highly immodest underthings...after all, she had thought, spies aren't spies without a few secrets. She finished up by buying a couple of the patent leather, big-buckle belts, one black, one red, that she had so admired since she was a child.

As each purchase was consummated, electrons darted. When a decent period passed after the last electron wave, Floyd sent on a message of his own: "the fish is in the net."

CHAPTER 19

Sarah went online to search "Israeli Secret Service." Back came "Mossad." Like the CIA, they actually have a website. Unlike the CIA, which sports a good guy facade with kids' games and useful information about places world-wide, the Mossad's website is brutally to the point. It was started in 1949 with a guiding motto taken from Proverbs 24:6: "For by wise guidance you can wage your war." It has a fearsome track record of bloody successes along with horrendous grisly errors, and an overt distain for international convention and law.

The website left others to detail its storied, violent past, declaring it could neither confirm nor deny tales of specific exploits. Sarah gasped at the disclaimer, because word for word, it was what had come from Floyd's mouth during the Fontainebleau lunch.

The screen shared some successes, such as prior recon that gave the Jewish air force its walk-off home run obliterating Egypt's air force in the first hours of the Six Day War. On the other end was Lillehammer, with six Mossad agents arrested after assassinating a waiter mistaken for a terrorist. There were reports of Nazis kidnapped in Europe, South America, and Africa that may or may not have been moral but were one hundred percent illegal. There were myriad assassinations, terrorists and others like the Canadian developer of a Super Gun for Saddam Hussein in "Operation Babylon." Ships sunk that may or may not have carried yellow cake from whence come nuclear bombs. French soil blown to bits in a Toulouse raid on a manufacturer of what might be an Iraqi reactor. A British citizen literally and figuratively "screwed" by a Mossad temptress who, as part of a team, kidnapped and smuggled him out of Britain so he could face Israeli charges of treason.

The Mossad on one hand, attempted theft of American nuclear secrets, while on the other alerted the USA to what became "9/11."

These people sent letter bombs to presumed terrorists without regard for collateral damage.

Forget justice. Mossad existed to terrorize terrorists.

No wonder Floyd chose the story of Gideon. In that tale, a small but dedicated group of well-trained, ruthless warriors did in an invading force of Midionites. She fully understood his message; if you are our enemy we will kill you by surprise. If you happen to be standing beside someone we choose to kill, then you're going to get dead too.

There seemed always to be proof of the deed but not the doer. Sarah recalled a recent news article detailing the morning rush hour explosive death of an Iranian nuclear physicist. In traffic, a motorcyclist assassin attached a magnetized bomb designed to explode inward. They were clearly OK with collateral damage.

She realized with chilling clarity they would kill at the drop of a hat; and would be ultra-pragmatic about the well-being of friends. Perhaps a lifeline if it didn't slow or inconvenience them. You didn't want to be on their shit list, but being on *any* of their lists was cause for concern.

"Secrets," she uttered aloud, and then continued in silent thought..."Everything is secret". Her old boss, the Vatican, markets the secret of life everlasting, while keeping its every move among the living a secret too. No fly lists are secret. Securities investigators don't tell witnesses that they aren't being investigated.

Most interviews with power centers or their minions end in disclaimers that the public is better off not knowing.

"Well," she thought, "I have a secret too. A big one. I don't know who else it helps but me. God knows who it will hurt. But I'm not telling anyone my secret until I get what I can!"

Then, as was her wont after a firm decision forward, came doubt.

If Mossad actions were directed against threats, why were they messing with the Catholic Church? More important, what would they do with, or to, her after her utility?

Also her wont, she was fearful, but also more alive than ever with a fierce tumescent fire, libido redirected, horniness of the jungle. She remembered the time she was hunting with her dad; watching the stag die, its eyes go lifeless, how she had felt both exhilarated and dirty. This was the same exhilaration now but not the least bit dirty.

She prayed. Not for divine inspiration to arrest her smoldering life force, but quite the opposite. Sarah thanked God for the gift of Floyd.

At that instant Sarah realized she had never properly been a nun. There could be no rapprochement.

Opportunity only knocks so often, and the sovereign State of Israel asking you to help possibly the finest "just do it" force on Earth ought to be viewed as such.

Of course, she reasoned, recognizing the knock was one thing, taking advantage quite another. She must figure out how best to help herself while being useful to them, and to do so in a manner that wouldn't come back to bite her.

Really, what could they want from her? It probably was just the computer. So she should withhold it as long as possible.

Peripatetic; she felt one minute euphoria, the next, paroxysmal fear.

Surely just one of their recon jobs! No, if this was about the computer, then they planned to have it. What had they said on their website? "...we encourage initiative, creativity, resourcefulness, and daring..." This had to be all of those. They didn't buy the property and then deed it over to her, well them, out of the goodness of their hearts. And they knew to do it so quickly; the ink on the excommunication wasn't dry when Floyd first called.

What if they found out that Ted knew about it? Damn, she never should have told him. Ted was a problem now, an impediment, a risk, maybe even a fatal flaw. She concluded that she had to make the play worth the risk and she had to move as far away from Ted as possible.

Back in bed. Lolling in tension-induced sweat, and coddling the sense of adventure, Sarah returned to the question Floyd evaded at lunch. "Had he…they…known enough, and early enough to have saved Therese?"

She understood from the website that Mossad missions were more important than random bystander salvation, which is what the entire convent must be to Floyd. She knew she had to know, fearing both his answer, and her response to the sure knowledge it might bring.

Fitful sleep. Her darkest dream had her naked in her own bed, Floyd atop her with one hand on her throat, the other brandishing a military knife. Awaking with a start she shuddered, then calmed herself with the sure knowledge Floyd would just cut her throat and be done with it.

She wriggled beneath the heated excitement of Floyd and nakedness and violence and power. Sure that once in bed with the Mossad, there was no going back, Sarah reasoned. She had to make the most of it.

She laughed aloud as it struck her that when the panties came off, so did the gloves.

Now on fire, she wondered if it was the money, the risk, freedom, or Floyd? She allowed that fire to consume her, and then slept blissfully.

CHAPTER 20

The credit card was like a magic wand; she waved it, and people gave her things. Things! The very antithesis of cloistered life! That made it sweeter.

No longer a nun by either vocation or inclination, it remained her cover, and there was her obligation to Sister Marie. Well, more than just obligation. She loved those nuns in a way, and enjoyed the delicious irony of becoming their guardian angel. But she was not one of them. Never truly had been.

Showered and pampered with creams and unguents, Sarah reveled in her newest joy. Jeans pulled gently tight over buttocks, pressing, caressing, she luxuriated in self-indulgence that, for the past few decades, had been sinful. Slipping the "Texas meets Paris" leather belt into place, then locking herself in its silver buckle embrace was a riot of naughty self-indulgence. Its heft, and stiffness slipping through her hands caused her to wonder, just briefly, how much pain it could inflict.

In the last two weeks she had spent more time primping, posing, and patting before her mirror than she had in total over the past twenty years.

Now with denims covering silks, Sarah slipped on the heels, did one last half-turn-over-the-shoulder inspection of her butt, and descended through the foyer, past her flock, directly out the door. No one uttered a sound. They knew their role; and had faith that their leader knew hers.

Sarah had convened an up-date session with the ladies of the convent, explaining only that they would not have to move, that the property was for their use, and that for the foreseeable future, food would be on the table. They had cheered, prayed, and bombarded her with questions. She had given no details, but had showed them the deed. In the same way she took half-answers from Floyd, they took half-answers from her.

When Sarah left 2200 O'Neill that morning, she walked to the bus depot to catch a bus into Marco, and exited the bus just a quarter of a mile from the "National" leasing office where she used her money wand to acquire the use of the sportiest little bit of transport they had.

In no time, she aimed her one-and-a-half ton haven toward Bigliardi's Grill House, where she took a table for four so that she could spread out her copies of the New York Times and Miami Herald for front-to-back perusals.

"Just coffee, fresh squeezed O.J., and toast please."

She didn't need to be in Marco. She wasn't there to meet Floyd or anyone else. She just didn't want to be trapped at the convent. She had dreams, plans, obligations, negotiations, and issues to address. 2200 O'Neill had brought her to this point, she thought, but God, it was boring.

Sarah wasn't sure how long she would stay away, or how she would get back after returning the car. Maybe she would just keep the thing. The ladies of the convent weren't going to ask and if they did, she just had to tell them she would make it all clear soon, and to please just be patient.

Fifteen minutes in, her concentration was broken as Ted crowded into her space. "Sarah, I've tried to get to you a hundred times. What, are you hiding from me, or did you lose your phone?" he asked with a nervous laugh.

She made her point wordlessly by picking the phone up off the table, examining it, then slipping it into her purse. "Did you follow me? How did you know I was here? I drove ten miles to be alone!" Ted ignored her and just continued.

"What's with the get-up?" he asked.

"Ted, this is not a good..."

"Well then, what is?"

"I don't know. I'll call you later, maybe tonight. Right now I have to go. I have a thing, you know, to get to."

He ignored her and plunked himself down. "Who are you? Where did you get that stuff? I mean, you look great, but...you've changed."

"That's right Ted. I've changed. And I came here to be alone, to get caught up on the world, to think. If I wanted to talk to you I would have called. So..."

He could feel his dudgeon rising, "That bitch, that Liberté thinks that I—we—you know because we're in cahoots. Or not really. I mean, she thinks I've been screwing you all along so you would help me steal that computer. Sarah, for the love of God, give her the damn thing. Or tell her you've got it. Please, tell her I didn't take it. Get her off my ass. She thinks I killed Therese to cover a theft but you can prove I didn't take the thing. If she's got the computer she doesn't have a motive, and I'm free."

"You're a smart man Ted. Figure it out. Wriggle off the hook all by yourself. I can't help you."

He was stunned. "What? Why? Because of the..."

"Sex? That would be a negative Ted. I did the sex, not you. Men are all the same. You're whiny, just like Jimmy."

"Who the hell is Jimmy?"

"Jimmy? He was my first, back in Minnesota. Then he thought we were you know, lovers, and I couldn't get rid of him. I never should have done this."

"What? The sex?"

"No! I never should have been a nun. There's more..."

"Us?"

She looked at him like he was an alien. "No, not like 'us.' We're not 'us.' This was about me...and them...not you. There is no 'us.'"

"Jesus, Sarah. This isn't some kind of high school puppy love bullshit. They want to charge me with murder..."

"Can't help, Ted. There's stuff you don't understand."

"What?"

"I can't..."

"You know what, I'm going to go to that bitch and I'm going to tell her what you just said. I'm going to tell her about the computer. You won't tell me? Well, you can just deal with her."

"Do what you have to do, Ted. Just do it somewhere else. I've got other things to do." With that, she slithered herself off the bench seat, primped that little primp that girls do, and then said, over her shoulder, "And Ted, don't call me anymore." Then off she went.

He tried to cling to her, sort of between a wounded dog and a dog in heat, but she brushed him off. Her impatiently raised hand stopped him.

Wounded as he was, he was still man enough to enjoy watching her leave. Then he sat at the table she had just vacated and grasped at the crumbs and lied to himself that she hadn't left him.

Buoyed by the exchange that any normal man would have taken for what it was, Ted felt a surge of hope mixed with relief and joy. He had seen her, talked to her, made his case. She would help. He would have her again. He ordered steak and eggs, and then fingered his way through all the news in both papers without reading any of it, until he found his blessed Sudoku game.

When Ted finished his meal and game, he picked up the phone, found Liberté's number in his call history, and pressed the green button, then immediately, the red. He owed Sarah 24 hours to come to her senses, and if she hadn't by then, he would sic Liberté on her.

Sarah had left him holding the bag for her meal too. Ted took that to be a good sign.

In fact, Sarah had decided that if she did use her money wand, that that might be a clue Ted could somehow use to learn more about her and her new friend. Since she didn't have cash Sarah just told the cashier her friend would cover when he left. It was a small thing, but it made her feel deliciously bad and that made her feel deliciously happy.

She swung by National and renegotiated the lease from one day to two weeks.

CHAPTER 21

Vestments of today's Roman Catholic Church are descendants of magisterial Rome. The empire didn't die, it morphed into the Holy See of the Roman Catholic Church and spent hundreds of years protected by barbarians to whom it awarded status of Holy Roman Emperor.

In a more recent deal with the ascendant barbarian of the time, Mussolini. With neither land nor population to speak of, the Holy See gained international recognition as a state. As a country with less land than a decent golf course and fewer than four hundred passports issued, it now has formal relations with 178 countries, the European Union and Taiwan, and even a "special relationship" with the PLO. Sixty-nine sovereign states maintain diplomatic offices to the Vatican. The Holy See holds observer status at the UN and the World Trade Organization, and sits on the International Agency for Economic Development.

The man at the helm is the Bishop of Rome, a.k.a. the "Pope," but for all practical purposes it's his Secretary of State, a.k.a. "Carmerlengo" or "Prime Minister."

He is the point man in matters secular, runs the Curia, a.k.a. "the bureaucracy", and holds the reins to the money. When a Pope dies it is the Carmerlengo who first checks to see if he's really dead by tapping the corpse' head with a hammer while asking it to wake up, then keeps day-to-day operations running while the shoes of the dead fisherman get snuggled into by a successor elected in a process convened by this same Carmerlengo. The smoke and mirrors rite of passage of infallibility ends with the white smoke announcing the process complete.

The Church is big business. Excluding the parishes, it grosses around $200 million a year and spends about $130 million to operate Vatican City. Estimates of net value, ignoring the art, are in the half-billion dollar range.

The Church may be the unrecognized inventor of a commonly used business structure, the franchise. The Master Franchise, held by the Holy See, licenses God to dioceses for distribution.

Each franchise eats what it kills after piecing off the level above. So loot from the faithful flows upstream as tithes. This arrangement generates Revenue from sales of eternal salvation and related indulgences, to around 1.2 billion souls by 408 thousand priests operating out of 270 thousand parishes bundled into 2,795 dioceses for administrative purposes.

The Carmerlengo runs it all. He's the Chief Operating Officer.

Over two plus millennia, the Church of Rome has conquered monumental problems, and has occasionally been forced to barter riches now and salvation later for protection by a variety of tough guys, Charlemagne being the first made emperor. The empire has been kept intact through ruthless destruction of any not bowing to it. If they weren't crusading against Heathens, Muslims, or different versions of Christianity, they were torturing any of their own acting outside accepted script.

More recently the church swapped barbarian swords for the power of the pen. Cleansing death by fire and mutilation replaced by legal process to confuse and confound a variety of claims, rumors, lawsuits, and the occasional sectarian investigation.

Notoriety of sex scandals demand print time. As revolting as molestation by wayward priests may be, there is a more hideous history of systemic malfeasance by the organization itself, such as co-operation with sectarian tyrants and concomitant theft of property. This history includes claims of complicity in Nazi murders and attempted genocide of Orthodox Christians, Roma, and Jews; laundering and redirecting Nazis and their loot; arms smuggling; and advocating insurrection. In one celebrated event, the Church paid investors and creditors of Banco Ambrosiano $241 million in settlements while denying guilt in the failure of that bank, the hanging murder of its President Roberto Calvi, and association with the mafia and drugs.

They also have an issue with human and employment rights in the modern world. "Isms" don't appear to apply to the Church in its dealings with, for example, homosexuals and women. It would be difficult to find any other employer getting away with ordering employees not to marry, and to fork over all earthly possessions and earnings.

The Master Franchiser has established sound protective methods against vicissitudes arising from these behaviors.

These, ignoring the technique of excommunication, fall into three categories: maintain alliances with secular alphas, compartmentalize the franchise structure so when bad stuff flies it doesn't hit the Master Franchisor, and critically, use the laws of man to protect the rule of God.

The organization whose apparent purpose is to find, deal with, and be governed by "the truth" has successfully defended itself from fact-based claims with arguments such as genocide and money laundering. These are found to be not court-worthy since they are political issues, relatives and descendants of murdered people are disallowed as plaintiffs since only the dead guy has legal standing in the debate, otherwise valid claims are deemed past their "best before date", barred by statutes of limitation. Finally, as a Sovereign State, the Master Franchisor is immune to all claimants who are themselves not a State.

A key player in the recent modernization of this strategy was Father Tomas.

He understood the genius of the three-part defense well enough to craft its fundamentals into something far more efficient. Over a period of twenty years of tweaking this and altering that, he brought each parish to the edge of financial ruin and therefore not worth suing. At the same time he amassed "Settlement Trusts" in obscure creditor-proof jurisdictions, while centralizing claims management to maximize defenses and make prosecution as difficult as possible, while denying ultimate access to money pot at the end of any lawsuit rainbow. His purpose was to dis-incentivize plaintiff lawyers.

It was done meticulously, and over such a protracted period, in increments so small it was like geologic aging; everything changed while nobody noticed.

He got to keep making these changes over such a long period because a succession of Fishermen and Carmerlengos respected his genius in making and protecting money. Corporate life is like pinball. The first prize for success is another game!

CHAPTER 22

Raised in Rome backstreets, as a ward of the State, Father Tomas excelled by dint of hard work and massive intellect. As a kid he had developed an interest in art and history, which he enjoyed to the exclusion of all else except his obligations to God and Church. His was an ascetic, almost monastic, life. No one could remember seeing his apartment. Located just outside the Saint Anne's gate, it might have been expected that an occasional late work session would spill over to his place for a nightcap. He never offered. No one ever asked.

Tomas' work consumed all his time and energy. He traveled incessantly and actually kept an overnight bag packed and ready in the office so he could go wherever needed on the spur of the moment. His days typically began at 4 a.m. While ingesting raw egg, nuts, and fresh fruit washed down with Aqua Pura, Tomas digested what he could of world and investment news through the Internet and hard copy, spending little time on the popular press, instead concentrating on subscription services. Evenings were spent reading business books, industry reports, and financial statements. His washroom library was art anthologies and medieval texts, in Latin, on all subjects centered around Rome, its society, and the history of its great families.

Although he ran many billions of dollars, his only direct report had been Sister Therese.

That was by special assignment occasioned by the remarkable rotating art lease program initiated by him some twenty years earlier. Portfolios were managed by outsourced advisors, each kept alert by competition among providers. Father Tomas required absolute secrecy from each of the fact of his engagement, amount invested, and compensation arrangement. He understood the improbability of continued first quartile performance, and tended to move money into second and third quartile short-term performers, and then out again when they achieved six quarters of top quality results.

None of the money Tomas ran was identified as "Vatican" money. It was held in trusts with bland names like "Cayman III" and "Davos B." His operators did not know he was a priest, they saw him only in lay clothes, and only in business surroundings. He did not party with them. All his advisors but one were based in major business centers of the world; New York, London, Singapore, Hong Kong. Curiously, none were in Rome. No one got close. Everyone remained immediately available.

No one but Tomas knew the totality of his empire. About 35% of the wealth he controlled was publicly tradable securities, the balance in bullion, real estate, and private company shares. He professed no faith in banks or governments; so assets safekeeping was through non-traditional arrangements. Gold bullion, for which he feared confiscation in the event of some global banking melt down, he kept in a vault under the Lateran Palace, well within the walls of the Vatican itself, watched by its very own police, the Swiss Guards.

The only other person who understood the intricacies of Tomas' empire was a lawyer named Lorenzo Mitachelli, who worked alone, associated with a firm known as the Parma Partnership. The fact that he worked alone meant no leaks, yet the association provided case-specific speed.

Tomas and Lorenzo first met during mandatory service in the Italian army.

A few years ago, another of Father Tomas' army buddies had taken his own life because of a personal financial crisis, and Father Tomas had insisted on special dispensation for his burial in holy ground. When in Rome, Tomas went once a week to pray at the tomb. Both the Carmerlengo and the Pope himself had asked Father Tomas if they could help him to come to peace with the tragedy. He had been grateful, but resisted help. Nonetheless, each had taken comfort in the state of his soul his pain attested to.

Tomas was his own trusted brand, and no wonder! It was understood that money management and claims management activities were in support of saving souls; he was granted dispensation from normal priestly duties.

Sometime in the 80s things that had worked for thousands of years changed. The world had shrunk, settlements and admissions of wrongdoing damaged the Church brand as never before. A small issue in one corner of the Globe became front-page news everywhere.

Historically, individual claims and legal process were not big issues for Mother Church in and of themselves. She would out-spend on defense, outwit on process, and out-maneuver on settlement. With individual claims, you at least had the final defense of the secret settlement. Even if it cost some money, the brand wasn't hammered.

The advent of the class action lawsuit changed all that. Now Mother Church faced professional milkers who would have at her teats; these she must smother. Professional milkers, the lawyers who take the big case, do so because of a huge payday. If you could decrease the certainty of that payday they would go away! The merits of any case were what they were, so the solution didn't lie there. Making process expensive and recovery of money well nigh impossible even if you won——there was the answer.

The old system was clearly broken and the status could not remain "quo."

It had been young Tomas who saw this, had had the opportunity to properly express it, and the energy to run with it. Settlements and admissions of wrongdoing simply had to stop.

His solution was a 180-degree about-face in strategy. Instead of insulating the core, Mother Church would gird her loins to battle any and all with her own centralized crack division of legal talent. While she was at it she would make it as tough as possible for valid claimants to succeed; she would kill their claims with process. Everything would become so protracted that the news would grow old, and the reporters would find something new to rave on about.

Thus, with Tomas as midwife, a new strategy was born in three parts: effectively bankrupt the franchises so they weren't worth suing, put the wealth into creditor-proof structures and havens, and defend all claims aggressively.

When Sister Therese met her violent end and the computer had disappeared, Tomas had advised the Carmerlengo on appropriate strategy consistent with this course of action.

His logic was impeccable; with the computer unaccounted for, the less publicity the better. The less that was said, the fewer people there would be trying to find or understand it. Sister Therese's entire "family" was right there in Rome, so that is where her final farewell and resting place ought to be. America was not terribly sympathetic to the Catholic Church, so plucking heartstrings wasn't likely to be productive. However, that order of nuns could be a story, the kind of crap the weeklies feed on. Therefore the best thing, given the "starve the press" strategy, might be to dilute the story by closing the place and spreading the women all over the world.

It's like the old axiom of industrial polluters; "the solution to pollution is dilution."

Within this context everything that had happened to the poor women down there in Ophrah made sense. Not ethically or morally, but most certainly pragmatically. And more than anything else, Father Tomas was a pragmatist.

CHAPTER 23

His rise had been meteoric, starting with a single suggestion. He was the tag-along when his mentor, the Archpriest of San Giovanni Laterano and Cardinal Vicar for the Diocese of Rome, one morning twenty years ago met his life-long chum, who just happened to be the Carmerlengo, for coffee.

Perhaps due to Tomas' presence, conversation was business. Tomas had remained silent while the senior prelates discussed growing secularism and the lawsuits it brought. They talked wistfully of the old days of respect for men of the cloth and the institution. During a lull, Tomas spoke up.

With due respect, he had wondered if the cache beneath the Vatican might not represent a means to two ends: make money, gain respect. Curious about the man before him as much as about any idea he might have, the Carmerlengo encouraged the young priest to continue.

Tomas had wondered if it might not be possible to share the art and artifacts with the world at large, and in so doing promote the aura of historic worthwhile while earning fees. When it had been suggested that Rome was already chocker-block full of art, artifacts, and patrons, Father Tomas had elaborated. He didn't propose another gallery or museum in Rome. He wondered if they might make some sort of deal with galleries and museums all over the world, some sort of rotating exhibits arrangement. Those institutions would get refreshed product on loan, and Mother Church would get additional grandeur.

The plan would export grandeur to those who could not, or would not, come themselves to the Eternal City. The two senior churchmen encouraged the junior, and, emboldened, he came up with his first brilliant scheme for monetizing assets without actually selling them.

He proposed they could get some number of institutions around the globe to prepay some amount, say $1 million, to be in the rotation for some protracted period of time, say 50 years.

There was silence when he dropped that on them. It had to be investigated.

Right there, on the spot, the young cleric was seconded to the Carmerlengo's office, to test the concept. His career in money was launched.

The six-month term became "for life," and "temporary" became "permanent."

Within the six-month test period, Father Tomas had been successful enough, and had shown enough initiative, that his entrepreneurial skills were established.

Preliminary records detailing art and artifacts were hit-and-miss. A middle-aged nun teaching art history at the Sorbonne was brought in to make sense of the records, and to make the exhibits interesting. That is how Therese came into Tomas' orbit. Together they worked like demons to compile interesting and diverse "shows" that could be sent out and back, and then somewhere else, on six-month rotations. Tomas had discovered two efficient channels to market participation in his program: the Association of Art Museum Directors and the

American Association of Museums. Through these he reached almost 20,000 potential clients. Given the need for appropriate "territories" in arrangements such as this, he inked two hundred lend-lease deals

within three years of that cup of coffee. It nearly killed poor old Therese, but it created a $200 million cash inflow. Tomas proposed those funds remain separate in a discrete arrangement, at least during the term of the program.

Through this fund, Tomas added investing to his portfolio of skills.

His art program was paying all its own bills and contributing to rebuilds of select church property in and around Rome.

After the first fifteen museum deals were executed, and the spectacular success that it would become was obvious, Father Tomas had made a new and different suggestion to the second-ranked man at God's Head Office; this was made at a midnight dinner at Il Convivio on Via Vicolo Dei Soldati, just across the Tiber Bridge from Castel Sant' Angelo. Tomas loved history, and the place reeked of it. Built as a mausoleum for the emperor Hadrian, later a residence of Pope Clement VII's mistress, it served to hide the Pope himself when Charles of Bourbon invaded.

Pressed for the reason for the meeting, Tomas explained the restaurant as a castle keep and a perfect metaphor for his proposed new initiative concerning the growing lawsuit issue.

Over dinner he laid out the hazards of the current situation, and the increasing difficulty to stay "on message" when the only product is your message; such is the destructive potential of global and viral press.

Over brandy they discovered his solution; centralized defense, immunized settlement funds, and poor parishes. If parishes were impoverished and debt-ridden, plaintiffs would be disincentivized. By the same token, cleverly jurisdictional settlement trusts engorged with money would tip the playing field in favor of the defendant.

Tomas had proposed that all Roman Catholic parishes borrow as much as possible against bricks and mortar and send it up stream to the settlement trust. The local parish would own a piece of the trust. The concept espoused that night took four years to implement, and not without a great deal of push back. In the end, $2.7 billion found its way into the care and control of the financial genius whose idea it had been.

But Tomas had not finished. As the parishes fell into line, Father Tomas put the finishing touches on yet his next fundraiser.

As he shared at a spiritual retreat for select personages, property monetization had helped the flock to their next step of personal sacrifice.

The numbers were impressive, and they rolled off Tomas' tongue with the soft assurance of the best Wall Street securities salesman. A good, committed pitch was contrived on the basis of an average of eleven ounces of gold donated per parish. Eleven was chosen as the disciple head count, minus Judas. The team had laughed at the twist as Judas settled for silver.

In any case, 270 thousand parishes each delivering an average of eleven ounces would amass a lot of gold. It made sense though, as the faithful had not really dug into their own pockets when the properties had been mortgaged. This would be a natural follow-on, allowing each of the faithful to make a personal sacrifice in the same spirit as the entire parish had just done. It was good, solid marketing.

Faithful the world over answered the plea. It came in many forms, from the virtually non-existent of gold wash costume junk given by children to the purest of 24 karat parsed from personal savings of the poor accustomed to wear their wealth. There was gilt, plate, filled, with a wide variety of karat weights. It took a year of weekly collections and blessings, so the "take" flowed steadily through secure transportation to a high-security refinery and smelter located just north of Rome proper. There, denuded of ancillary gems and stones, it was concentrated into its precious components, such as gold, silver, and platinum.

Treasures of the faithful were then exposed to the fire and brimstone of modern alchemy; cupellation to melt and separate precious from slag, melted down the totality, with the non-gold materials floating on the molten gold as slag, then 90 minutes of chlorine gas to render the gold 99.5% pure, and finally to electrolysis for two days for virtually

100% purity. Re-melted, it was poured into bars, weighed, stamped, and stored.

The work had been done by a private company that had been around for over fifty years, recently acquired by a senior technician. That man, a certain Luigi di Parma, paid $25 million for the business; the money arranged through a Luxembourg bank with guarantees provided by a Maltese merchant banker. All done through the divine intervention of Luigi's best friend and old army buddy Father Tomas.

Given their relationship, and the proximity of the plant to Vatican vaults, along with the obvious efficiency of the single supplier relationship, it made sense that Luigi got the job.

The deal was unimpeachably typical; half a percent of market value of the gold plus retention of everything recovered from slag and electrolyte slime. No one cared how profitable the deal was to Luigi. No one knew he was doing the work.

The program proved immensely successful, collecting 2.9 million ounces of pure gold. At 400 ounces per bar, it produced 7,250 bars. It took Luigi almost four years, running 10 Wohlwell cells flat out.

Each bar was assayed and certified by Luigi before the Vatican crest was melted on and the bars delivered to the Vatican vault prepared for the purpose.

When gold hit $2,000 an ounce this hoard was worth just under $6.5 billion. Father Tomas arranged an offering of Vatican Gold Notes. Seven hundred and fifty thousand notes were sold at par, raising $1.5 billion in cash.

The notes were redeemable in series, starting five years out, at 20% per year. In other words, they were illiquid for between five and ten years. What made them spectacular was the guarantee. They were principal protected notes. Redemption value was the issue price plus 50% of the up-tick in gold between issue and redemption.

The issue took 30 minutes to fill. When asked about redemption risk to the Vatican, Tomas had explained that the issue was small relative to the total holdings of the mineral.

When all was said and done, the three major programs plus sale of the gold notes had resulted in $10.4 billion of new money for Vatican reserves. Well, not exactly. It disappeared into secret settlement trusts, and thus unaccounted for in Vatican financial statements.

CHAPTER 24

Once or twice a year, Father Tomas would pack his bags and fly to Milan, rent a car, drive about an hour north to the Swiss border town of Chiasso, and check into the Centro Hotel Garni. He was heavy-laden but took only the clothes on his back. Upon return the bags were empty. He travelled under an assumed name. His car, food and lodgings were paid with a debit card drawing on a nominee account in a domestic bank funded by a Cayman blind trust.

Chiasso is infamous; cheek-by-jowl to Italy, catering to legitimate consumers of cigarettes, gas, and the legendarily discreet Swiss banking system, Chiasso has a darker side. It meets the needs of less legitimate pursuits; smuggling in and fencing of diamonds, passports, credit cards, even guns.

Tomas travelled to Chiasso as a vendor.

He typically sold six or seven, never more than eight items, each of fabulous intrinsic value yet offered at massively reduced prices demanded by black market middlemen.

He dealt with only one man who called himself Medici. Tomas didn't want problems, and Medici was reliable. Tomas also liked the idea that he was communing with the great medieval family.

Getting the last dollar out of any one piece wasn't critical; he had an endless supply. He called his goods "Curia Curio"; lifted from Vatican archives, crypts and vaults. He had the keys, it was easy.

Ultimately Medici got himself arrested. Tomas had been forewarned. In his day job, he was briefed on a variety of cases as items of antiquity were wrested and returned.

Venerable institutions like the Met, Getty, Boston's Museum of Fine Arts, even Princeton had repatriated items of doubtful provenance to places like Italy, Greece and Egypt.

To Tomas' mind it was all part of this insufferable movement toward political correctness, as if some judge could turn back the hands of time! Since World War II much had been written about Nazis, Jewish property, and the Vatican. But, he had thought, how was that so different from Venetians pillaging Istanbul? Virtually every tourist attraction in the place had once been looted? Or, maybe the Spaniards ought to give back everything they took from the Incas and the Aztecs. Half the antiquities in Britain were stolen from Frenchmen during the Hundred Years' war.

It wasn't like they were even being restored to rightful owners. A goddess recently court-award to the town of Aldone in Sicily...what right did a town have to it? A family? Maybe. A person? Yes! Who even knows if somebody in Aldone hadn't stolen it, or pillaged it from some other town?

Tomas concluded these analyses the same way. People and families, had rights to property. Towns didn't. Cities didn't. Churches didn't. That's why his actions weren't theft. He was trading what was his...his family heirlooms. His birthright.

Medici had loved dealing with the man he knew only as Enrico. Goods from this enigma were instantly movable. They weren't "hot" in the conventional sense of Interpol lists or cold files. No buyer of any item sourced through Enrico complained. Each piece came with a concise, informative descriptive detailing "who" and "where" of origin, backdrop to its history, school and style, and defense of proposed value.

Each write-up was by Sister Therese. Not so for each item's provenance.

As Sister Therese had processed bits of antiquity, she had stored information germane to it and other pieces in a computerized database. Each specific piece she allocated to one of the following: "Add to rolling exhibits in the art lease program," "place on exhibit in a Vatican display," or "return to storage."

It was from this last category that Father Tomas used unfettered access to pilfer inventory for these pilgrimages of illegality.

There was an equally useful source he also accessed. When antiquities went out on the now twenty year old art lease plan, they did so on a six-month roll-over plan, to exhibits new and marketable. Items were always routed through Sister Therese, who religiously pursued feedback on item-by-item success, and occasionally new bits of history. Pieces that were either not well received, too fragile, or about which new information indicated the need for further study, were removed from the rolling displays.

This was Tomas' other cache.

The nun would complete her assessment, update the catalogue, and move on. Then Tomas would raid the vault, help himself to a duplicate, a forgotten, or a "retired" piece. He used Therese's notes to select, document, and to forge final provenance.

Documenting provenance required sophisticated chicanery. With the advent of UN rules governing antiquities, major institutions eschewed anything lacking in proven provenance; that solicitude altered the market size and acceptance. Tomas used Therese's notes but edited most recent provenance records by establishing former owners from among the dead.

He selected people with dark, mysterious pasts from dark, mysterious parts of the world. The more reclusive they were, the better. Buyers needed proof to defend title and that did the trick.

Each bill of sale to Medici was backdated to a date before the demise of the man or woman claimed by Tomas to be the vendor.

It worked for years, until Therese went to a dinner party in the Florida swamp and came face-to-face with one of her blessed artifacts.

She had e-mailed Tomas immediately then blathered on about leaks, scandal, stolen treasure. She had proposed police involvement, but he calmed her, obliged her to wait while he got to America, so they could sleuth further on the Q.T.

Therese was murdered to shut her up. She got the knife as retribution because her meddling had screwed with Tomas' program.

Tomas needed the money from those antiquities. It maintained an expensive breeding operation.

Four appropriate vessels of procreation were kidnapped two years prior, and now aged twelve, were ripe to be bred.

Obtaining them had cost a considerable sum of money, keeping them even more so. Soon there would be breeding and harvesting costs. The mafia is expensive. Years earlier, God had sent a young penitent Mafioso to Tomas' confessional for absolution. There in the friendly confines of dark confidences, The Holy Father had pried enough from the hood to know two things; the hood could never rat on him, and the hood could do the doing for the most awkward part of Tomas' plan.

That plan required four virgins of good Italian stock to carry Tomas' seed.

Four ten-year-olds just disappeared. There was a fury of investigation, a storm of fear. Within eighteen months the ripples settled, funeral masses said, and the world moved on. Accepted as dead, the virgin vessels ripened in rigid, lonely captivity at an abandoned castle in the north of Corsica.

The time was close for those vessels to fulfill destiny. Father Tomas would arrange to disappear, then reappear as his very wealthy alter ego. He would "adopt" the virgin vessel babies and raise them to their proper place in society.

The vessels themselves would, of necessity, be slaughtered along with the team of caregivers. He would use the same modus operandi as with Therese; the hood would kill the others, then he would dispatch the hood.

Tomas regretted the need, but knew he was no monster; he was the corrective arm of justice, of retributive justice long over-due.

Years earlier, when he first laid eyes on the medieval portrait of Ranuccio Farnese, his life had begun to take on purpose. His calling had required sacrifice: his, theirs, and others' past and future.

Now, as he sat looking at the quiet waters of Lake Como and listened to wind in spars, waves spanking boats, the man any sane person would call demented and delusional lifted blood-red wine to toast forbears, and whispered the words of his oh so many dreams, "Cum tristitia hoc facio ad meliorem gloriam familiae meae."

Absently, he noted that, as with every time he saluted family past and future, his penis became engorged, and throbbed with lust as it never had for a woman.

CHAPTER 25

Sarah spent hours wrestling with her two conflicting roles, spy and mother hen. She concentrated on what could be good, refusing thoughts of the Mossad as murderous. Inkling by inkling, she concluded that Floyd was an arm from God, sent to do good, and that God demanded she be in league with him. However, survival of itself, and certainly not the amassing of money, was ignoble. She searched for ennobling sacrifice; for a Greater Good.

Sarah began to think of herself as newly minted leader of a miniature country. No one cared what happened to the citizens of her little country. They were foreign to everyone; Catholic but expelled, devout in a secular world, unsustainable without an infrastructure of support, strong of character but weak of means.

Her identity was her work and her work was saving her Order, the people and its essence, its value. If they were to have a future then they must have a purpose, a vision, a reason to exist.

Floyd thought she was Ruth. Who was Ruth anyway if not a woman in duress because of the way her society treated her gender? Ruth survived and prospered because she was true to herself and because she met her obligation to those dear to her who desperately needed her help. It was the concept of Ruth that permeated her thoughts as she walked alone, more and more often, in the garden by the swamp.

Sarah began to feel hatred for the unnatural cruelty of her enslavement. Faith in abstracts became a dedication to building something concrete. Her glory in the Lord became a search for glory in people. Devotion to sacrifice became a search for her place in the world. Her legendary focus on the needs of individuals became a focus on needs of the world.

Her calling? Liberation. Her flock? Womanhood. Her enemy? Not the devil, rather whoever or whatever threatened or abused any of her flock. Therese, God, Floyd; they were giving her an opportunity beyond measure. She must not, would not, fail.

She was to be Ruth to all women.

That would require a great deal of money.

A plan began to hatch.

It was born of the union of pain and opportunity; the pain of Therese, the order, and herself; and the opportunity of Floyd.

He, or those he killed for, would do a lot for her, particularly in the way of money. While she did not completely comprehend all of their drivers, the signs were all mercenary. There was the credit card, the dinners, the Fontainebleau, the deed, the loan.

How far could she push? And for what?

Sarah had chosen a life of service and remained ironically true to those roots, but only to the transcendental; not to anyone on Earth. She wanted to serve, in ways broader than her Catholic cage permitted, in ways for which she would gain glorious recognition.

She needed to test the edges, to find Floyd's limits.

She knew there was a cost. Pipers get paid, but dreams flounder when dreamers dwell on costs. They would be what they would be.

Sitting alone and staring into the swamp, the first brilliant flash of genius came. She was a woman. Ruth was a woman. She had gender-based issues. Ruth was the same. Ruth prospered by staying true to herself. Sarah would do the same, by the same route. She would make the men help her, and help all the women suffering from the unfairness of it all. She would be a modern Ruth.

The women of the convent were her immediate citizens, but the women of the world were her focus. She became energized. She would share a dream big enough to get all she needed from Floyd, and use what she got to make the dream a reality.

What Sarah had learned from recent experience was that weak women are gratuitously crushed, and that a great deal of the weakness of women was imposed through worldly custom and its institutions. God was irrelevant in this. She determined that whatever their individual God, every woman on Earth was a member of her flock. She was being offered the chance to help every woman on Earth.

But it would take money.

Her mission was no longer about God. It was about women, all women. It was about empowerment.

Sarah had a new purpose. No room for mourning or fear.

Purpose brings plans and designs. Plans and designs bring momentum; the trickle of concept becomes the stream of reality, then the river of momentum that carries all along with it.

Once she had the germ of her idea, she saw answers everywhere. Her dreams became focused thoughts broadened to include example after example of transformative, heroic women, not just Ruth. At some level she envied them. Consciously, she studied them, across religion, geography, and discipline. She internalized the Meirs, Bhuttos, Ghandis; even the Deborahs, the Cleopatras, Boadicia. It was remarkable how many of these women had died by the hand, or at least the action, of men folk!

She puzzled over Ruth and Jezebel. Both dedicated to their people, both captives in deadly alien environments, both magnificent. One despised, other glorified.

There were so many scientists; a nun like Hildegard of Bingen and the frisky gambler physicist Emilie du Chatelet who made Voltaire the man that he was, but whose fame was not recognized as hers. Marie Curie who won two Nobels but was allowed only to work under the aegis of her husband. Rosalind Franklin who discovered the double helix but died of cancer for her efforts while Crick and Watson got Nobels. Jocelyn Bell discovered pulsars as a grad student but the Nobel went to her male professor.

And now the activists of her own day; Tawakkul Karman of Yemen who at just 22 years of age operates the group "Women Journalists without Chains," Leyman Gbowee of Liberia who led a peace movement of Christian and Muslim women to halt a dozen years of male carnage, and Ellen Johnson Sirleaf, also of Liberia, who is now President. All three Nobel Prize winners. All three people Sarah wanted to emulate. All three were people she wanted to know.

On one of her swamp walks the ex-bride of Christ put land into the dream. What about a thirty-acre campus right here, focused on women: their needs, their aspirations, their role in the world? What if she could build a center here where they could all come, share, be? Would that help them, and the other women of the world? Could a center become a focus for change across the globe?

Sarah began to dream of herself as one of the most powerful people on Earth, the leader of the women's leaders of the entire planet.

She would need big money.

Sarah knew that Floyd and his team were using her. Their interest was not some esoteric trip of innate charity. These people kill people, she thought. Being in bed with them was neither without risk nor cost. She could only get what she wanted if she gave them what they wanted.

They wanted that damned computer. Well, not "damned," she ruefully reminded herself. If not for that four pounds of historic Intel, then she would not now be dreaming dreams of greatness and glory.

She inherently understood two things: these people could get that thing with or without her unless she utterly destroyed it, and that people, well one person, had to disappear for their plan to actually work. Investigations continue until all wrapped up and tidy. They were going to kill someone when they stole from the thief, as surely as day follows night. It was the same thing for the computer; someone had to take the fall for its disappearance.

It made sense that the same person would "wear" the murders of Therese and Leroy. She knew the obvious choice for the box job was poor Ted. If it wasn't him, then it might as well be her.

Sarah felt the pain of this realization as more an ache than a sharp, searing, stabbing thing. She sort of knew the outcome was inevitable, so compliance was more about survival than anything else. Not her survival though...the survival of her dream!

She sort of knew that Floyd's buddies must have her under surveillance. Really, if they had infiltrated the Vatican, how tough was it to watch one little ex-nun?

Through this logic, Sarah arrived in a conveniently comfortable place. If "it" was going to happen anyway and she couldn't stop "it", why not go with the flow and make the best of this situation? Her dreams had made the best of it look pretty damn good, morally as well as in terms of personal gratification. Her bread was buttered; her bed was made. It was now more about the dream than anything to do with Ted or Therese.

Sarah meandered.

The gate would go there, the office complex here, maybe an outdoor auditorium for arts and argument. Housing was tricky, because the young entrepreneur knew she needed the good will of the town of Ophrah...so she would house VIPs only. The rest could go where they might, as long as investors picked up on it. She needed to talk to them. She needed plans. There were so many approvals. How do you build five stories up on swamp? God, they had to park. What is the ratio of people to poop? Do you rent space to retailers or keep it all for the foundation? Do you become a landlord or a trustee of a common tenancy? She needed help.

She needed money.

Could a compromised divorcee of God command enough respect to pull it off?

Could she slough Ted off? Would Liberté let that happen?

The plan came to Sarah in vignettes, but over the two days Floyd had given her to think, the picture was clear enough for her to express it in words. Floyd would hear it first. The dam in the stream was funding; blow that dam and the river could flow. Floyd was her dam buster.

Her plan was to foment a thousand revolutions through millions of devotees. She would recruit, train, mobilize, fund and lionize warriors for change in a thousand different communities.

She would need money.

As far as she could tell, inequality was the barrier; if women were equals then they would no longer be enslaved. They could bear witness, say "no," demand education, marry as they would, survive the death of a spouse, and earn an income, fettered only by their own limitations.

As far as she could see, religion was used the world over to enslave half the human race. It wasn't some supreme being doing that. It was men perverting the Supreme Being, turning it into a stick with which to beat and a yoke with which to fetter. Her flock could believe whatever they wanted, as long as they were free to adopt, deny, or alter how it would affect them in their own stay on Earth.

Huge. Expensive. She would need money.

She waited anxiously for the next call from Floyd.

It came three days and nights after the Fontainebleau lunch.

She took the call breathlessly, wanting to share her plan, to enlist his help, to truly whore herself out to her cause.

He agreed to meet. Not for lunch, just a walk on a very public beach in a very public place. She wanted to change the rules.

They met on the jetty at Venice, he with two coffees, hers mixed exactly to her taste.

She told him her plan. There was to be an institute for women's issues. It would be built right on the site of the old Convent...all the capacity thirty acres of land could deliver.

There would be a shrine for poor dear Therese, but not as a fallen Catholic victim, rather as a symbol of all abuse to all women suffered all over the world, through all of time.

She would need a lot of money, but then there was to be $10 billion; she aspired to use maybe a billion.

He didn't say "No," but he did say now was the time to talk turkey. They found a bench.

That is when and where Floyd explained to Sarah what had to happen.

The theft from the thief had to be clean; no one could ever ascribe it back to his people. The best way to make sure of this was to leave no evidence. They couldn't just steal the money; they were going to have to "disappear" this person ...to have him vanish without a trace. That way, the myth of a successful theft run by him alone might be perpetuated.

And she had to deliver the computer, now.

Murder, calculated and with consent, was a big step. She waivered. He plucked her back from the brink of indecision. "Sarah, this sort of thing is like sex. You always remember your first. Difference is, with sex, your first should be with someone you like, maybe even think you like, but murder is easier if it's someone you really hate. Do you hate anybody, Sarah...I mean *really* hate?"

"I don't like the bishop, but I don't hate him enough to kill him. No, wait, yes there is one person. I honestly think that I could kill the son-of-a-bitch that did that to Therese. I think I would love to take a knife and cut his..."

"OK! Enough. You don't have to do any of that, Sarah, and believe me, you really don't want to. But you see there are people who don't deserve to live. Right?"

"Just one that I could kill."

"And you will give me the computer?"

"Will you give me the money?"

"Sarah, it's not my decision on the amount. But I am sure we can give you a lot of money. After all, we're not paying you with our money, it's coming out of the Church's pocket! Will you be able to deal with that?"

Her positive response was a simple, harsh laugh.

"There are details to be arranged, Sarah. I will call you in the morning to book a time and a place. We will deal with the money issue then. It's not about "if," but rather how much. It would help me to help you if I could tell my people with certainty about the computer."

She blurted, "I have it. I took it that morning, first thing, before I called anyone or tried to help the woman." She shuddered in a spasm of grief, and then continued, "At first I put it under the mattress and then in the trunk of the convent car, where the spare tire goes. I just wanted to protect my church. Then the bastards did this. It's not there now though."

He moved quickly to envelop her in an avuncular hug, and whispered, "Thank you for trusting me. We will do this thing together now. And I will show you now that I trust you Sarah. The man you most hate, the only one you could kill, is the man who is stealing the money from the church...the one we will "disappear."

She pushed him away and demanded to know.

"It is Therese's old boss. The man who hired her, and for whom she worked all those years. He had all the access. He was the one she contacted a day before she died. It was the man who had all of you excommunicated, who sold your land. It is the man we have been following for fifteen years. Father Tomas."

CHAPTER 26

They were mongoose and snake. Every move a jab. They circled. Weapons were words. It was all about wits and survival. This had been inevitable as each was feasting on the same flesh; Liberté was pulling it apart it while Sarah was sucking it dry. They had to collide.

It started in Walgreens, thrashed its way to the bench outside Liberté's office, and ended with a truce at the gates of 2200 O'Neill.

It began in "Feminine Products." Liberté was examining some strange new device with which to plumb her depths for even greater hygiene when Sarah tried to slither by unnoticed. Mongoose Liberté engaged, "Ah, there you are. I've been meaning to track you down. Got a moment?"

Fight-or-flee hormones surged in the snake, she coiled for battle, furiously tasting the air, "For you? Sure. What's up?"

"I've noticed a bit of a change. Well actually a couple. You're not doing any teaching I guess. Did you have to stop because of that excommunication thing? I notice the nuns working at the health clinic. Are the others still at school, or…"

"I've got new responsibilities now, Liberté."

"Oh. I see. Well I guess that explains it. How are you feeling? Any after-effects from that drug? How's Ted? Here, just a minute while I pay. Can we talk for a bit? Are you in a hurry?"

Snakes don't leave exchanges with mongooses until one is dead or both are too worn out to continue.

"Sure, I'll just wait outside." The snake slithered out feeling the nauseous after-effect of flight-or-flee response. She barely had time for burped relief before the mongoose was on her again.

"Where were we? Oh yes, how's Ted?"

"I have no idea Liberté, and frankly my dear, I don't give a damn!"

The mongoose smiled brief acknowledgement at the stab at humor, then jabbed again, "His nuts are in a noose Sarah. Everyone wants me to just arrest him and have the whole thing done with."

After awkward silence, the snake hissed, "But…"

"He's as dumb as a post. He actually thinks he can schmooze me. And when he's not doing that, he's checking out my ass. He loves the attention he gets from me, which is dumb in its own right, and he still doesn't have a lawyer, which is beyond stupid. I don't have that much experience, but guys that act like that are either so tough, so vicious you can't believe it, or…they didn't do it and know you'll figure that out."

After another awkward silence, it was the snake's turn, "And…"

"Everything we have on Ted is circumstantial, except one thing."

"What?"

Liberté chose her words carefully for the next move, not a jab but a thrust designed to wound.

"The only hard evidence," she allowed herself a smirk for the pun, "is that you both agreed. Both you and Ted said the same thing. That you banged him."

Sarah knew instinctively that monosyllabic wouldn't cut it, "I already explained that. It was a lot of things...anger, rebellion, that knife stuck in Therese..."

"I know. It's in my notes. But as Ted might say, a crime is like Sudoku, it isn't solved until all the pieces fit."

"So what doesn't fit?"

In the kind of feint any mongoose would be proud of, Liberté let that hang as she changed the topic, "You used to be such a frump. Where'd you get the new stuff? That belt is very un-nun-like. More like Paris chic."

The snake was ready, "You would be amazed at the generosity of people. We've been getting care packages ever since the article about e-squared...excommunication and eviction. Believe it or not, this stuff came in the mail!"

By now they were on the bench. The mongoose stretched, then jabbed again, "OK. So let me tell you where that puts me. The person who last saw the victim and the victim's property now seems to have a few bucks and she admittedly fucked the guy who actually knows how to kill people. In my book, you look like the bitch who dreamt it up and used sex to get Dumbo to do the deed. I think you're guiltier than Ted. Funny though...I'm also sure in my own mind that Ted didn't do shit. Which means that the sex thing and the apparent money thing are loose ends. What would Ted say? You know where they don't fit, but you don't know where they do."

"So...?"

"For now the only thing is the Big Bang. He's circumstantial. You're circumstantial. Come on, I'll walk you home. I want to see that donated stuff for myself."

And so they walked, at first in silence with Liberté wondering if this last bit was a jab or a thrust, and Sarah knowing she had won the exchange because of the mountain of donated food, clothing and money that had been flowing in for days, some opened, some not.

It was Liberté who spoke first, "How do you feel now about your... I guess it's awful. Have they talked to you any more? When do they want you out of there?"

Sarah decided she would forgo any conversation about leases or what not. "I dunno. It hurts, but I mean, God's still there."

"You know, you might be right. Remember the last time we talked? I was talking about how the geniuses who say science explains everything now say they can explain about 5% of the whole damn universe. They call the other 95% dark matter and dark energy?"

Sarah felt relief that the conversation was turning from pointed fact to general philosophy. "I do. But they seem to know a lot more than nothing. I mean, they can make the lights go on, get to the moon, predict earthquakes...but that's sort of like the God squad. They can make a lot of sense, but in the end, they don't have the answers. Maybe you're right. Who cares?"

"I know I do. I was raised to believe, then convinced not to. They don't actually know squat. You're as right as they are. Your people say they have faith in what you don't know and the scientists say they have faith in what they do know."

"Ya, well, they're not my people!"

"True. Sorry."

"It's OK. God isn't the church. It's funny, really. The church is just a great big business. It's like pyramid sales; they retail salvation. The margins are incredible! It's a great product too. Trust me...us...we know about heaven and hell. You'll see. Just one catch: you don't actually get to see how smart we were until you're dead and can't report back on "the product." No calls on the guarantee from the hereafter. Then there's the warranty. If you go to them with a problem with their product... like a death or disease or a war or a famine, or someone can't cope, or they're starving... they tell you it's your own fault because you're inherently bad. It was Adam's fault and you inherited it... and they ask you for some money to see if they can help you to solve your problem... yours, not theirs.... They have a beautiful no-refund policy, and what a brand! Nobody kills in the name of Adidas or Campbell's soup! They don't actually even pay the staff either, or give them a pension."

"So you're rethinking all that creationism crap? I mean even more than last time?"

"I'm rethinking everything."

"Funny, so am I. I know what I know, and it's at odds with what justice, law, and good government wants to do. Church, the law... bullshit. It's people...not all of us, each of us. I have to do what I have to do."

By now they were among the tribute flowers. Sarah led the detective to the mountain of clothes, and stood silently as it spoke for itself. Her suspicions not allayed, Liberté nonetheless knew her notes must refer to a plausible alibi for Sarah's new look.

As the mongoose prepared to disengage, once-was spirit deep within the snake came out, "Do they call lady cops "Dicks," too? I love you, but you really are being a dick, you know." Then she said, "I hate this."

"Me too."

Liberté turned to leave. Sarah talked to her back, "This will pass, you'll see. When it does, we can be...like we were...friends. You just go on being a dick, and when you find out I didn't kill anyone..."

Liberté spun on her heel. "That's half of it. If Ted gets hurt and he didn't do anything and you knew — then you and I are...kaput. More than that, I'll never stop until I get to the bottom of it and put you where you belong...make no mistake about that." She completed the three-sixty and strode off.

On her way back to the station Liberté played the exchange over in her mind. She knew Ted didn't do it but thought he was an ass. She really wasn't sure how dirty Sarah's hands were, or even what she was into, but wanted to believe her because she liked her. Whatever Sarah was up to, maybe it didn't involve Ted.

When she got to the bench she had earlier shared with Sarah, Liberté sat in the afternoon sun and wrote up her notes. That done, she stretched and closed her eyes for a minute.

The image that came to her was not comforting. She saw herself naked on a rack in a torture chamber, right at the point where the next click of the gear would tear her arms right out of their sockets. In the flicker of the ghastly fire in the brassier she could see just enough of the executioner's face to recognize the District Attorney.

She shook herself to snap out of it, arose, and returned to work.

She now understood justice isn't just, law isn't moral, and that justice and morality consume people. And not just the people in the dock either, but also the people whose job it is to get them there.

Liberté had another fleeting thought: guilt isn't really black and white, or good versus evil; it could be kind of a nuanced thing. Whatever that woman, her friend Sarah, was up to, Liberté knew it couldn't just be evil, it had to be nuanced. Every ounce of her fiber told Liberté the nun had a secret...a big secret...but she didn't kill Therese to steal a computer. But she sure had gotten some money, or whatever money could buy.

For her part, snake Sarah went straight to her office, where she took down her messages from voice mail. There were five, but only one mattered; the one from Floyd.

CHAPTER 27

Sarah crawled into bed, beat her pillow into sleep shape, pulled up the blanket, wriggled to fetal position, and closed her eyes; her brain would not stop. The Mossad is the big leagues. This was for keeps.

That computer had tricked her into a vise. She had tightened it herself. Lying now in bed, Sarah felt the crushing of its jaws. The killer might kill her, or the Mossad might. In any case they were clear in their position on collateral damage.

Once of no further utility, they would not owe her a second thought, but they had enough on her that they owned her.

If she went to the cops…to Liberté…all she had was a solitary clue in their murder investigation. At the least that must be public mischief or evidence tampering. At worst, she was a co-conspirator with their only suspect, Ted.

After what seemed an eternity, Sarah rearranged herself, willed her mind to "off," closed her eyes, and damn it, there was Ted. He appeared as claimant in some demonic court to which she was now called to give evidence to convict him of something egregious enough that the penalty she must impose would be warranted.

Tomas was just a name and Floyd was absent. Just Ted.

How had she arrived at this intersection of demonic and dangerous?

A flight of fancy saw her as older, elegant, and stately. The Matriarch. The Mother. Not just of a convent in a Florida backwater, but of something grand, big, important. Then back to the awful specter, not so much a vision as fear for the Ted she could see and of the Tomas she could not.

Her trip to Matriarch would pass through murder, betrayal and theft. Floyd had been clear, "You are either completely in or you are completely out." She understood, and hated him for the choices it forced. Unimplicated would be an intolerable loose end for the Mossad. A fragile alliance of short-term expedience must be forged to permanence in the hell-fires of murder and betrayal.

After an hour of flipping and flopping on the issues and bedsheets, the benighted nun arose, bundled, and stole quietly to the common room, the scene of the murder, and there sat before the communal computer console, where she proceeded to move at the speed of electrons through history and geography.

In no time at all she looked into the face of the alleged monster, Father Tomas. His unblinking stare froze her, much like a cobra. Each time Sarah left the image to read about the man, the image drew her back. So she just stared at him.

It came to her that his deeds did not matter, just hers. Could she deliberately conspire in this man's death? No! Not her! Not that! Every ounce of her roiled against it. Now, sure of her decision, she could look dispassionately at the image, but then her mind clouded in the memory of butchered Sister Therese. Tomas disgusted her. Floyd disgusted her. With the weight of the world as she knew it resting on her shoulders,

Sarah logged, then nodded, off. Ten minutes later she awoke with a start and returned to her bed.

The console catnap and the walk up to bed had the poor woman, once again, wide awake.

She felt for Ted, but like a puppy. A big, drooling, stupid, fawning, hopelessly loyal puppy. The thing about puppies is, cute and cuddly though they may be, they are betrayed by owners all the time. Dogs get put down to save on veterinarian fees. They are left to die in fires while owners escape. They get destroyed because people move, or have a baby, or buy a new carpet.

Thinking of Ted as a puppy changed everything. And what changed for Ted changed for Tomas too.

Years of study; the Bible is loaded with duty death. Flat on her back at about three in the morning, staring into the darkness, the "no-choice" became the "Hobson's choice." The generality of the "Greater Good" obtained purchase and began to grow.

It subsumed personal glory to noble sacrifice. Ethics are a "Greater Good" formulation. Sarah did what countless others have, and doubtless will; she arrived at the self-righteous reasoning that the necessary trio of theft, murder, and betrayal were the "more ethical" choice.

The human mind is a beautiful thing; by logic it can create and then alter ethics, then use altered ethics to eliminate self-doubt, guilt, sin… conscience.

Sarah concluded that murder isn't so much the taking of life. Everybody dies. Murder is a timing thing.

That led to the fabulously self-serving analysis of the question, "what kind of life was left anyway?" For Tomas, disgrace, and perhaps a life on the run.

Ted was, of course, different, but logic is strong medicine! She reasoned the big dope had placed himself in "prime suspect" territory and was bound for the pen regardless of her commission or omission. She wasn't really the one hurting him. His life was irrevocably altered, with or without her.

Next to these rationalizations, theft was nothing.

Finally she slept; deeply, serenely.

The woman who awoke was harder than before she had gone to bed the night before.

In the light of day, rationalizations were suppressed. Sarah went to breakfast firm in her support of traditional values, troubled at her thoughts during the night.

During breakfast she received a private message from her body, a stabbing chest pain and swirling vertigo. Bathed in a cold sweat she felt her heart race. A covert pulse check confirmed that. She knew this was not a heart attack…but manifestations of serious stress.

At the prayers ladies of the convent still said, every other person in the place basked in beatitudes and the safety of blind faith, except Sarah, who burned with thoughts of intrigue and murder.

They rose to sing, she sat and wept.

The singing stopped, and a comforting hand held her shoulder. Her flight of mind thus broken, the abbess-elect sniffed, wiped back the tears, stood erect, and bade them continue. They did, but with eyes only for her.

She felt their gaze, but felt never more alone in that group with those secrets. She was prisoner of it all…regardless of how she proceeded.

Private prayer brought Floyd to mind. She escaped to what passed for a garden, and sat staring through the only angle providing just a glimpse of Desultory Bay. In her abject loneliness, she felt frantic for friendship.

Liberté wanted to trick her. Floyd was using her. The nuns relied on her. There was no one else. Ted was her only real friend.

Sarah made her way to the sanctuary of the office that was now entirely hers, and picked up the phone. She got his voice message, and left one of her own, "Ted, this is Sarah. I know you have been trying to get me and I am so sorry for being unavailable. I want, no, *need* to talk to you Ted. Today. Please meet me at Sharky's for lunch Ted. Noon. I am sure you will get this message and am sure you can meet me. It is important. I really look forward to seeing you, Ted."

The light on her cell phone blinked hypnotically, incessantly, demandingly; it was a text from Floyd. Could she please meet him and his associates at the Fontainebleau tomorrow? They had booked a suite where they could meet and a room for Sarah so that she need not worry about driving back to Ophrah late at night.

People wrestle with issues, but more often than not let events decide by carrying them along as a stream might guide an unpiloted boat. Sarah returned a text that she would get to Miami today, a day early, so please make the reservation for two nights, and went to prepare for her trip.

At noon, as Sarah pulled onto Tamiami and headed toward her destiny, Ted rolled up to Sharky's feeling a mixture of relief and apprehension.

He got a table in a private corner and waited. After an hour, he left. He did not call Sarah. He had no need. He knew that what had been was no more, and that what would be, would be awful.

Meanwhile as Sarah hurtled toward destiny, she continued her rumination on morality. First, the score card. She had already broken four of the commandments; adultery, theft, false witness, and greed. She was on her way to a council of murder. Five out of ten. Several of them more than once. In under a week! Now the rationalization; is adultery truly adultery when the marriage wasn't human, and alternatively, if it was then was God a polygamist? She didn't steal, she put into safekeeping. She didn't covet for herself, she offered what was offered by the Mossad to the use of women. Bearing false witness was bogus anyway; if you committed an untoward act then lying about it was a derivative crime...protected in USA law by the Fifth Amendment and not relevant to God since he saw all anyway and she could deal with that through confession.

The fifth was tougher. Murder.

So she began. So many killing acts; unabrogated statistical death rates at intersections, cost-benefit analyses of HMOs, military assessments, acceptable civilian collateral damage, state-ordered execution.

Much killing is non-specific; nameless, faceless victims. Or sanitized by process. Side effects of crime or rage don't count, because they are unplanned.

Rare indeed are face-to-face, planned killings; acts of love, hate, or expedience, requiring the perpetrator to come to terms with the deed, to justify it, in advance.

Decisions, justifications, and mortal sins don't happen in a vacuum; streams of consciousness in streams of events. The most common practice of humans in such moral dilemmas is to let the event stream override the consciousness stream.

So it became for Sarah. Whatever she might or might not do wouldn't change the outcome. Floyd's gang could do Tomas, get the loot, with or without her.

Aware also that she might become a loose string for them to nip and erase. The complexity of complicity might actually be her protection against Floyd. Self-defense isn't murder, and is not a sin.

Tomas was a dead man anyway. So her decision wasn't even about murder. Or betrayal.

Ted was different.

Here were clear moral rights and wrongs. Clear weights for each side of the balance. She followed the course of thousands before her; cognitive dissonance.

The basic tenet is, "I am completely justified in wronging you because you caused it...my action is your own fault."

Viewed through this rationale, Sarah saw herself as victim, Ted as a stupid, bombastic and unaware author of all the trouble she now faced. If he got hurt, then it was of his own doing. If he had kept his nose out of it and his mouth shut, then the police would by now have come and gone, and that would have been it!

If Ted hadn't been so smart, hadn't confused things, there would be no Floyd. No offer of complicity. No implied threat to her own existence. Ted was now the reason for Floyd. Whatever steps she took were Ted's fault, and at Ted's peril. She was Ted's victim. She had a God-given right to protect herself!

The decision was easy.

Suddenly aware she was far above the speed limit, Sarah slowed down and, checking her bearings, realized Miami was almost upon her.

CHAPTER 28

"Life…" thought Sarah…is an interesting term. In her case it meant linkage…duration in the now and the hereafter. In the case of Father Tomas it meant an end to his duration in both. For Ted…the waste of incarceration.

If Floyd's gang was going to "disappear" Tomas, she thought, then the computer was the endgame. They needed a scapegoat, and she was glad not to be their first choice. It had to be Ted. If the cops were already going to nail him for two murders he clearly didn't commit, why not help to nail him for the computer he didn't take, as well?

This they would do. She was sure of it. She was equally sure that she wanted to somehow make them pay for all the pain her moral compass had been forced to endure. An antidote, if not a cure. Retail therapy.

Her chariot swept onto the Fontainebleau grounds, and she into her Bay Front room with the aplomb of an heiress. It took minutes to book services at Lapis.

Sarah would receive a complete assessment, learn womanhood outside the cloister, and primp. She would even wax "down there," in for a penny, in for a pound. Apparently it would take some time, she was told four hours for the overhaul.

They were waiting. There was the assessment of skin and colors, a bit of herbal tea, then a shower. She had no trouble with the near-nakedness of depilation by wax, and actually found it exhilarating until they ripped the first strip off.

Her visceral scream alerted the attendant of torture that in this at least, she was still a virgin. She only screamed once though. Then took it as a form of penance for Ted.

By the third strip, Sarah was re-convinced that she was involved in heroics of a different level, Ted a regrettable yet unavoidable bit of collateral damage in her war on behalf of women.

The pain of exfoliation comforted her. Her wax was the hair shirt floggings of yesteryear.

Then it was her hair, mani-pedi, a light sushi snack, bathroom break, Swedish massage, and bed.

The make-up, the war paint, would be tomorrow at three.

After breakfast in her room, and some planning with the concierge, she was off.

Eight minutes north by cab, she arrived at Bal Harbor Shopping Mall to begin an orgy of Neiman Marcus. Diane von Furstenberg beckoned not once but thrice; chiffon, raw silk, and a somewhat staid hounds-tooth skirt and jacket ensemble.

Minolta three inch, open toe, nude patent leather shoes were perfect for the afternoon meeting, so she got them plus a black version, one pair of flats, and a set of fashionably edgy boots "good girls" would not have been caught dead in until four years ago.

The matching Valentino shoulder bag for the "nudes" was like armor. Victoria's Secrets became hers, lovely silken secrets that teased her body and touched her mind. She loved it.

Everything she acquired fit nicely onto that lovely little debit card. Everyone she bought from undertook to have the goods in her room at the Fontainebleau within the hour.

Throughout, she thought not once of Ted, Tomas, Liberté, Marie, or Therese.

That changed in the cab. A rumbling stomach. Waves of vertigo. Inexplicable dew in the fleece of her neck.

The symptoms grew through the rigors of makeup.

Although the beautician laid on more advice than chemistry, Sarah heard none of it. She fought the urge to vomit. As she was handed her gift bag of future beauty chemistry, reality struck her consciousness with absolute clarity.

This grand excess, this mad rampage through the shops, was by design. She was their whore. Obscenely bought and paid for.

It was a startling realization that when Floyd had first given her the card, this was his plan. He knew her buttons before she did, and had been pressing them all along.

But, she reasoned, if not this way, they would have found another. She assured herself of her cause. Her cause. The vomit reflex subsided.

As she had shopped, the stream of transaction-inspired electrons kept Floyd up to speed. He had known of her arrival the day earlier, and now watched as the fish leapt, finally and absolutely into the boat. There would be foreplay, but Sarah was his.

CHAPTER 29

At three-thirty Sarah was back in her room, alone but for the mountain of purchases. She felt a twinge of panic hoping Floyd would be as good to his word as she to hers. She saw herself as a great warrior, and today's meeting the real beginning of her campaign. The die was cast. Warriors don't wallow in self-doubt. She must don her armor.

Sarah unpacked, hung, stacked, or folded as appropriate.

Which armor? The professional look of hounds-tooth.

That drove the other armor; the panty hose would be "nude," the shoes black. The undies were problematic. She fussed, fingered, went with what she knew. Beneath the regal exterior she would be comfortable with a standard issue convent bra and panties.

She loved the lady in the mirror, even liked the hint of panty-line; it said "traditional". Mummy would have approved. But she wore no jewelry; she'd overlooked it in her acquisition orgy. What the hell?

There wasn't time for that now. She called the front desk to confirm tower and suite number, and then sallied forth.

At precisely 4 p.m., Sarah knocked. It opened immediately.

This was not to be a twosome. Floyd had a friend, whom he identified as Sammy. Sarah was sure that his real name wasn't Sammy, just as she was sure that Floyd wasn't really Floyd.

For an instant she was the fish in the boat. All her dreams, all her aspirations, lay in the hands of these two. She assumed Sammy was there because of the money negotiations, but since she didn't know for sure, she would let Floyd play captain, praying there was to be no gaffe hook.

The suite was amazing. She didn't notice. The view was a heavenly seascape vista. She didn't notice. Clear from briefcases where Sammy and Floyd chose to sit, she took a seat opposite.

Wordlessly, Floyd poured, creamed, stirred, delivered, then sat.

"OK" he began, "This is a big day for all of us Sarah. And none too soon, I might add. The target is getting ready to run, so we need our deal settled right now, here, today."

Sarah wondered if the change in demeanor was due to Sammy, then realized she didn't care. She was here too for the money. Curious though, "How do you know he's getting ready to run?"

Floyd looked briefly to Sammy who nodded slightly.

"Good question. Father Tomas has been to see the same lawyer in Rome he has used for years…who prepared all the paperwork on all the settlement trusts, his arrangements concerning a gold refinery, even the arrangements for the bullion itself. He is to return on Monday to sign transfer documents and finalize a series of offshore trusts and bank accounts that a forensics team couldn't unwind in ten years or break in two hundred."

"How do you know all this?"

"His lawyer is, how shall I put this…in our debt?"

"So you need to get him after he moves the money, and make him move it to you?"

"That would be so 70s. No, Tomas is going to sign a lot of documents on Monday. Two of them are all we care about. He won't know he's done it."

Sarah felt sick. They were telling all to imbue her with enough guilty knowledge to hang her if need be, and she didn't even know their names. They had a knife ready for her, just like Leroy had for Therese. They just hadn't stuck it in. Her crotch pulsed unpleasantly. Involuntarily, Sarah crossed her legs as tightly as the table permitted. "Go on."

Floyd studied her quizzically. "That's it. What comes after? We're really here to talk about money. Money for you. Have you given it some thought? The computer is worth millions to us Sarah, not hundreds of millions."

Floyd looked down, Sammy smiled, and Sarah's fist hammered the table. She unwound her crossed legs and rose in a furious release of pent up nerves and anger. "You, you, you bastards! And you..." this while pointing at Floyd, "You play me like some kind of fiddle? "Millions not hundreds of millions?" she sneered. "If I don't get what I need, what we agreed, then you can forget the computer. I'll destroy the damn thing!"

"Calm down Sarah!" snapped Floyd. "We've been pretty good to you, wouldn't you agree? You've got your place. I said "millions" Sarah, not "nothing."

"You let me believe. I trusted you!" Then, struck by the reality of Sammy, she turned on him. "It's you, isn't it? This one" gesticulating toward Floyd, "reels in the fish, then you..."

"Shut up Sarah!" barked Floyd. "This is a negotiation. You want more money. We may be able to do more for you. But we're gonna want more from you. Is the computer even here?"

"Of course not! Look what's happening now? If I brought the thing with me, God knows what you'd do. Fuck...!"

"Sit down, you stupid bitch!"

That was like cold water. She sat. Floyd continued, "Pull yourself together. Sammy, you come with me. I have an idea. Sarah, just stay where you are. We need a few minutes." With that the two men retired to the bedroom on the other side of the suite. Sarah strained for snippets but went unrewarded. What she did hear was Hebrew. After the eternity of maybe three minutes, the men reappeared and resumed their seats.

Floyd began, "OK, so Sammy and I have talked. He agrees that the work you want to do is important. I reminded him that whatever we pay you isn't coming out of our...us. But it isn't going to be a billion."

Aware that as much explaining as Floyd said he'd done couldn't have been accomplished in their three minute huddle, and that she was being played, and that this was a negotiation, she said, "Fine. Five hundred million."

"Two hundred and fifty."

"Three-fifty."

The men traded glances, and then Sammy made one of those "after you" gestures in which he waved Floyd toward Sarah, and then sat back. Floyd winked at Sarah. She did a double. He winked again. Floyd began, "There is a catch. You've been great. But we have a problem. When this goes down there's going to be a lot of pissed-off people. They all need answers. We need to give them answers."

"I know. You kind of told me that when you said Father Tomas had to be, what did you say, *disappeared*?"

"True. Sarah, there are two loose ends here. I mean beyond Tomas. The computer needs to be accounted for...someone has to take the fall so people can close the book. And then...there's you."

The pulse below thundered as her face paled.

He continued, "But relax. We have a solution. If you agree we solve both problems."

The pulse still thundered. She did a little hand waggle that meant, "continue."

"I need you up to your ass in this so I know you can never talk to anyone about any of it. Do you understand?"

Sadly, she did. "You need me incriminated. If I agree to be a criminal and I give you that thing, then I can have the three fifty. Right?"

He nodded. "So what's the crime? What do I have to do?"

Floyd took the great big breath that deep sea divers do, then dove in, "We need to close the book on the computer. You are going to deliver it to us. Then we scrub it...no memory, no prints, and then we dump it somewhere that it can be found..."

"That's it?"

"Then we box Ted." Her look meant she didn't understand. "We frame him. He takes the fall."

"Are you nuts? That would be motive. They'd pin murder on him. He'd go to jail for the rest of his life. No, they'd execute him. Florida still kills people."

For the first time all day, Sammy said something, "It's not easy making three hundred and fifty million dollars. You can be in or you can be out. Right now."

Her gut twisted in agony as his knife penetrated her soul. She wanted a toilet. She didn't move. They waited. The silence was deafening. She felt tension rising unbearably in the quiet. Their gazes lased straight through to her. A clock in the corner ticked. She stood. They stood. She reached her right hand across the table. Floyd took it in his. She whispered, "You have a deal."

Sammy didn't shake. "Get it now."

She nodded and left.

CHAPTER 30

Three hours to drive to the bus station at 2250 Peck Street in Fort Meyers, turn the key in locker 4020, retrieve the computer, and return to the still-available parking spot at the Fontainebleau. She heard several times from Floyd by phone and PIN, asking about her progress. The door ajar, Sarah entered unannounced, and wordlessly placed the computer on the table. All three paused for a moment, and then sat, mutely staring at the object of this covert affair.

It was almost religious, the computer a sort of Ark of their covenant. It held secrets, antiquity, and now bore witness to more crimes of blood and betrayal. It was both awesome and awful. Each of the trio was for the moment oblivious to each other or anything else.

Then Floyd handed Sarah an envelope, gave her a minute of perusal. She looked up, having read the details of location and time for the money transfer, and said, "Thank you…I am sure there will be no problem," as she pushed it right to the very bottom of her Valentino bag.

"Oh ya, here's your phone." She held the blackberry out but he didn't take it.

"No. Thank you. I want you to keep that phone Sarah, and keep it on at all times. It is only for our communication, that is all. The debit card is for your use for the next ten days, to a limit of twenty-five grand, and then it will be dead. OK?"

She nodded. Not sure what else there was, but sure there was more, she sat in a mournful sort of silence. Then, on a desperate whim: "Isn't there another way? I don't want to kill Ted. He just doesn't deserve that. Can't we find another way? Please?"

Sammy began to drum his fingers on the table, then stopped and snapped, "The way to hell is change and added complexity. As far as I can tell, the man's an idiot anyway. If we had set out to box him we could not have done it any better than he already has! They're most likely going to charge him anyway; they have to close the book on the case, they don't have anything or anyone else. He's already screwed. Forget about him. Grow up. Earn your money."

Then he heaved himself to an erect position, and came around the table to tower over her. "I wonder how things go for you now, if the police come to some knowledge of the kind of money you've been throwing around. Or that you took the computer before the dead woman was cold and never told a soul. Oh, here's a better idea. Call whoever you call at the Vatican and, if they even speak to you, tell them. I'm pretty sure they don't issue some kind of blessing or whatever. Maybe you're a bigger idiot than numb-nuts. We're your only friend, the only one giving...I repeat *giving*...you 350 million dollars so you can chase a pipe dream, and you want to screw around with us? And make no mistake missy; if you're not our friend, you're our enemy. There isn't any in-between! Got it?"

Sarah broke, and began to heave great sobs. Floyd scowled at his partner, came around to sit beside her. "Listen to me, Sarah. Here, turn your chair so you can see me." She did, and he continued, "You're not killing Ted, he is. All by himself. And besides, if I told you that you could save four young lives by sacrificing one more than half over, would you think that was a bargain you could make?"

Sammy rose in protest, but the trained assassin motioned that he sit. There was expectant silence, then Sammy's nodded consent.

Floyd returned his attention to Sarah, "Do you remember a thing that happened about three years ago in Italy? Four young girls from blue-blood families went missing and were never found..."

"Sort of..." she shrugged.

"Sarah, you don't know everything there is to know about your Father Tomas. He is completely crazy, and stealing ten billion was only part of his insane plan. We're not entirely sure what his plan is, but we do know a lot. For years he has been contributing sperm... he's got the stuff banked everywhere...they are identified as only for safe-keeping for some Cayman trust and his name is always fake. We know this because we've been following him for a long time."

Sarah was no longer weepy. Her eyes huge, mouth agape.

"OK. So the second thing we know is, your Father Tomas made a deal with the Mafia, and on his behalf, they kidnapped those girls! We're pretty sure that's why he was doing the little pilfer jobs. He needed money to cover some of those costs. The big money for the kidnap was paid by making a bad loan that got written off out of one of his trusts."

She said, "Your lawyer again?"

"Right. The third thing is, we have an idea where those girls are."

She rose in a rage. "You know? You didn't turn the bastard in? You didn't do anything to save those girls?"

"Sit." She did. "Sammy said it earlier. Grow up. We have a job to do. We don't hurt the innocent unless we have to, and if we can without impunity, help someone, sometimes we do. But we have a job, a mission, and we are never going to sacrifice that for some off-plan rescue. I'm a daddy Sarah. I don't like it, but its life. We sort of know, but only Tomas can tell me precisely...if I ask him...not simple when you're disappearing a person. So now, Sarah, you get to make your choice."

"What?"

"Fuck Ted, maybe save the girls. Save Ted, for sure fuck those girls."

"Huh?"

"The clock is ticking. When we disappear Tomas, my guess is the money dries up, the clock hits zero, and those girls vanish forever. They're being kept by mafia types."

"What was he thinking?"

"Not sure. But I'm guessing that with the money, old Tomas planned a big family, and wasn't sure he'd be young enough to still have swimmers. I figure he plans to breed the girls, and once that's done, they're dead anyway. Do you get it? If we have the "I's" dotted, then we alert authorities who can save the girls. If not, then we can't take the chance. So you make the decision Sarah. Do the girls maybe live or for sure die?"

"Where are they?"

"You are way better off not knowing."

She looked at him long and hard, then nodded, "Yes. The girls must be saved. I agree. Even if Ted Coulson has to die. I need the washroom."

Three flushes and a lot of tap water later she returned, calm and somehow visibly older. She poured herself some water, then slumped into a couch in the sitting area. Floyd sat across a coffee table from her, and put his briefcase in front of him, on the table.

"You have made a good decision Sarah. Thank you. There is one more thing on my agenda. Are you up for one more shock to your system?" Her thin smile indicated she was.

"We have something here for you. Something that will for all your life remind you of us and what we have done." He reached into his briefcase and pulled out what to Sarah looked like a jewelry gift box, placed it on the table in front of himself, where she could see, but not touch, it.

"We wanted to find something that told the whole story. Nature contrived to a great human purpose; something demanding of explanation but silencing with awe. Something with both our purpose and our background. Timeless. Beautiful. Deadly."

Already bought and paid for, Sarah sat in anxious anticipation, waiting to know what more they seemed to want to pay. He continued, "*Physalia physalis*. Man O' War." He pushed the box across the table, and sat silent as she opened it, and gasped.

"My God," was all she could manage. The box contained a most wonderful arrangement of sapphires, gold, and diamonds. The diamonds shaped like an umbrella, with yellow gold loops coming down from it, each encrusted with maybe eighteen little sapphires. Articulated stringers also fell from the umbrella top, also made of gold, and carried some kind of other stone. "What is this? What does it mean? My God, it's beautiful."

"It is a Man O' War. The guy who made it was very famous. It's a Tiffany exclusive."

"Oh."

"I will explain. There are so many levels really. First, the Man O' War is symbolic, right?"

"Right, but..."

He never really stopped, "You see, in biology the Man O' War is more properly called "*Physalia physalis*" and it's not just one animal, it's a bunch of them working together to survive. One completely separate group of them makes up the floatation part, some others do the stingers, and digestion is done for the group by another completely different set of individuals. These things not only survive, they prosper, because they work together and aren't even remotely selfish or territorial; therefore they can make it in the most dangerous environment in the world...where everything is preyed upon...sorry, no pun intended! Please, take it. Put it on."

She did, but with a gnawing in her gut and a very wet nape of her neck. "It's a jellyfish?"

Visibly annoyed he spat, "No, not a jellyfish. A Man O' War is different," Then he seemed to catch himself, took a gulp of air, and continued, "and second, it's uniquely Jewish. The guy who designed it was this guy, Schlumberger. The piece is actually called a Medusa but that's just a Man O' War stage of life. Schlumberger's dead now, but he made the original for Tiffany because a member of the Mellon family got bit by a Man O' War and the Matriarch thought it might be a nice way to remember the event. A bit weird, but there you go!"

By now Sarah had the Medusa stuck to her brand new suit, and while she was wondering what all this meant, Floyd continued, "Anyway, we thought the moonstones in the stingers were symbolic because the Judean calendar is lunar. With me?"

"Stunned but yes, I guess," then in a subdued voice, "Medusa. How appropriate."

He came close and his tone changed, neither engaging nor exasperated, just a touch threatening. "Sarah, we, you and me, this, we are all linked now forever. I want for you a long life and to remember us...and our bond. Yes?"

She thought, "Yes—bought and paid for." She said simply, "Yes."

Before this Sarah had believed she was playing with the fate of others. This gift and its presentation startled her to the reality that it was her fate now in the offing. She must take it, she knew. But just as surely, she knew she would never wear it. It meant she was a killer and a spy. It meant she was no longer free. It meant she was in league with...

It was Sarah that broke the silence during which she had been allowed to absorb all that the gift meant. Feeling very small, she ventured, "You think of everything...you knew that night...when Therese..."

Both men stood silently, each carefully scrutinizing his shoes. She had her answer. Therese could have lived. These people were completely ruthless. An ally today, but tomorrow? She shuddered involuntarily. Quietly, as to not awaken a sleeping ogre, Sarah gathered her things and left without another word.

CHAPTER 31

Within minutes of her departure, the computer was expedited to an encryption lab in no way associated with MIT, yet a proud user of that institution's hardware and software; an employer of some of the best computer tech brains in the world, unaware their numbers included undercover spies.

The device was quickly disassembled, with the hard drive and memory card compromised for simultaneous multiple access to its private secrets while protecting those secrets from erroneous damage or willful self-destruction.

Within an hour analysts broke the encryption code, developed an algorithm, and saved millennia of secrets to their own secure system. Two hours more saw those compromised secrets of art and artifacts starting to be pored over by a hundred experts in twenty disciplines, located in five cities on three continents.

Within eight hours a top secret electronic dossier had been compiled and forwarded to the team captain in Jerusalem. He perused it quickly, and then called the private number of the office of the Prime Minister. Twelve minutes later the head of the country and the head of the country's spy network conferenced. Only ten hours after the redhead's clandestine delivery, treasures of and crimes that had now borne witness were assessed, prioritized, and planned around.

The team of art historians, numismatic experts, religion historians, architects, antiquarians, Egyptologists, gemologists, anthropologists, materials daters, and Talmudic scholars expressed awe at the quality of Therese's work. Elements of their grand tradition lay exposed before them; some expected it, others were shocked.

Before them lay disclosed the secret Templar fortune. It was moved by hook and by crook to the bowels of Saint Peter's Rock, carrying with it a great mass of Jewish history, picked and axed from David's famous temple.

Roman legion plunder of Egypt, Persia, Greece.

Crusaders with lust for blood second only to lust for salvation and loot; plunder off countless dead holding unsanctioned versions of God.

Letters, bones, weapons, coinage, jewels. Documents and pronouncements of and around the emancipation of Moorish Iberia, annihilation of Longue d'Oc Cathars, Baltic sword-point conversions, the rape of Christian Constantinople.

Some of it was real; coins, jewels, parchments. Others were suspect; Joseph's coat, Moses' rod. Some was creepy; skeletons of butchered enemies, schismatics, rivals.

Thanks to the quality of Therese's work, re-cataloguing to provable provenance and identification of cultural treasures had gone quickly. The authors, true to academic roots, referenced their awe at her work.

Their dossier proposed repatriation to the care and control of Israel, of items of Jewish social, religious, historical relevance. Bones were not interesting, jewelry was, but only as it related to their culture. They were to reclaim, not to thieve.

Thus the dossier proposed keeping the ancient scrolls that first recorded mystic secrets of the Kabala and the crowns of Jewish kings, but not the mountain of booty from Alexandria.

It claimed Maimonides' notes, but not medical texts wrested from the dead hands of Druid teachers in Arles.

It listed frescos removed from Cleopatra's palace in Alexandria but ignored the work of the magnificent Muslim mathematician al-Khwarizmi.

It listed coins from the periods of enslavement in Persia and Egypt, but only samples, not the entire cache.

They did want Joseph's coat, not because they believed it was as claimed, they just held intellectual curiosity what it in fact might be.

The dossier claimed five thousand specific items, but that included each coin and jewel, so it was quite a small list of troves, each of value beyond price.

Master spy and Head of State reveled in mutual admiration, then got down to brass tacks. The original plan was theft of money Tomas stole, use of it to buy claims of Jews dispossessed by Nazis implicating Rome...then, with status as a State, to sue the Catholic Church.

For years Church defense had been lack of plaintiff status; as a sovereign state The Holy See was unassailable by such mortals. However, claims pursued by Israel as "holder in due course" would be heard.

The irony of the Church's money purchasing claims was delicious, especially as it would take the Church from unexposed to doubly so; her money to buy claims, more money to settle those claims. A bridge too far, that plan had been shelved as economically rich but politically bankrupt. The replacement strategy was to use the recovered money to cause and fund an omnibus settlement between the State of Israel and the Vatican. Absolution for Rome, money for heretofore impoverished claims, Jerusalem as arbiter of all.

Secrecy was deemed a safer protocol than transparency, an approach consistent with global modern government doctrine.

Sarah, her demands and her future, were at issue. A demanding little thing, and what they call in spy circles, "a loose end." If they did away with her they would save $350 million with no chance of future embarrassment.

But the State of Israel only countenances extinction of enemies, not friends and allies; it was ruthless, but not willfully treacherous. Besides, the decision not to sue the Vatican meant returning money beyond reasonable claim settlement amounts. Whatever Sarah got would just be an expense. Money they didn't care about.

If she succeeded in her "girls" club of the world, all the better.

The Prime Minister joked that Sarah could help emancipate Haredi women. That brought laughter, followed immediately by fingers to lips signaling, "Let's keep this secret."

Floyd had reported having a good leash on Sarah and possible uses for her in the future. She was smart, feisty, controllable, rich, possibly powerful, and, compromised. An asset. An upside, with a limited downside. She would live.

After adjournment, the Spy Master called Floyd on the secure line. For a briefing ending with, "And yes, deal with that money transfer business, the $100,000 to what's his name...at his bank. Make sure there's a memo on the transfer an idiot couldn't miss. Banker's draft, move it four times."

CHAPTER 32

Orphaned as a toddler in a tragic car accident that had taken both parents and his older brother, young Tomas grew to manhood as ward of the State. At age fifteen, a school project introduced him to the famous medieval portraitist Tiziano Vecellio, known to posterity as "Titian," and through him to Ranuccio Farnese.

Ranuccio was twelve in 1542 when captured in oil on canvas by Titian. In every detail, the spitting image of Tomas. Hours were spent in front of a mirror comparing his own countenance to the work of Renaissance antiquity. Tomas had even used double mirror technology to reverse the image reversal. By night he studied Ranuccio's portrait; by day, the history of the boy in the portrait and of the boy's family.

Tomas had immediately concluded his genes and those of the boy were of a shared pool. It grew to an obsession; Tomas knew himself to be the reincarnated Ranuccio Farnese.

The reincarnate Cardinal of the Catholic Church, Prior to the Knights of Columbus in Venice, Administrator to the Archdiocese of Naples, and twice the Latin Patriarch of Constantinople. He was grandson to one Alessandro Farnese...Pope Paul III.

Reincarnate of the grandson of the Pope that began the counter reformation that, through the Council of Trent, made the Catholic Church pretty much in its modern mold, oversaw da Vinci's Sistine Chapel ceiling, made war on Protestants and Lutherans, commissioned the new order of the Jesuits, awarded North America to Portugal and Spain, approved enslavement of blacks, bred four bastard children, and then conferred benefices in the form of erstwhile Church property and domains upon them. Grandad made the Farneses rich and powerful, contemporaries, essentially equals to Medicis and Borgas.

One of those bastards married an Orsini; Ranuccio was one of three sons born of that union.

Ranuccio's brother Alessandro and grandpapa Pope came to Tomas in dreams. Every visit ended after they intoned his Latin paean to murder, "Cum tristitia hoc facio ad meliorem gloriam familiae meae," which translated means, "I do this, sadly, for the greater glory of my family."

Tomas' madness initially made itself manifest as curiosity about art, matters ecclesiastic, history, and Latin. The middling, diffident student became a star. Those present at his valedictorian address applauded long and hard at his remonstrations to his relatively untutored classmates to learn and to love their personal histories.

Tomas adopted the baser elements of his forbearers. He was the toxic cauldron in which ancient Borgia, Medici, and Farnese villainies brewed thoroughly modern medieval evil. By fifteen, young Tomas settled on his vocation; recapture the wealth and glory of his former self, repopulate the near extinct bloodline. He would use the tools of his forbearers.

Upon graduation, young Farnese did his mandatory military service for the required two years. Uncharacteristic of men of his generation, he re-upped and spent four years in special ops, in strange places doing strange things. He was discharged with honors, and a record showing five sanctioned kills.

There were considerably more notches on his belt, and one enduring friendship.

As a retired officer with an undergraduate degree, Tomas/Ranuccio completed a two-year business degree in one year, heavy on finance.

Now ready for his life work, Tomas began regular confessions at the Basilica di San Giovanni in Laterno. The old building bears scars; sacks, fires, earthquakes, history. It is the epicenter of the Latin Church, holding within its walls the mortal remains of six Popes and the heads of Saints Peter and Paul.

Tomas conspired to confess only to the Cardinal Vicar himself. This required his military expertise in stealth and planning, and bore fruit shockingly quickly. Confession turned to counseling, hence retreats, finally a suggested vocation.

He was, courtesy of his mentor, on a fast track in the very center of God's head office on Earth.

It took Tomas ten years to achieve the critical point of departure for his life's work. At age thirty he became a deacon; by forty and by then Father Tomas, he sat for the first time at his desk at the Holy office of the Apostolic Camera. That is, he went to work at the central board of finance in the Papal administration.

CHAPTER 33

Tired, hungry, frightened, and grieving, Sarah fought to keep her eyes open. Liberté's assertion of faith as driving on a two lane highway kept her focused. At just past one in the wee hours, she collapsed into the safe haven of her own bed.

She tossed, turned, shifted, and pummeled the uncooperative pillow. At five she gave up trying.

Tea and toast were taken alone in her office, door closed, drop-ins dismissed. She ran a gamut of fear over Sammy, the guilt of Ted, and shock at that breeding pen.

There was a mountain of mail, but she didn't care. She sat, paced, sniffled, almost called her Mom, drifted from thought to thought, and did nothing.

Finally she attacked Floyd's document. It told of a lawyer named Irv Solomon, whom Floyd had engaged on her behalf to establish a charitable trust in the Cayman, Alcazar Trust, according Butterfield's banking requirements: to facilitate the $350 million. The money was to come in the form of ten different anonymous donations, each through different banks and in differing amounts.

She had no doubt the money would come when they had done for Tomas. She had no doubt this Irv Solomon was one of theirs. She dialed, got his voice mail, hit zero, and talked to a secretary named Doris, who made an appointment for Mr. Solomon's office for the following Thursday at 10 a.m.

The delay was necessary to assure everything preconditioning the flow of money was complete. Vertigo.

Off the phone, Sarah realized she wanted more than anything to talk to Ted. She really didn't have anything she could say to him, but had to see him.

His voice thrilled her even more than hers thrilled him. Lunch at Sharky's.

Instant regret.

As was her wont, she took her angst to the end of the garden, stared into the primordial swamp, prayed for the osmosis of its simple logic.

In the swamp one kills or is killed.

Warn Ted, be destroyed.

Apologize, be destroyed.

Explain, be destroyed.

Mention the four girls, be destroyed.

Survive, make history, not become a footnote of it.

Ted was to be consumed.

Also from the swamp: she, Sarah, an apex predator. Strange, tumescent heat in her loins.

Turning from the swamp, thoughts leapt from the inhuman darkness of nature to the nature of human darkness. She now assumed that by noon on the day of Therese's death, Floyd probably had her under surveillance. She couldn't risk seeing Ted even if she wanted to.

Her next thought was that if they knew so much about Tomas, they must have surveilled Therese. They probably watched her murder. She clasped her hands to still their tremor. The swamp. Fear. She had been lucky; when she moved the computer to the car the Mossad spys must have missed her because they had vacated in anticipation of a rash of police.

What if the church learned of her role? Excommunication might be inconvenient, but it wasn't death. If Liberté found out any of it... In the swamp, paranoia is a tool of survival. Everything threatened. Everyone threatened.

The apex predator clawed for what she had been. The little girls gave her purchase on moral high ground. She wouldn't...*couldn't* risk the lives of those girls!

She called and cancelled lunch. Ted wanted to know what she had wanted to see him about in the first place. She equivocated. He became frightened that there was something he needed to know that she was now withholding from him. He was fine with not meeting, it might have been a bad idea, but he begged to know what was so important.

Telling someone, whom you have previously told you have things to discuss, that it really wasn't anything important and that you should forget it doesn't sit well with a person looking at a prison sentence. Ted became angry, sharing distinctly inelegant references to Sarah. She hung up.

CHAPTER 34

Floyd's analysis of Therese's demise was spot on. Therese attended the party at Mr. Tamaros', her host proudly showed off his collection of antiquities, including a five inch gold and lapis scarab brooch he had only recently purchased at auction. It was reputably from the time of King Tutankhamen, and offered for auction by a dealer in Switzerland.

Sister Therese had immediately known the item belonged in the Vatican. Not six months earlier, she had done the write up on that very piece. The good woman did exactly what she ought; contacted her boss.

He had insisted they correspond by Blackberry PIN. Had she known modern technology as well as she did antiquities, she might still be alive. A major selling point of the Blackberry is secrecy of PIN transactions. Securities dealers forbid its use as it has been used for nefarious insider trading, and repressive regimes forbid its use as it doesn't allow them to spy on their citizens.

Chaos is reordering. Chaos is change. Chaos is a force. Chaos was rampant.

Tomas was making mistakes, even as the Carmerlengo defended him against a barrage of questions from jealous and concerned curia denizens. It had been Tomas who had handled public relations after Therese's murder, and everyone questioned the no-funeral move. It had been Tomas who pulled the trigger on the excommunication.

Others agreed it might have been Latae Sententia as Father Tomas held it to be, but it could have been Ferendae Sententia, with the force of a real hearing, or not a schism at all. It had been Tomas who forced the hasty sale of 2200 O'Neill.

That was the single act that caused the ripple that caused the wave that went rogue and began to sink Tomas' boat.

People doubted motives as well as judgment. Increased caviling about ungoverned acts. The same questions from so many different thoughtful and esteemed colleagues of the college, a college of which Tomas was not a member, forced the Carmerlengo's hand.

He called Tomas in for a chat to explain face-to-face the accountability changes being made.

Different forces in Ophrah. Money from tourists and pilgrims. They would stay longer, spend more, if only they had a place to stay and things to do. Homes became bed and breakfasts. Men of the swamp became tour guides. Hunters operated safaris. Sharky's even offered a buffet. Strange men in suits, driving fancy cars, surveyed property.

Forces act on other forces. In Ophrah, economic forces bore on legal forces. Chief, judge, district attorney all owed paychecks and aspirations to votes. Balancing public demand for speedy conviction with a plaintiff's right to fair play and personal aspirations. Something had to give.

Floyd was a force. With a team. There were four of them; one female, three male, all trained and field-tested in state-sanctioned murder.

The team began rehearsals for what would be a ballet of death in secret, in Beersheba even before Floyd arrived on the military jet that left Berlin a scant twelve hours after Sister Sarah departed the Baie Suite. Floyd had personally requested the team; this would be their fourth operation as a unit. En route to Berlin, he had mapped out the generality of the assassination, had forwarded it by secure transmission. Prior to embarkation from Berlin he spent an hour in secure Internet conferencing, consumed a military ration and heavy dose of diphenhydramine, and chatted briefly with his wife and the twins, careful to deny them any information of his whereabouts or plans. He then squeezed aboard the Mirage 2000 which carried fuel instead of bombs and missles so it could make the 2500 mile flight, mach 2 non-stop. Five minutes into the flight it arrived at 60,000 feet, and five minutes after that, Floyd succumbed to drug-induced, much-needed sleep.

Yet another force. As Floyd winged toward Beersheba, politicos convened to argue who, what, and how concerning the huge amount of money their angel of death was to deliver. Hawks pitched the original plan; buy claims then sue. Doves vetoed that approach as unacceptable public relations risk. The middle carried the day, but insisted on the Hawk backup as a threat to help negotiations. The compromise was to approach the Holy See on a safe pretext, restore to them enough money to assure survival, and in the process get returned to Israel's possession those parts of its history now known to be resting in the sacred vaults of Saint Peter's Rock.

Liberté wrestled with internal forces. As much as her masters craved a closed book, she craved truth. She knew Ted wasn't completely dirty and Sarah wasn't completely clean. She, the lone bastion for a man she could not stand, was consumed with ambiguities around the ex-nun, whom she liked and admired.

Fact is force. A new force emerged. A First Bank of Miami clerk showed his manager a deposit order. $100,000 was paid into Mr. Coulson's account. The quantum triggered a hold as assurances were sought that the money was not about blood or drugs. The transfer was from Butterfield in the Caymans so highly secretive of source. The transfer memo said only "re: computer." The manager called Head Office. Head Office called the police.

CHAPTER 35

At 5 a.m. Father Tomas' cell phone winked news of the arrival of a message. The Carmerlengo. "See below. Come ASAP."

In the normal course, Carmerlengo inquisitions were easily managed. Whatever the issue, Father Tomas simply inferred risk to the financial side of life, launched a complex diatribe, obtained a testament of continued support, and got out as fast as he could.

Not this time.

There were no pleasantries. No background. Just specific questions about the gold notes. Exactly how did the guarantee provisions work? Upside be damned. The notes were issued at $2,000 an ounce and gold was now hovering at $1,200, a 40% reduction, a loss of $800 per note if redeemed. A total of 750,000 notes were issued, so right now Mother Church was sitting on a loss of $600 million. Was this correct?

Parishioners had been talking. The Securities and Exchange Commission had taken up the issue and was rumored to be preparing for a full investigation. In spite of himself, Father Tomas couldn't help a tiny inside smile..."They think that's a problem? Just wait!" Putting on his game face he intoned there was no problem. He explained that the notes weren't due for another couple of months and only a fifth of the issue came due at that time.

The penny dropped, "Il Papa has taken advice," said the Carmerlengo, and then he read, "The Church must prepare to answer questions and to do so from a base of knowledge much greater than simply referring everything to one man. Father Tomas is instructed to meet forthwith with a team from the Prefecture for the Economic Affairs of the Holy See.

They will prepare a full report. If this is done well and quickly then perhaps the Holy See will not be obliged the inconvenience of fighting an audit by outsiders. Church affairs are like the knees of virgins; they must remain closed tight."

"Tomas, you have served your Church and your God well, but that service must now be altered. It will be quite impossible to put you in the position of answering questions to our enemies who seek only to discredit...us...by discrediting you. It is better if ignorance of specifics permits the luxury of plausible denial.

I know this is a shock and that you have your ways. Change can be difficult. Tomorrow you begin transfer of responsibility for all the funds. For the benefit of your own soul, we instruct that within a week you begin a private pilgrimage of faith, to visit the holiest of holy places on Earth. During that pilgrimage you are ordered to one year of silence and complete anonymity. You will deal in cash and carry no modern communication devices. No one is to know where you are or are going, or to hear a single word from your lips, unless it is a final confession in the final moments of your life. Do you understand?"

The Carmerlengo stood. Tomas knew he was dismissed. The Carmerlengo silently embraced him. Tomas knew it was forever.

Tomas was unfazed. These orders were remarkably close to his own plan. It had just moved up, and only a little. He would have to be much more careful though. Planning and execution is much more complicated under suspicion, and Tomas had no doubt this was about suspicion. And distancing; any perceived impropriety on his part could alter it all and ruin his life's work. Questions, answers, prying, explanations, altered signatures. A week? Screw that. What had Il Papa said about virgins' knees? That vicious little bastard was trying to pry his open. He would leave this very night.

Tomas now saw danger everywhere. Was he being followed? Was his phone tapped? Had his room been bugged? The Carmerlengo's was a big step. Clearly they no longer trusted him, so he ought to assume they suspected something. But nothing like what he would now do; if they had, they would have clapped him into ecclesiastical irons right away.

Three cabs and one bus later, Tomas felt secure enough to make a single call from a pay phone.

Two more buses and the shopping was done. Tomas was packed with all that he needed and no one had seen it happen. Another bus, a cab ride, and a twenty-minute walk took him to the garage where Luigi had died. The priest-turned-fugitive placed his travel kit in the tiny trunk, relocked the rusty old door and left.

One hour later, Father Tomas entered the law offices of the Parma Partnership to meet with lawyer Lorenzo Mitachelli.

The papers were as per his instructions. The settlement trusts were to be liquidated, cash transferred to Butterfield bank. It was all straight forward as Father Tomas was sole trustee in all files. Mitachelli, a crusty seventy-two year old, advised the money couldn't move until the following day, but with all the documents signed, it was a mere formality.

Tomas shook the offered hand and left.

Mitachelli waited five minutes to frustrate any unplanned disclosure that might result from a client re-appearance, then dialed.

"Hello, this is?"

"Floyd."

"Bird's in flight. All as arranged. Money to your account tomorrow. Please instruct concerning the gold bars."

He hung up, shredded the paper. Five minutes on, those shreds entered the Eternal City sewage system and were forever gone.

Blissfully unaware of the fatal wound his plans had just suffered, Father Tomas employed consecutive cabs to return to his office at the Vatican, where he marshalled documents for the meeting ordered to occur the next morning. Two bemused Swiss guards puzzled how he'd escaped their watchful eyes, and determined it best to keep it to themselves.

That very day, in a deserted castle in the north of Corsica, four twelve-year-olds were segregated, each to a separate cell. Each was bound and gagged, knees forced, repeatedly raped with basters to inject previously banked semen. The procedure was to be repeated daily until conception was validated.

CHAPTER 36

Finally panicked to appropriate action, Ted yet again acted without counsel, turning instead to Liberté. He had at first thought her a foolish enemy, and now his friend. "Oh, come off it! You're trying to make "9" fit where "6" goes!"

"Huh?" replied the exasperated detective.

"Sudoku" he said, a little hurt that she hadn't caught the reference cleanly.

Liberté just shrugged, "OK, Ted, give it to me again then."

He emitted a long, frustrated breath, tired of endless, unheeded wisdom. Now frightened, his exasperation conveyed long over-due angst.

The huge deposit in his account? That could not have been Sarah on her own. She had an accomplice...or someone else was out there. This one, Liberté, would see the light, but Ted was at a loss as to who the accomplice could possibly be. No bravado, now thoroughly unnerved.

He'd kept Sarah's secret, and that sleeping dog hadn't bitten either of them until now. But this was different. She, or whoever, was out to destroy him. If the cops connected Ted to the computer, they would have the missing piece: the motive.

Unless Liberté believed his story, he was done. In his own career he'd taken down countless perps for much less.

"Sarah took the computer from the dead woman and she hid it."

'So you say, now.'

"Look Liberté, if I took the thing, why in the name of God would I sell it, like now, and have the money ear-marked and sent to my goddamn bank? I know about money transfers and limits and reporting. You do. I do. Anybody that can read knows about the limits to catch drug money. So did the people who sent the money. So they even put a memo note on the transfer 'full payment for computer.' I mean, really...come on..."

"I can agree that it's a dumb mistake. That's how we catch bad guys. They make mistakes. You need a lawyer. I'm not even sure I shouldn't just read you your rights right now, and slap your ass in jail."

"I don't need a lawyer. Guilty people need lawyers. I didn't do anything. She did."

"You've been warned."

He couldn't stop himself, "I don't know exactly how this went down. I'm pretty damn sure Sarah didn't kill the old woman...that Leroy guy did, and whoever killed him is long gone. But when Sarah found the body, she saw the computer and took it. She told me...do you understand? She told me it was to keep it safe for the Church. Maybe she thought that. But look around. Look at her clothes, the way she comes and goes, car rentals, you name it. Out of nowhere the nuns own the place they were supposed to get thrown out of. None of it makes sense unless..."

"Unless?"

"Someone shows up. Someone with a lot of money who wants the computer. They buy Sarah off."

"So why pin it on you, Ted?"

At this point he was flummoxed. "I don't know. Unless...yes...I do know. They want everyone to think I did it so they'll stop looking. This is part of a bigger plan. This is just the first square in the Sudoku."

"Ted, shut the fuck up about Sudoku. I swear, one more reference out of you and I'll arrest you for...I don't know...being annoying."

Ted correctly surmised that Liberté's turn of attitude meant she was buying in to his argument.

"So you see, right?"

"I think you have a case for reasonable doubt, but that's for court. As of right here and now, I'm a cop, and I'm looking at a guy with motive, means and opportunity."

"You're arresting me?"

"No. Not yet. I'd guess you've got a day at the most. I'm going to have to tell the DA. He can make his mind up."

"But..."

"But? Kiss my ass! Do you think you're the first suspect with a theory? Shit, Ted, they all have a theory. And you know what else Ted, they all get helpful, like you right now, when the noose starts to tighten. You're beyond stupid Ted. If you heard what you say you heard come out of Sister Sarah's mouth, and you didn't say anything, then you're already a guilty man. You aided and abetted after the fact...of course that assumes she actually said what you say she said. Right when it's crunch time, all this evidence shows up. Nothing I can corroborate, just hearsay. No Ted, you're just like every other slime ball; the minute we get close, you have a million theories. Get a fucking lawyer. The only way to save your ass is to get Sister Sarah to tell me that she took that computer from the dead nun...from Sister Therese."

This presented Ted with a problem. The redhead wasn't talking to, taking calls, returning texts, even getting caught in the same room with him. "That's a bit of a problem..."

"I know," said the cop. "Must be tough on your ego."

"Huh?"

"Well, you were good buddies...then you weren't. Let me see, when did things go bad between you two?" At this point she threw her hands up in the universal "stop" gesture, chuckled and said, "She hasn't had sex in maybe twenty years, and after you boink her once she wants nothing more to do with you. What are you Ted, a lousy fuck? Or does she know something about you that spoiled your little love affair?"

"I didn't fuck her, she..."

"Right!"

"Besides, what does that have to do with anything?"

"Let me explain. Here's a scenario. She tells you that she took the computer, and you tell her it's worth a fortune. All hell breaks loose with the people in Rome and now she needs money, so she comes to you and you sell the thing, but not for enough so she gets mad and here we are."

"That's ridiculous."

Now Liberté was angry. She started finger stabbing his chest and snarled, "I'll tell you what's ridiculous! A woman got killed because of secrets in a computer. I'll tell you what else is ridiculous! A grown man, a cop...*ex-cop*...finds out a stupid little woman withheld information from me, doesn't tell, screws her, takes her money, then expects me to believe anything he says. Either get that bitch down here to confess right goddamn now, or get a lawyer. I'm finished with both of you. Now get out of my way."

With that she pushed past Ted, and left to the sanctity of the women's washroom.

Sitting, staring at the banal blankness of the stall door, Liberté came off boil, and thought. There was no doubt now that Ted was a liar. When he disclosed Sarah's secret about the computer, he proved it because he hadn't told earlier. However, what Ted had said about the money transfer did ring true. The size of the transfer was sure to garner further examination, and the notation had to have been designed to set Ted up. Ted had lied by not telling, but that was all he had lied about!

So that left the redhead; first on scene, now cavorting with cash, and not close to forthright. She knew Ted was right about the sex too; the only reason they did the deed was because she wanted to. Sarah had said that herself that day in Sharky's. Who knew her reasons? Maybe she was rebelling, like she had said; maybe she was roping Ted into her nefarious plan, her little web. God knows she wouldn't have been the first or the last vixen to spring a panty trap. Maybe she was celebrating her newfound badness.

Didn't matter.

Liberté knew her superiors wouldn't take on God and his team. Of course, Sarah was no longer on that team, so maybe she could get broken to a confession. It was worth a try.

Liberté was sure Ted was an idiot, but equally sure he wasn't evil. Her gut told her that. The same gut told her that Sarah had many more answers to give, but she wasn't sure what the questions were. The only person who could tie Sarah to any piece of this whole mess was Ted, and he was the prime suspect—a liar either way, and fighting for his life.

If Ted went down, it would include the murder; they could work it as a contract with Leroy co-opted as Ted's proxy.

If Sarah went down it would be relatively minor, maybe theft, perhaps obstruction of justice. The stakes were so high on the one side, and so relatively low on the other that Liberté felt obliged to act as Ted's ombudsman in the decision to arrest or not.

CHAPTER 37

The team waited. Five strong, the wheel man the only local. A business trip, in and out, under a day; by this day's end Father Tomas would be gone. Without a trace. They arrived the day before, separately, in different transport, unarmed, with false I.D.

Each to a separate hotel, room service, sleep, isometric fitness, assignment step-through, weapons cache retrieval, weapons breakdown, covert phone engaged, local newspaper for cover.

Electronic surveillance details of Tomas and the garage. Background of the car; prior owner Luigi de Parma, an estate sale managed by Mitachelli. Fifteen minute surveillance reports. The reminder, silent kill and removal: no trace. A disappearance.

Preordained stations surrounding kill zone, radius one mile, perimeter patrol, crossing patterns, wordless team encounters.

Fleeced

Review of specifics; if the target arrives in daylight, a single assassin within, if in the dark, permit ingress and then swarm assault. Reduced chance of fatal mistaken identity.

Electronic confirmation; night job protocol.

Within the garage, the vintage MGA that had carried Luigi to his maker awaited its next eternity traveler; as Tomas had left it, but it was now with the distributor cap disengaged, removed.

Carrying only a briefcase, the target passed from street lamp pool to street lamp pool, striding purposefully until ten feet from the kill zone. He stopped briefly, quickly surveyed the scene to assure privacy, missed the ten eyes not thirty feet distant, ingress. A brief quizzical start at the ease of the rusty lock response.

Starter motor music cued assassins to begin the dance. One went to the getaway Suburban, another to the delivery van hearse, three to the kill zone. Silence. Two assassins huddled briefly in front as the third went to the rear to snuff any chance of escape.

A pause. Tomas cursed, slammed the door of the MGA and emerged from the claustrophobic confines of his mechanical setback for fresh air, to consider options. They pounced.

The two at the door shoved the target hard, back into the garage, aiming flashlights to blind, stun. Tomas fell back onto the grill, reflexively used it to advantage. Like footbal linemen and trained assassins, he loaded his total weight onto the car, rolled hard left, dropped to one knee to evade the angle of obvious first restraint, sprang quickly back to his feet and hard into the side wall to avoid being outflanked.

The assassins spread out to maximize situational control while minimizing the potential damage of any lucky shot the target might take.

The target recognized the professionalism of his own training, knew the outcome in this mode, altered his tack to a new defense.

Floyd, one of the two covering the open door, stood directly before the target, and demanded, "You are Father Tomas?"

Tomas raised, straightened to his full 6'1", pulled his cuffs down, rearranged his jacket, and sternly averred, "No. This is Ranuccio Farnese. I command that you obey me. I am your better."

This startled Floyd. Those hits that survived long enough to know it was a hit normally went wide-eyed craven.

Floyd raised a hand to stay his team. The inevitable delayed.

"You are not Father Tomas? I am mistaken?"

"I am Ranuccio Farnese. The world knows me as whom you seek. I lived five hundred years ago, and am reincarnate, on a critical mission. As your better, I command your support in this campaign. Much relies on me. I am among the living to right wrongs to my familia...to bring Farneses back from the dead. I have reclaimed the inheritance of our forbearers...will reestablish the line...peers to Medicis, Borgias, Orsinis...Farneses from the darkness into the light. I command that you guard and protect me in this mission. Farneses do not forget their friends. You will be justly rewarded, will want for nothing. Perhaps your daughter will carry for me the Farnese seed and you and I will live as brothers.

For the first time he could remember, Floyd was nonplussed. All he could muster was a weak, "Say again?"

With the urgency of the situation apparent to him, Tomas explained his heritage as papal grandson, his task of redemption and reclamation.

Floyd seized the opportunity, "I understand sir. You are of noble blood and purpose. We must consider this. Your seed, you said? Surely not to the rabble."

Tomas, now insane with purpose, "Correct, my brother. You understand. Only noble Italians may thus serve. It is done."

"Done? Who? When?"

Tomas drew back from the brink of disclosure, "You understand, sir, there are things you must know and things only I must know."

Sensing angst among his own kill squad and the need for efficiency of deed but also time, Floyd took one shot, "This plan...it is so...so profound. How can you do this?"

The mad man gambled, "I will show you. They are not far. My people found a place...an old air base in the north of Corsica..."

"Your people?"

Tomas laughed demonically. "Of course a team. Mercenaries are so expensive. I have had to..."

Floyd now knew all. With luck some might be saved.

Floyd raised his right hand in a signal Tomas and the kill squad understood. He slumped. Assassin Sasha, positioned behind the target, struck. The syringe pierced his neck, flirted with vessels, nerves, spine.

As Sasha pressed the syringe piston, Floyd pressed "Call" then spat, "Corsica, North, old air base, mafia guards."

Ten ccs of pentobarbital, the elixir of python death, began its work. In seconds Tomas' current and past worlds coalesced. Into the body bag, then the hearse.

The hearse carried the bipedal viper one way, the SUV ferried the kill squad the other, the garage was left locked, devoid of all traces of Tomas.

The hearse took twenty minutes to deliver the package to the waiting hands of an undertaker previously compromised in a Mossad sting. Tomas' remains underwent double incineration, were then swept into a cardboard urn, and surrendered to Floyd.

While Tomas returned to dust, Floyd had dropped kill squad members at separate locations, driven to the Trajan Market mall, parked the SUV beside a white Volvo, hence to the mausoleum in that Volvo, in a rental...this time from Eurocar using separate I.D.

Once he took delivery of the urn, Floyd drove to Piazza Farnese, descended the river steps to the Tiber, and there beneath the ancestral city home of the once-was Tomas, just south and across from Vatican city, dropped the last scintilla of the madman into the river. Gone. Without a trace.

By the time Floyd got to his hotel room, Corsican military had identified and begun surveillance of the Farnese breeding pen. Within 24 hours, three girls were restored to their families.

Five mafiosos and one child died in the liberation assault.

CHAPTER 38

Sunlight pushed out the night. Liberté, at her desk since midnight, looked up, then at her watch, saw it was 7:30 a.m., and felt the grit of sleep starvation. She had rehashed every piece of evidence; witness notes, forensic reports, photos. Darkly puzzled by Ted and Sarah's various statements; he saying too much, her too little. Three realities crushed in on her; Sarah knew more than she was telling, Ted didn't cause any killing or mutilation, and she was out of time. The brass was not going to back off. Their facts weren't any more legitimate than her feelings, but the bit was in their teeth.

The phone. The sheriff. She was needed upstairs.

The honest servant gathered files, packed them in an evidence box, heaved it into a cradled hold, and trundled awkwardly toward the stairs. Forced to shift the weight, Liberté abandoned the load; if she was going to convince anybody of anything, specifics would be distractions, and bad ones at that. She would take only her eloquence. Use real truths to dismantle half-facts.

He was not alone. The sheriff, the judge, and the district attorney awaited. Motioned to a seat by the sheriff, she sat, noting diverted focuses of the other two. Diverted glances could mean they were now embarrassed and about to come around, she dared hope.

That was immediately dashed by her boss's next utterance, "We've had enough. It's time, Sergeant. You're costing money and time. That son-of-a-bitch did it. We have prepared an arrest warrant..."

Liberté began her practiced refrain, "All we have is circumstantial..."

The DA cut her off, "Sergeant, it's done. Case closed."

Fatigue overcame caution. She lost it, "Really? Who do you three think you are? Judge, jury, maybe executioner...or maybe just three blind fucking mice?

The sheriff jumped in, "Tell ya what, Liberté. I know you been here all night, so I'm going to kind of forgive that little outburst. I know you care and all, but we all do. And that man did this thing. Half the damn jails in this country are full of people convicted on circumstance. It's not your job. It's out of your hands..."

"Listen," she interrupted, "I swear to God I'll go to court as a witness for the defense."

"That would not be a good career move."

"Whatever. If telling the truth is a bad career move for a police officer, then I'm probably in the wrong job."

The unspoken truth was that Sheriff Smith didn't want to lose Liberté. She was a damn fine cop, and besides, she put up with stuff other women might not. This political correctness thing was a pain in..."OK, OK, OK. Liberté, give it your best shot. Convince us. Right now, right here. You got a pickle up your butt I see. Y'all been here all night. You look like shit. Get it all out then go home, get a shower, get some sleep. Probably best if you're not here later anyway."

She looked from face to face, slowly. Then rose, poured a blessed cup of coffee, channeled Clarence Darrow. Clarity infused her mind. Focus on only one thing. Pressure the weakest link. Explode the myth of "circumstantial". "OK, so, there's another person as circumstantially guilty as Mr. Coulson. Think about it. We need motive, means, and opportunity. No one thinks Ted, er, Mr. Coulson pulled the trigger. They think he conned Leroy into it and then offed him. Right?"

Sherriff Smith nodded. The others stared impassively. She continued, "OK, so the computer's the key. Right?"

Same reactions. "Well, here's the thing. There's one nun over there that sure as hell isn't acting too angelic! That Sister Sarah has been spending some serious cash, and I have not heard a word from her on how she got it. Oh ya, I've asked, but it's always vague. If I were going to third-degree anybody, I think it would be the nun. In any case, she confuses things. The computer was supposedly stolen to make some money. No one knows where the thing is but only one person is flashing Benjamins."

The DA interjected, "Two perps don't mean I don't take down the one I got dead to rights."

Liberté gave no reaction, kept her eyes on Sheriff Smith.

The DA continued, "So that's it? He had GSR, she didn't. She has some money, so she planned a murder, then killed a guy herself? What'd she do…plant the money in his account?"

"Why not?" responded Liberté while continuing to pinion her boss. "Let's look at that. She has lived in South Florida for over a decade now, and a lot of her work has been with the poor and the pathetic. She had as much chance to find a Leroy as Ted, er, Mr. Coulson did. And I betcha don't know that little Sister Sarah grew up in an outdoor paradise, up in Minnesota, right by some of the best hunting in America. She told me herself. We dined one night and she told me about her youth as a tomboy, with canoes, and fishing, and yes boys, guns! Sister Sarah is, was, a trained markswoman! GSR, the lack of, may exonerate her from the shooting itself, I don't know, the rest of it looks iffy, and we already bought his explanation of his GSR. I don't know how she moved the money, but if she could do all the other things…"

Judge Jeb was twitchy, "Sheriff, you got a damn case here or don't you?"

Liberte was on a roll, and kept going, "So the nun knew about the computer, she could handle a gun, she would have been able to find a Leroy as easily as the next guy, no question she could come and go as she wished in that building…and then…she was first on the scene. She's the one who said the computer was gone. Maybe it wasn't gone until she took it. The whole show didn't start until she pressed, "Go." I don't know what she did before she pressed, "Go." Maybe she took the thing before Leroy even got there! Then she waited for Leroy to come back to meet her, killed him, came home, and "discovered" the body! That fits too!"

Liberté then hit them with her newest fact. "I interviewed Coulson again. He's been a lovesick puppy so he sat on some important facts… you know…to protect his lover. That's over now, he knows she's moved on, so he's ready to talk…to protect himself. I have what amounts to hearsay evidence but I believe it. Coulson told me that Sister Sarah told him that when she found the body in the first place, the computer was there…that she took it to protect it from the public eye, hid it under her mattress. We did a once-over but no in-depth. So maybe the bit about protecting it was a lie. Maybe she planned this whole thing, and then had a minute with Ted, er, Coulson, and got caught up in some post-coital sharing. I don't know, but I believe she said it."

The DA jumped in, "We can't use that! All it means is that a guy's feeling the heat and trying to pin it on someone else. If it gets out, it means you didn't do your job so well! As for the rest of it, look, this here's all circumstantial…"

Liberté scoffed, "Uh-huh. Every bit of it. The stuff on Sarah, the stuff on Ted. That's right, sir. If you're gonna bring in one, shouldn't we bring in the other? I mean, hell, they seem to know each other. The whole damn town knows he did her. What's good for the goose is good for the gander. You can't say one's guilty and the other isn't. Maybe he didn't fuck her, maybe she fucked him. Maybe she's doing a box job on Ted…um, I didn't mean that as a joke. My point is, we just don't know who did it. It might have been Ted. It might just as well have been Sarah. Or it might have been someone else. We don't know, and if that's true, we can't just put some poor slob on trial for his life. We gotta keep looking."

The DA had been waiting long enough. When she stopped for air, he jumped in, "Well I'll be damned. We got us a situation, don't we? Sherlock here wants to tell us that she can't find us a killer and he's right here in front of us!"

The judge nodded. The DA continued, "Little Miss Perfect here clearly doesn't get it. We all got ourselves elected to find killers and get 'em off the street, not to mollycoddle 'em and worry about what we can't do nothin' about."

Sheriff Smith and Judge Jeb looked at each other in silent assent, as Liberté stared in disbelief. The DA went on, "I get paid to convict and I'm here to tell you I can convict that feller. Everyone in this room, except for Miss Perfect, has to prove that he's doin' his job. The whole town knows who done this, except for Miss..." he just waved contemptuously in the direction of Liberté. "I'm not goin to tell 'em they was wrong, and I sure as hell ain't gonna tell 'em I...we...were wrong! Sometimes you go with your gut. This Coulson fella did the deed."

Liberté felt like she was spinning...dizzy. She was sure that if she stood she would fall down. These clowns were prepared to convict Ted, at least to the perils of a trial, and maybe to death because they didn't want to do their jobs?

Sheriff Smith raised a cautioning hand and began, "First off, she's "Liberté" or "Sergeant," or "Sergeant Alvarado" to you," this while pointing at the DA. Then he turned and directed himself only to Liberté, "Sergeant, you are not the only person on this team. You are part of this team, not all of it. What you say has some merit, I daresay, but there are other considerations here. I think you may be too close to this. Anyway, it's about community. Our community. We gotta get this thing behind us and quick. Fear is a bad thing for a community, and a worse thing for the folks supposed to make problems disappear. Thing is, folks think the nun's a hero, and I for one ain't gonna tell them different unless I'm damn sure, and you didn't make me damn sure. Sam here says he can get a conviction. That's his job, not mine. I'm supposed to help him make his case…he's says that's done, so Liberté, it's done. I'm not taking on any hero nun, and who else ya got? Some theory that some unknown person from Italy…you know…the Vatican, might have, maybe, for perhaps…not happening girl. You said your piece, now back off!"

She didn't. Furious, she rose, flushed, "You all ought to be ashamed. You'd put an innocent man in jail to save your own butts? Good thing the Marines don't fight wars like that! You're supposed to make the place safer, not seem like it's safer. The whole bloody country has jails full of innocent people. Thank God for DNA. At least some of them are getting out because of it. And every one of those people were like Ted. Someone thought they could convict, trick a jury with fear and innuendo, and bad facts, and lies…."

"Whoa, girl," interjected the judge. "We're not on trial here. And don't use this DNA stuff because, and I thank God Almighty for that, we can deal with facts here, and not some obtuse science shit that everyone believes but no one really understands. Facts are he did it. Facts are Sam here can prove it. Facts are you don't have a creditable alternative. I gotta get some breakfast, this meetin's over. Sam, where's that paper?"

Liberté turned white, "What paper?"

Sheriff Smith passed a document file to DA Sam, who gave it a once-over, then handed it to the judge. He also gave it a once-over, then fished for a pen to bind the warrant with the force of law. Liberté repeated the question, this time in the shrill squeak of fear looking for confirmation. The three men rose. The judge and DA brushed past Liberté and out the door. Sheriff Smith put his hand on her shoulder, and gently but firmly, pushed her back down into her seat. "Liberté, that was a warrant for the arrest of Ted Coulson. I'm going to get a black-and-white to pick him up right now. We know his habits. He'll be at his breakfast at the wharf. You are going to stay right here, Missy. I am going to get some food at Sharky's, and get caught up on the news."

CHAPTER 39

Fear overtook anger. Fatigue overtook fear. Liberté succumbed to the wreckage of emotional and physical exhaustion. Her eyes burned like desert skin. Swallowing hurt. Her lower back screamed for relief, while her shoulders ached the agony of prolonged stress. Grit and sweat conspired to chafe her folds, and her skin crawled. This couldn't be happening. Her career, and Ted's life, destroyed. After five minutes of hellish solitude, she stirred and slowly, unsurely, descended to her corner.

Ted had come to her as a last hope. For him, financial ruin, death, and prison. Prison, for an ex-cop, perhaps the worst of all of it. Estranged now from his sister, abandoned by the system he so trusted, deceived by that whore. Finally, failed by her. She could not let this happen.

With demonic sudden purpose, Liberté realized she could not now fail him in the only way there was left to help...to just be there.

A spasm of white hot terror bolted through her.

Ted might very well choose death by cop. He had nothing, nobody, no-where to turn. Only her. All those guns. One sudden move. If he had a gun... Nobody in that black-and-white would hesitate...or maybe they would...then would Ted force his execution, suicide, whatever, by shooting at them? Was her failure going to cause death? To whom? And to how many? Only she could stop it, and only if she got there before it was too late.

She had sensed the quiet, utter exhaustion of the man. Now she understood its meaning.

He had nothing to lose by dying; yet so much to lose by living. Only she could save him. Or them. No one sent to arrest Ted deserved to die. If they did, it was her fault. She couldn't let it happen. She had to be there. Maybe she could reason with him. Or them. Intervene. She would do what she had to, even if it meant harm to herself...

Collaring the first Uniform she saw, pulling him to a car, she ordered him to go full speed to the wharf. While he drove, she dialed.

First, Ted. After the three-ring maximum and the laid back "Please leave a message," she shouted into her mouthpiece that he must be calm, do nothing, she was on her way, and this could be worked out.

Then, Sarah. Straight to voice mail. She began to explain, got mumbly, and signed off with "If you have one ounce of decency left in you, get your ass down there. He's a fucking human."

Then she was silent, staring, thinking, gathering herself. Reminding herself no cop is safe to themselves or those around them when they've "lost it." Was she a danger? Had she lost it? Would she do something wrong, regrettable, hideous?

Another darker thought. Her voice message. What if Ted heard it? Knowing he was doomed, determined to take persecutors with him? Policing 101 teaches surprise and overwhelming force to assure peaceful ends to volatile beginnings. She had broken faith with the men in blue on the wharf. If Ted shot one of them because of her warning, then that man's blood would be on her hands.

"Fuck."

The Uniform looked at her mutely. Had he been more experienced he might have ordered her to stay put, or kept her away from the wharf. But that was not to be. By the time they arrived, the woman who had come to save Ted realized she probably...might have to kill him, or have a policeman's death on her own conscience. The steady hand becomes the itchiest finger.

The cruiser screeched to a halt behind the others. She leapt quickly out, elbowed her way through the ubiquitous crowd that only tragedy can draw, into the knot of officers immediately behind the District Attorney.

Sensing her presence force of purpose, the officers separated like the Red Sea. The DA shook his head at her. "You were warned. Get back. Get out of here sergeant. You shouldn't be here." He pushed her hard enough that she staggered back into the friendly arms of uniformed cohorts.

She wrestled violently from their grasp. In that split second the DA had moved forward toward Ted, two uniforms in tow for safety and formality.

"Wait!" screamed Liberté. "You don't understand. He's desperate. Suicidal. He might have a gun. Let me talk to him. He knows me, he trusts me."

The Uniforms looked briefly back, and then into guard lock step, each with a right hand to his hip, each unleashing his gun.

Reacting now more than thinking, Liberté bolted forward and to the side so that she might see, intervene, connect, let Ted know that she was there and that he wasn't alone.

She arrived at the fore precisely as they came within Ted's unadulterated line of vision.

There he was, same seat, same table as all those yesterdays.

Today was different; his food uneaten, Sudoku untouched, and mug full. Nature communed noisily. No one heard. No one took note. Ted was all there was.

Ted ached in his soul; his solitary comfort was the hard cold polymer handle in his pocket. His fingers probed, fondled the Glock.

Vaguely aware of his calm, Ted now yearned for the quiet solitude of oblivion. He would make them do it!

The only person who might care was Mariah; he reveled briefly in the guilt she would carry to her grave. He visualized redemption once they all learned the truth. Vignettes crowded in; Therese, Liberté, the money, Sarah, the computer.

Sarah? Which Sarah? Ingénue or witch? Confidante or bitch? Gentle disciple or vicious cunt?

His entire life a joke, his death, this great staged event of his, a hideous farce.

The posse pressed forward.

Ted pulled the gun from his pocket, placed the muzzle directly into his throat aiming up through his mouth and brain.

The posse stopped.

He saw Liberté crashing toward him, wanted to see more, say something, explain, make her understand his pain. He needed to live.

Immediately recoiling from his intended final act, Ted stepped back and in so doing stumbled. The maw of weapon dropped from him to the crowd of anxious, armed police.

A single shot crashed through flesh, bone, brain, instantly consigning him to history.

One gun smoldered ephemeral residue of death.

Liberté's.

She did to death the man she came to save. In the instant of his stagger, her fear for her brethren won.

Different circumstances, yet the same dilemma as for Sarah, with the same lethal choice.

CHAPTER 40

Time and bullets don't go backward.

Friendly arms broke Liberté's collapse. Someone held her hair away from her vomit. Another took the gun, bagged it.

From some removed out-body place she sensed it all, seeing only that last, stunned look on Ted's face.

Gentle hands pulled her to her feet, to a chair, wrapped her in a blanket. A napkin daubed vomit from her mouth and chin. Hot coffee. Kneaded shoulders, cooing that it would be alright, assertions she had only done what she had had to do.

She bawled.

Sheriff Smith bustled over to order her to snap out of it. She did.

Quiet now, she stared at the husk in numb disregard of all else. He was altered, and seemed shrunken, grotesquely akimbo.

Liberté pushed away, strode alone to the parking lot where one of the new cabs prowled, got in, directed the driver, drew her phone from its holster, typed "Sarah," pressed "Call."

Sensing she must, Sarah answered. When Liberté told her that they needed to talk she agreed. When Liberté said it had to be now, Sarah said, "As soon as you can."

CHAPTER 41

The convent door opened silently, the two women passed wordlessly through the foyer, down the center hall, and into Sarah's private office. Liberté started, "Who the fuck are you?"

Sarah: "Why are you here? Is it..."

"Yes. Ted's dead. I shot him."

"Did he..."

"No, he didn't try anything. They think he slipped. He had a gun. It was reflex. But I killed him! I went to save him, to stop him from being killed by some trigger-happy idiot. I knew he was suicidal. He told me he wanted to end it. I knew he couldn't. I begged the DA, but he just had to have a closed file..."

"So it's not really..."

"Shut up Sarah. I know you had that damned computer. So how much money did you make? Is that how you saved this dump?"

Sarah stiffened. "You should go."

"Relax," spat the cop, "you're safe. Nobody wants to say we drove an innocent man crazy and then killed him. This Goddamn place can't think beyond the money they're making...not a chance they're going to risk that by making their fucking hero a...what are you Sarah? A thief? What else don't I know about my BFF?"

Sarah collapsed into a guest chair, chin on chest, silent but for breathing.

"Well?"

"Liberté, you didn't kill Ted. Neither did I. Ted did it to himself. Honest to God, he was too dumb to live."

Liberté collapsed into the other chair. "What? What are you saying?"

"Ted didn't get it. He didn't know how things work. He was in his own little world. He was...naive."

"That why he slept with a snake?"

Sarah shrugged, "All I know was that he thought it was love. Love had nothing to do with it. Besides, that didn't get him killed. If he had shut his mouth about all his theories, and had just let you do your thing, he wouldn't have ended up as number one suspect, would he?"

"We really didn't have anything until the money showed up. Whoever did that killed Ted. Who did that Sarah? You?"

"No, but I know how it happened."

"How?"

"Don't you get naive on me. I can't tell you, but it's big, and the people aren't people...it's...spies..."

"So, I'm supposed to believe..."

"Believe what you will. That thing was loaded with information people were willing to kill for. *Did* kill for!"

"So there are more dead guys? Does the F.B.I. know about this?"

"It's not about America. It's international. And no one's going to tell Interpol. Nobody wants the rest of the world in on any of this...shit."

"So, let me get this straight. You know the "whos and the hows", but it's not your fault?"

"Uh-huh. Just like with you. We're pawns, just pawns. You can learn the game or get killed by it. I have it figured out. Ted never did. I just hope for your sake that you can. I know you're not stupid."

"How did you buy this place? Where did that credit card come from?"

"None of your business, officer. We're done here"

Silence for the eternity of a minute. Liberté rose, walked to the door, turned back. "Sarah, all I know is you are front and center in a lot of shit that's killing people. We had our chance, you and me. These people won't hurt you, and I won't work with them anyway. I'm gone. I never want to see your face again."

She left.

CHAPTER 42

The ex-nun stepped from her shower, arranged a towel turban over her coif, and studied her naked body's reflection, even using a second mirror and ninth grade physics to get a good look at her rear end. She liked herself, and resolved that the tyranny of wax was worth the pain.

She luxuriated in skin cream here and face cream there. Not yet comfortable with color on her nails, she nevertheless buffed them to a high gloss, applied just a touch of glisten to her lips, passed just once through her lashes with mascara.

The silk! Bra, panties. Such joy. The former fitted, the latter designed fundamentally to privately cosset, tease. So very privately.

After much testing, Sarah decided on the tweed ensemble. The Medusa? She couldn't, but she did tuck it into the jacket pocket, usurping the place heretofore held for her rosary. Finally, three-inch black patent leather Pradas, and she was off.

The trip into downtown Miami took almost two hours, but she made it on time, parking at 200 South Biscayne Boulevard in the heart of the business section. A quick look in the rear view mirror confirmed she belonged. Her watch said that it was time.

Sarah entered the building with wild expectation of her new life. She pressed "30" where the name "Solomon, Schwartz and Baum, LLP" was specially engraved, and rose to her new state of grace.

When she asked for Irving Solomon, Sarah was deferentially whisked to a huge room with an ellipse of a table surrounded by maybe twenty luxurious leather chairs, and array of electronics that she had no idea about.

She had barely time to help herself to coffee when a man entered, beckoned her sit behind an imposing documents stack.

He told her the terms of his engagement had been clear and that she was his client, that he had no conflicts. She clutched at the broach.

When Irving finished his diatribe and pushed what he called an engagement letter toward her, Sarah asked if she might make a quick call.

He left for the five minutes she needed. Upon his return, she advised she had hired her own attorney, a Mary McGrady of McGrady & Kline, just two floors down. The constating documents for the Cayman Trust were all in place, and she was on her way up.

Solomon now excused himself, and after five minutes, returned. "I talked to...Floyd...the man you know as Floyd. He said to tell you that you are a wise woman. We are to do as you direct."

Mary McGrady and Irv exchanged warm greetings; they had met often, held each other in utmost esteem. As Mary unloaded her document case and replaced those prepared by Floyd's choice of lawyers, they chatted about the weekend; every so often she stopped to explain an item she was delivering.

When Irv wondered if he should review the tendered documents, she confirmed she was content with that but as happy, if it was OK with him, with an undertaking, already prepared and on one page, to the effect that all was correct and complete, holding Solomon, Schwartz & Baum harmless in the event of any deficiency.

He opted for the undertaking, leaving only mutual releases and the transfer of $350 million into the McGrady & Kline trust account, a twenty-minute wait for bank confirmation of the transfer, then the departure of the two women from the board room on the 30th floor to the board room on the 28th floor.

The room at M & K was in the same vein as that of SS&B, with more people around the table.

Clutching, again and oddly, at the broach, Sarah began her career as Chief Executive Officer of the fully-formed Women's Institute for Female Equality ("WIFE").

Her first act in this capacity was an around the table talk-and-tell to introduce team members to each other. Some three hours later, she shook each by the hand and thanked them for their commitment.

During that three hours development team members Government Relations firm Claxton Byrne, Town Planning Inc., and architects Shromski and Little, were tasked to redesign the thirty acres in Ophrah into an appropriate campus for WIFE.

Preliminaries complete, Sarah invited the team to drinks and dinner at Morton's; they all knew the place, all agreed to be there at 7.

Silently and seamlessly, at some point during the three hours just elapsed, an M & K clerk wired banking instructions previously approved by Sarah. The $350 million in WIFE became $300 million. The new numbered secret account in a separate discretionary trust with Sarah as sole trustee swallowed up the $50 million.

Sarah drove directly to the Fontainebleau, where, now known and greeted by name, she checked into her Baie suite. A dozen blood red roses and congratulatory note greeted her, courtesy of Floyd.

This break, intended for private rejoice, became crushing loneliness. She had not, and now did not, think once of Tomas or Ted. Nor for her family of sisters of the swamp. Only Liberté. She wished Liberté were here for, could share in, this. Time and chance estranged from the one person she felt was truly her friend. She drowned the ache in action; lists of "to-dos", and the agenda for the dinner at seven. If they were going to have the campus up and running within two years, there was no time to waste.

At six, Sarah dropped by the hotel business center, commissioned a computer, employed directions earlier provided by Mary McGrady.

In seconds she arrived at a Lichtenstein bank account of a Bermuda trust. There it was. $50 million. Whatever else happened, Sarah had her golden parachute. She touched the broach in her pocket.

The team arrived at Morton's at precisely 7:05, and was ushered into the private dining room antechamber where cocktails were offered along with canapés. Thoroughly enjoying the role, Sarah did not arrive until just after 7:30, made a grand entrance and "did" the room, with a private word of welcome to each team member.

After thus gracing each guest with alone time, during which she reverted in form to deeply interested nun Sarah, she gave the go-ahead to her maître d'; he popped and poured two bottles of Cristal champagne. When all were flute armed, she raised hers and declared, "Welcome midwives. Si Deus fecit, Deus fecit omnes...If God made one, then God made all! Salut." All raised their glasses wondering what she meant. After the meal they found out.

As coffee was served, Sarah reached into her Valentino and pulled out a fat 8 ½ by 11 manila envelope, opened it, retrieved some notes for her own use, and then passed the pile of two-pagers to her right. Each guest took one. Their leader began.

"As all of you know, I am sole trustee of a charitable trust that has been endowed with $300 million of capital. The work of the trust is to help women the world over, regardless of color or creed, to break the bonds of slavery by their men folk. The work of the Women's Institute for Equality, otherwise known as WIFE, unless and until we agree on a better acronym, will be conducted from a campus we, all of us in this room, are going to create on the thirty-acre site of the once-was convent of The Order of Saint Mary the Virgin. It will feature a memorial to the late Sister Therese that is to be paid for by the town of Ophrah, but it will be, oh, so much more."

She paused, sipped, and then invited the table to take a minute to look at the sheets she had passed out.

The gasps were of people about to make a great deal of money. She coughed. They shut up. She continued.

"The first page is a very rough diagram of what I want you to help me build. It is a plot of the property at 2200 O'Neill that I will convey into the trust. There, just inside the gates you can see the shrine on the right, where my dear Sister Therese was taken, then, just past a smallish parking area, a 50,000 square foot office tower to house public areas and meeting halls on the first floor, four floors of sublet space to governments and NGOs, with the sixth devoted to UN ethics committees and initiatives. I am pleased to announce that the State of Israel will be our first tenant and has pledged that when the place is built, they will take one unit on the third floor.

Farther into the property you will notice a residence for...well...me, then a dorm for the staff, and finally, where the land turns to water, a museum of natural history. I am happy to tell you that the Smithsonian has given me preliminary thumbs up on some sort of working relationship on that."

Another sip, pause, then, "To paraphrase a man of many years ago, $300 million ain't what it used to be. This plan won't work without financial backing from grants, co-ventures, and tenant rents. My job, with the able help of Mary McGrady and the people of Claxton Byrne, is to finance this great endeavor. It will be up to Julius Shromski to get the place planned and built. The accountants are to help in each and every way any of the rest of us require. Please, I am your project manager. Everything is subject to my approval. Are there any questions?"

Her audience could see gold. This project full of fee potential. No one would play naysayer. You were on the team, there was no sense playing yourself off it right before the game even started. Each knew they owed Mary McGrady a large debt of gratitude.

There were no questions. Sarah hadn't expected any. She closed with an invitation to chat among themselves, proposed a schedule of one-on-one meetings to start at 10 a.m. the next morning in the Baie suite, then made her exit, and headed directly to bed and the deep sleep of happy fatigue.

    The next day, after the one-on-ones, Sarah employed the debit card once more, to check out, the dinner having been charged to the room. Then the mogul returned to Ophrah to begin a new life of grand pomp and ferocious circumstance.

CHAPTER 43

Inured as they were to his comings and goings, minions of the Medieval Palace, Charity Offices, even the Commissary just inside the Santa Ana gate, had no personal attachment to Father Tomas. His treks between office and apartment were remarkable primarily in that no one noticed. Until the infamous scuttlebutt suggested a fall from grace. Now people were no more sensitive to the man, yet sensitized to his presence.

When he failed to show up by 11 a.m., four hours late by his own standards, a deacon was sent to check in on him. Tellingly, this mission was preceded by a frenzied search for his exact address. No one had been to his place, no one knew precisely its whereabouts.

The deacon knocked hard and long, then reported his failure to make contact.

No less a personage than the Carmerlengo ordered that Swiss guards enter the apartment immediately, ostensibly out of concern for the missing priest. While the guards didn't want to think he was dead or dying in there, the man who ordered them in wouldn't have minded such an outcome, even a blessing, or perhaps an intervention.

It took considerably more effort to get in than anticipated, but with skillful deployment of plastique, the reinforced steel door was breeched.

They were shocked.

This was no normal housing, let alone for a man of God. What should have been a living room was more like the nerve center of a major military/finance operation, with time zone clocks across the main wall just below the ceiling, a bank of phones, three different computers, an industrial size shredder, a high-speed scanner/printer/fax, and a single high-backed leather executive chair. Blinds pulled fully, indirect LED units the only source of illumination. The electronics arced in a semi-circle before the chair, wiring connected to a single continuous input panel installed at floor level in a circle beneath the command center equipment it fed, and through which the world and Tomas apparently communed. On the long wall, beneath the clocks, hung four stock market monitors; one each for New York, London, Shanghai, and Tokyo. On the far wall, reverse to the kitchen, hung two TV monitors, one silently streaming BBC World, the other Bloomberg.

The bedroom was a single military cot, made as for inspection, and a single foot locker, also meticulously arranged with spotless items of personal apparel. The fridge was full of only four items: bottled water, freeze-dried military rations, cream, and pre-prep coffee packets. Cutlery was limited to a single set of knife, fork and spoon. There were two glass tumblers and a couple of coffee mugs. There was also a Moka brew pot. That was it.

No art adorned the walls of the nerve center. There wasn't any room! But the rest of the place sported a number of what appeared to be prints of a medieval portraitist. Two stood out. One was a child of maybe fourteen years of age who looked just like one would imagine Father Tomas at that age. The other a medieval pope sitting with two younger men, and one of whom, once again, looked exactly as Father Tomas must have looked in early manhood.

It creeped out the hardened soldiers, but it was nothing compared to their next find.

The only paper files were a foursome of blue, green, yellow, and white. Each held series of photographs of a naked girl, recording an evolution from immature youth to ripe early maturity; each file label had a single name; Medici, Orsini, Pamphilis, Borghese. The photos preceded pages of data, gathered month by month on each girl, describing health, activity, diet, water intake and output, progression of each girl's menstrual cycle. Each file included an ancestry chart going back as far, in one case, as 1433.

One of the guards, raised on a horse farm, muttered, "My God, these are breeding files."

A single pad of paper bore witness to yet another important story.

Evidently Father Tomas had searched church archives for names of abuse claims against American nuns. A series of names were crossed off, stopping just before one Leroy Washington, his last known address in Miami. Beside the name, a phone number, date, time, an address for a Dunkin' Donuts shop in Miami. Elsewhere on the page, flight and confirmation numbers.

The guards immediately called for senior input; they knew they were witnesses to something horrific, beyond their bailiwick.

Swiss guards are not police. They work for one man. The Pope. They sensed ramifications far beyond the law.

One team of Cardinals descended on Tomas' operations center, while another established a command post to assist deliberations on how to proceed on what was found.

Experts couldn't crack Tomas' entry codes, so the PR machine of the Holy See had, for the present, to wing it.

It was clear to all that Father Tomas had had dealings with the man who had murdered Sister Therese and who had then apparently offed himself. It was also abundantly clear that Father Tomas knew things about girls who had been kidnapped some number of years ago, from very influential Catholic families.

The Cardinal committee immediately concluded there could be no "Vat leaks." If Father Tomas linked the Church to kidnapping and murder...at least in the case of Emmanuel Orlando, it had been 25 years before the leak. Kidnap? Theft? False accounting? Securities Fraud? Murder?

They had to say something yet tell nothing. Everybody's best interests were best served by meticulous and absolute cover-up. The law is the law, but when one is charged with the well being of God's church on Earth, one grants oneself some leeway.

Whatever Tomas was up to, it wasn't on the Church's behalf, so they really had no moral stake in the game. They couldn't help Leroy because he was dead. Well, actually they could, and should, cause prayers to be said for the man. That didn't need to be global. An e-mail to the bishop in Miami obliged him to include references to Leroy as a benighted sinner, in the same "pray for the following" way in which they already covered poor old Therese.

The girls they rationalized differently. To go public now or even just to alert the police, would not help the victims. After all, three were home now and out of danger while the one who perished was beyond their help, at least in this world.

As for the parents, it would be awkward to say the least, to explain to a major contributor how one of her own had kidnapped and apparently raped their child.

Such a disclosure would bring not a whit of comfort. Only resurrection of the panic and pain that the ordeal they once suffered was now behind them.

No good would come from disclosure, but probably much unwelcome mischief.

The men of Saint Peter's rock took the pragmatic route.

CHAPTER 44

The day after Tomas met Floyd and oblivion, an unsolicited notice suggesting theft of a huge amount of pure gold from the Vatican was anonymously delivered to the Questura di Roma-Centralino, with a copy to the Guarda di Finanza. These disclosures brought police and financial regulators to God's Earthly Head Office.

Each began a kid glove investigation. Swiss guards were left out; initial calls were directed to the office of the Apostolic Camera, thus to the immediate attention of the Carmerlengo. They were courtesy calls to alert more than an investigation. Help was offered, intervention unforced.

The financial regulator did seek formal confirmation that the gold notes, by definition a public offering, were secure, in good standing, and the issuer was willing and able to meet liquidity obligations imposed upon it by conditions of the notes.

Notwithstanding his admonition and dismissal of Father Tomas not forty-eight hours earlier, Carmerlengo's first instinct was to involve him.

When told Father Tomas was unaccountably absent, Carmerlengo felt the first thrill of fear. He called for an internal accounting, audit, and confirmation.

When told the gold was all in place he demanded random bar assays.

The first test of pure gold is simple. Having first measured it, you then toss it into water, and measure the amount of water displaced. That, compared with a standard, will tell if it's pure or not. It was off just enough for doubt. Further tests proved disaster. Each bar was 90% tungsten with a thin skin of pure gold accounting for the final 10%. That meant that 90% of $6 billion was gone; $5.4 billion of God's treasure had been stolen.

The anonymous note proposed the thief was the long-dead Luigi di Parma, the man for whom Father Tomas had so grieved. The anonymous note claimed that Luigi had not acted alone, but at the behest of Father Tomas. It claimed, moreover, that Father Tomas had then murdered Luigi to cover his tracks, perhaps also to alleviate the pain associated with shared spoils.

Not only was a huge amount of money gone, but also, the backing of the gold notes issued under the auspices of Father Tomas was not there; Mother Church not only didn't have her gold, but, net of the $600 million of surface gold, she was now light by $900 million on the guarantee reserve to which investors could already be entitled, should the notes be deemed in default.

The Carmerlengo faced two truths: his tenure was about to end, and his successor would inherit a major crisis of…faith.

Later that same day a committee of two agreed on two absolutes: Carmerlengo would keep his job to avoid further roiling the troubled waters of speculation, and, that Mother Church was once again to follow dictates of that great thinker of antiquity, Eusebius, in guarding secret truths against the slings and arrows of the unwashed. It was essential, dogmatically correct, to obfuscate, to lie.

The committee of two agreed on priorities; maintain the calm of ignorance among the holders of the notes, find the money, insulate the Institution from the apparent crimes of Father Tomas, and if possible, find the perpetrator. They weren't sure what they would do with such a find, as silence was imperative, and there would be but one way to that assurance.

The matter of the police inquiry was of little consequence. In both law and practice, Mother Church is beyond the reach of the law; besides, she had done nothing wrong.

At its essence, the nature of the crisis was clear: money and public relations.

The first fires of public speculation ignited spontaneously directly in the Questura di Roma-Centralino, through one set of loose lips to the ear of a calculating lover. The indiscreet disclosure, first learned at dinner, made the broadsheets by midnight.

The committee of two quickly determined the appropriate redress. Denial. That would buy time. Thus, their first Eusebian release; the gold is safe in our vault, the man with all the answers to every question is on retreat to the Holy Land, and he was to be given the duration of his retreat to heal his soul. He would be back in two weeks, so please, relax, and pray for a happy recovery of his earthly calm. Don't call us, we'll call you.

Two weeks is not a lot of time, and to furtively plan on such scale as required, near to impossible.

Somehow, reasoned the Carmerlengo, the gold note investors must be convinced, induced, to hang onto them, not to present them for redemption. That required doubts to be assuaged and a strong incentive provided in order to tease investors with sufficient hopeful greed to overcome reality-based fears; they must continue to hold those notes.

In normal course, the notes were scheduled for redemption over a period of up to five years. As long as they were not found to be in default, the Church had only to come up with about 20 per cent of the total outstanding, or $300 million within the next couple of months. That could be done; the thieving pig had left $600 million behind to cover his crime. If they avoided default then the vault had them covered for two years' worth of redemptions. If they could convince people to hold half of the currently redeemable notes, then the $300 million cash demand would be more like $150 million.

It was still huge, but maybe.

Then a brain wave. Carmelengo could use settlement trust funds established by Father Tomas to fund the redemptions. He fired off a memo to the Prefecture for the Economic Affairs of the Holy See asking for details on how, how much, and when he could access those funds. That done, he fired off a second memo, this time to his secular public relations advisors, convening a meeting to discuss alternatives.

He personally favored a deal where the investor got 25 or 30 percent cashed out and agreed to renew the note for five years, with a bonus of a deferred 10 percent bonus gain on the upside and a capital guarantee on the downside. As he liked to say, "A problem deferred is a problem solved." He just needed to have the settlement trust money, and he could make it all work!

Then came the call from the Prefecture for the Economic Affairs. "Yes the trusts had been audited and found intact… No, the assets were gone… The money had been legally transferred, over the signature of the sole trustee, Father Tomas… Three days ago… .No, the transfer was complete and could not be voided… No, the transferee had forwarded the money upon receipt, and no, it was beyond trace… Oh yes, on a hunch we checked the Museum Program Trust… Same thing. Gone."

The Carmerlengo collapsed into his chair, and stared unseeing at the wall. Father Tomas had walked away with $200 million in Museum Trust funds, $2.7 billion in Settlement Trust funds, and $5.4 billion in gold; $9.3 billion. Plus the $1.5 billion from the sale of the notes. They had been robbed of $10.8 billion.

The man the Carmerlengo had called "friend," whom he had nurtured and protected, had ruined him, and probably the Church. An institution that had survived countless wars, myriad schisms, and two thousand years of demagoguery might be taken down by this...Satan.

The Carmerlengo's furious contemplation was interrupted by his aide, who announced a "must take" phone call; it was Israel...the Prime Minister!

"We have a situation Father. No doubt you are aware; Israel has eyes and ears everywhere. We have learned things about issues the Vatican may have and think maybe we can help. I decided to approach you directly in the interests of time, to avoid rumors, and perhaps worse."

Sweat poured from the Carmerlengo's brow and pooled beneath his waddle. He was boiling, light-headed, sick. His phone hand trembled, the pencil snapped. "I am grateful for your call Mr. Prime Minister, but at a loss..."

"Yes, yes," intoned the voice from Jerusalem. "Of course. You have only just discovered a situation involving a priest of yours, this fellow Father Tomas."

"Please continue."

"My people tell me this priest has gone rogue, stolen money. We can help."

"I confess, we only just now found that Father Tomas is not here. Really all we know is what we have heard from the press. Do you know where he is? How can you help?"

"Father, we have a man in Rome waiting to see you. He will tell you everything and maybe we can help you with this. He knows all the details. Shall I have him contact you?"

"Yes, please. I can call him."

"No. He will call you. Please tell your people that you are expecting a call in five minutes from a person named Floyd." The line went dead.

The Carmerlengo sat frozen. He smelled rat. Intuitively he knew the offer of help was not gratuitous, but until he was better informed about their agenda, he had best keep this to himself. His own survival, let alone that of...he dared not think it...depended on knowledge, a plan, and decisive action.

"Decisive" and "Committee" are mutually exclusive. He was alone, isolated, adrift. His chest hurt.

Five minutes can seem an eternity. He heard the phone ring in the outer office, and suddenly realizing he had not warned his aide, yelled rather shrilly, to permit a call from someone named "Floyd" to get through. In an instant he was ear to ear with Floyd, but only for a moment.

Floyd instructed him to get to the front gate of the French Embassy Piazza Farnese, in ten minutes. And to bring no one.

Who does this? No longer overheating, but with a tight throat, throbbing temples, and sharp gut pains, the Carmerlengo got moving.

A foreign Sovereign State knew more about his predicament than he, and was behaving in a clandestine manner. He knew he needed help, but feared the price.

Knowing he had to play along for the present, and that he didn't have control was in a sense a plan, and with a plan comes calm.

CHAPTER 45

It took exactly ten minutes to get to the French Embassy. The Carmerlengo paid the cabby and waited. Like many clinging to reality in the midst of the surreal, he paused and took in the detail of the place with focus like never before.

The building was one of Rome's most impressive bits of renaissance architecture, originally the home to the medieval Farnese family; Father Tomas' last name was "Farnese."

At the instant of this revelation, a cab lurched to a stop in front of him, and a nondescript sort of fellow stepped out, offered his hand and pronounced, "Hello Father, I'm Floyd."

They walked in silence through Farnese Park and down to the Tiber, where Floyd directed them to an empty waterside bench, the location from which Floyd had so recently launched Father Tomas. There, among the sightseers, before the same river of the Caesars, Borgias,

Medicis, Farneses, and Mussolinis, the Christian priest and the Jewish spy talked turkey.

The man who had so relied upon Father Tomas now came to know him; learned his delusions, deceptions, and perversions.

A good, honest man of true devotion to his God, the Carmerlengo was sickened as Therese was explained. When the spy interpreted her mutilation as a deception meant to confuse committed by a ruthless psychopath, the priest required time to compose himself. The wind-up of the convent, the excommunications, the denial of the shrine was given perspective and the priest permitted private disgust at his unknowing acquiescence. Leroy was explained as a benighted victim of an unhappy incident, on record as a late-in-life claimant for sexual transgressions who Tomas set up as part of the theft and mutilation.

The spy explained the Luigi di Parma part. He told of how a military brotherhood became a cabal, how redirected Settlement Trust money funded the purchase of the refinery, how Tomas orchestrated its bankruptcy to bury economics tough to explain, and to validate an apparent suicide. Yes, Tomas had murdered his best, his only friend. He had used diethyl ether instead of chloroform as it is quickly and fully metabolized leaving no trace, and the MGA because modern emission standards make carbon monoxide poisoning too long for an efficient murder.

The priest sat aghast, moving only enough to recover the rosary, and to clutch it as a drowning man might a rescue rope.

Floyd skipped the story of semen deposits and virgin breeder slaves, moving on to money. He explained the realities of single trustee arrangements, the economics of banks, and the jurisdictional impact of financial havens.

During all the explanation, the Carmerlengo listened intently, asked myriad questions, searched frantically for an inkling of a plan to somehow turn this to his advantage.

"How is it you know all this?" The answer was a shrug.

"Do you know where the money and the gold is now?" The answer was a shrug.

"Why are you telling me all this?" The spy replied he had been sent to offer to help.

"How? Can you help us get the money back?"

"It depends. Most likely no, but we can maybe help solve the problem it causes."

Sweats, palpitations, a splitting headache. The poor man rubbed at his temples without relief.

"So you are here to help, but you can't tell me if you even know where the money is. An hour ago I was talking to your Prime Minister. What in the name of...what do you want? You know more about what's going on in my, um, office, than I do. How?"

The spy shrugged, "Look Father, I am not a diplomat, but it seems we have a bit of a situation here. You must remain calm. May I get you some coffee or water?"

"Just talk."

"Very well. You have lost more money than you can afford, and it appears there is a great number of people who want their money back on those, what do you call them? ...gold notes. We might be able to help you. But first, please consider this question of mine. When does the act of robbing a grave become the honorable profession of archeology? When does theft cease to be theft? When does the finder keep and the loser weep? Let's say, hypothetically, that someone stole something from you, like the money in your pocket. Then, also hypothetically, let's say that I took that money from the thief. Is it yours, or mine?"

The Carmerlengo was visibly agitated, "Don't quibble. It's my money. So you return it to me."

"OK. Do I get a reward?"

That put the good Father over the top. He leapt to his feet, bent over the nondescript protagonist until nose to nose with one comfortable in the knowledge of ten different ways to single-handedly and instantly kill him, then spat out, "You want money? You want a finder's fee? What in the name of God do you think you're doing?"

Floyd's response was flat, uncompromising, deadly, "You don't want to do this Father. Sit. And leave God out of it. Your God has already troubled my people enough."

Resigned, the priest sighed, then sat. Floyd continued, "You have a problem, I don't. People want answers from you. Not from me. They don't know I even exist. I, we, have gone to a good deal of trouble to meet here today. We didn't do it to not help. We came to help. But, there are some issues we need to clear up while we do that."

"Out with it. How much flesh…"

"Bad, Father. Not funny. That play did a lot of damage. You really do want to be very careful here."

A vision of a cat batting a doomed mouse flashed through the priest's mind. He knew he was the mouse, that the cat was playing, and fate was not within his control.

"I am truly sorry Floyd. That wasn't Freud. It was just a figure of speech. Believe me…"

Floyd reached around the priest and hugged him with what seemed a friendly embrace. "Thank you Father. I know you are a good man, and a smart one, and that we will be able to help each other."

The spy walked to the coffee vendor, looked around and said, "Latte, two sugars?" The priest nodded, pensively wondering, "Mary, mother of God, what does he not know?"

Respite of the initial sip. "So Father, we agree. Stolen money must be returned. I can agree. And when it's big money, maybe a reward. Good?"

"This is your show, sir, so why don't you just tell me what you want."

Floyd downed his coffee, pitched the cup into a nearby bin, and continued. "So let's follow the logic one more step, Father. In my hypothetical example, let's say that some of the money stolen from you wasn't yours…it was someone else's. Do I give it all to you, or just yours, and maybe I give to the other guys what you are holding for them?

The Carmerlengo was not stupid, in fact he was extremely bright, and the lights were now on. Headlights. "I could argue that with you, but you have an agenda. Why don't we just let you say how it's going to be? Shall we?"

Floyd knew that the Carmerlengo now saw clearly where they were going, if not where they would get to.

"Right then Father. I am told that with interest, and costs, and what not, up until your unmanaged rogue murdering psychotic priest took off, there was maybe $6 billion owing to dispossessed Jews who didn't seem able to cope with your God's justice done the way you practice it here on Earth. We thought we could help to resolve this. We deal with them, hold you harmless forever for everything before now..."

"So you send back the rest?" The priest allowed himself some hope, calculating.

"Sort of."

The hope became pounding chest and temples.

"We think a reward is good. We think 25 percent."

"You want 25 percent of $2.4 billion? You want to keep like 700 million dollars?"

"No, not at all. We want to keep like $2.3 billion...25 percent of what we found."

Now timid, the priest ventured, "So we get...nothing?"

"Nothing? We are restoring to you the ability to settle a very large, very old, very ugly score. That is not nothing! There were costs you know. Our organization has been following this psychopath for years. There were lots of people to pay. Our people. Maybe some bribes.

Here's the deal. Subject to one other matter, we take care of Jewish claims against you, we get all our costs covered, and we get a reward. You get exactly what you need to keep all those gold notes out of the way."

"We only get $1.5?"

"Father, you get to tell the world all is well. You get to put the whole thing behind you. We help you to look like... heroes. And no. You end up with $1.5 billion, after you take the real gold off the fake bars. Yes father, I knew about that. We can do arithmetic. With the residue he left, and $1 billion from us, you are as well off as you have any right to expect."

"You said subject to...what does that mean?"

"Apparently there was a computer. It might have been hacked into, Father."

The Man of the Cloth twisted the rope of his salvation...his rosary. It snapped. He looked at it dumbly as a child does at recently sundered china.

The spy continued, "It is possible that provenance detail of much you call 'yours' tells otherwise. The beautiful thing about your collection, all the art and the artifacts, is that you have saved them and kept them in good shape, maintained them...like in trust. The bad thing is that all you call 'yours' was someone else's before it was 'yours'. And it wasn't archeology Father." So far, few have successfully been able to draw lines well enough to obtain restitution. The good thing is that now, through this computer, you have done that. The provenance of every piece in detail! We think the art should stay safe with you, Father. We don't want to make trouble for you, and we don't really care who else does or doesn't own it...except what is ours."

"You want my art?"

The cold, flat tone returned "No Father, I want my history and my past returned to me...well, us."

"And..."

"And we will do two things. First, we will give you back your computer. Second, we will destroy our copy of the disc."

"You know everything about me, us, it. Surely to God you know I can't just say yea or nay. I have to go back to my people..."

"Of course, Father. I don't have a time line. You do. I believe you committed to redeem some gold notes in about two weeks didn't you?"

"I see your point. Let me talk to my people, then how shall I contact you?"

"You won't. I will call you tomorrow morning at eleven o'clock. If we're going to pull all of this together and get you where you need to be, a lot of things have to happen, so time is not a luxury you can afford."

With that, both of them stood. The spy offered his hand and said, "You are a good man Father. This is a nasty bit of business, but it could have been worse. We are helping. Father Tomas would not have done as well by you as we will. Your organization is important and we respect that. One day you will thank us."

With that the spy was off. The Carmerlengo looked heavenward for but a moment, and then turned back to watch the departure of the spy, but he was gone.

CHAPTER 46

What was "Number Two" to do in this situation? He had to report to his superior, Il Papa, but couldn't just go with the problem. He must also be ready with suggested solutions. He knew, because if he were not politically astute he wouldn't be "Number Two" in the first place, that he could have no confidantes. To do so would broadcast his failure in all cases and dilute his success if a way out of the mess manifested itself.

Surprisingly, in search of guidance, the Carmerlengo turned to Father Tomas. Not in person, but through review of past experiences, and imagining what Tomas might have done, had he been available, loyal, and appropriate. The irony was not lost; to escape present perils he must channel a psychopath.

First, a clear problem definition, then strategies to either win outright, or put as good a face on them as possible.

He must marshal every tool, including faith among the flock, general unawareness of Church finances, power of moral suasion, enlightened best interests of secular leaders. Floyd himself had said he was there to help.

So, thought the Carmerlengo, if Floyd preferred to bleed the cow, he didn't want to kill it. There could never be the gap, the hatred, begun in Empire times, festered through the millennia, exploded in anti-Semitic Europe. No sane Jewish leader would participate in bankrupting Saint Peter's rock.

There it was. He had a plan, a way out of this fiasco. He asked Number One to meet.

It went remarkably well. Both Prime Numbers agreed the offer on the table was actually workable, but could be improved. Number Two obtained discretion to give what he must to get the most. Once they knew what cards they had, they would deal with the flock.

Floyd called as and when he said, agreed to meet in the same place, same time, tomorrow.

This time Floyd arrived first. This time the priest got the coffee. This time the priest did the talking.

"Floyd, we want to thank your government for its help, and you for your role. Please forgive my manners during our first meeting. You are not the problem. We are grateful."

"You are most welcome, Father. So, we have a deal then?"

"No. But we do have a sort of an agreement to agree, and now we need to button down details."

Through the entire adventure with the nuns, the assassination, and the first round with the Carmerlengo, Floyd had never experienced loss of control. He felt a shock of excitement.

"I beg your pardon?"

"Floyd, we did as you proposed. We took the time to reflect on your offer, and as good as it is, we know you want to do better."

Floyd started to talk but the Carmerlengo gave him the palm up international sign for silence, "You cannot be seen in any light other than a good one, and we can make sure that happens, but not if we're getting screwed. You keep 5 percent as a commission and deal with it any way you want. We get $2 billion returned, you keep $435 million and pay whatever expenses you ran up in this whole sordid matter."

Now it was Floyd's turn, "Are you nuts? Your whole premise is that someone tells the great unwashed anything. Are you seriously thinking that's a good idea…to tell the whole world you cared so little for the security of Church money that you let one thieving priest take it all? If that's what you want to do, go for it, but we're out. No deal. We'll just keep all the money. You can say anything you want, but we'll deny it. I'm out of here, Father." With that he rose, walked to the curb, and as the ubiquitous cab showed up, turned to the priest, "If you don't stop me now, we're done Father. Is that how we leave this?"

It wasn't. The cab dismissed, and Floyd back on the bench, he continued as if nothing had happened. "The world can never know. We don't want to be heroes. We want you to be the hero. We want the Holy Roman Catholic Church to publicly settle the morally valid claims made against it by Jews, through a deal with the State of Israel. That will be a huge public relations win for you, and a very popular thing for my government with its people. Same thing goes for your offer to repatriate items of art and artifact for which you have maintained safekeeping for the past some two thousand years. It's a magnificent gesture of goodwill, even friendship. This will give you a boost. Us too."

At its essence, what the spy and the priest were doing was negotiating a business deal. Large or small, the weird thing about deals is they are usually quickly agreed upon in principle, recorded in minimal verbiage. It's the mandarins, the lawyers, accountants, bankers, regulators, boards and the like that take the time and documentation. Secret deals between accomplices with no obligations to third parties can be completed even faster, with no bits and pieces, no paper trail.

Thus was this. Right there beside the coffee wagon, on the banks of the Tiber, on land that was once Farnese estate, the deal was struck, exactly as initially laid out by the spy. Except that the $1.0 billion to the Church would now be $1.5 billion. Both left happy, the priest because he had managed to keep $600 million free and clear of what he needed to pay off the gold notes, the spy because he had been authorized to go to $2.0 billion.

CHAPTER 47

An array of functionaries sprang into action. Pens whirred. Spin doctors spun.

The two sides of the monstrous tug-of-war now pulled together in an uneasy alliance with each attempting to maximize its own ends, yet limited by need to accommodate the other.

For the Israelis, it was pretty much all upside, although there would be questions from the floor of the Knesset about how to divvy up the money, and how the deal all came down in the first place. Much would be made of the lack of debate prior to making the deal. The religious right and moderates would clash over the significance and propriety of every settlement with every dispossessed claimant. Ultimately, it would be essential to share the halo of this victory with political enemies or suffer through intolerable debate on every ounce of minutia. But, in relative terms, these were good problems, the problems of shared victory laurels and managed modesty for political gain.

Not so much for Mother Church. This really was a sow's ear! The embattled vestigial of the long-dead Roman empire was now reduced to the necessity of assuaging fears among investors, making sense out of stewardship decisions, avoiding self-incrimination, and keeping the flock in tow. There could be no disclosure of theft, murder, abuse of sacred practice, incompetence, and the potential financial collapse.

Then there was the business of agreeing with each other's version of the facts.

Both teams quickly agreed that no one was served by disclosing nefarious elements. Both sides understood that Father Tomas would go unmentioned.

The Jewish team wanted credit for settling the claims, so it was agreed that Rome would get credit for gifting the artifacts.

Since each had to approve the wording of the other's announcement, it became appropriate to make joint announcements. Since they couldn't agree on whether those announcements ought to be made initially in Rome or Jerusalem, they made them simultaneously in both.

It was further agreed that maximum goodwill accrued by allowing some time to pass between the two announcements; thus the settlement announcement would come first, and ninety days later, the artifacts gift.

Rome would deal with the disappearance of Tomas unilaterally, subject to prior approval of the text by Jerusalem. The same went for the gold note redemption issue.

First up was the announcement regarding the gold notes.

In the securities business, major announcements are typically made after the close of financial markets. That's become increasingly tricky in a world shaped like a slightly pregnant peach, because there is almost no time when all markets are closed; somewhere, it's tomorrow. "Closed" in London is just getting rolling in New York. When New York closes for the weekend, it's midafternoon in L.A. "Friday" in L.A. is "Saturday" in Tokyo and Shanghai.

Convention has it that financial disclosures are made after the close of business in the local market, and delivered to news services on the understanding of no public release of information until after the close of the North American markets.

Following the dictates of perfect markets regulation, at nine o'clock in the evening on Friday the 13th of November. Just fourteen days after the discovery of Therese's remains, Mother Church issued a press release to the financial media in which it confirmed its intention to buy back the entire issue of gold notes at the issue price of $2,000 per ounce, notwithstanding the current price of gold of $1,200, nor the Vatican and legal requirements to offer on only 20 percent of the outstanding issue. Funds had been deposited with its agent, the Union Bank of Switzerland; investors could deal through UBS or through their own broker. The notice went on to detail an offer of settlement in cash or by replacement certificate providing for the original capital guarantee of the $2,000 on a five-year term, with half of the gain over $2,000 for the account of the investor and the other half for Saint Peter's team.

Ninety-nine percent of the old notes rolled into the new.

Next up was the settlement of the holocaust-related claims. In a prepared statement broadcast simultaneously in Jerusalem and Rome, a joint communiqué was read at twelve noon, Rome time.

It announced that the Holy Roman Catholic Church and the State of Israel acting on behalf of Jews wherever they live or lived, had utilized the procedures of class action settlement to arrive at a mutually acceptable resolution of all claims by all Jews against the Church, directly or indirectly, arising from any matter whatsoever, in the period ending at the date of the announcement. While the Church was saddened by the plight of the claimants and delighted to be able to put these matters behind all the parties for all of time, she nonetheless warned that the settlement was in no way an admission of guilt. It went on to define the omnibus settlement ceiling of $6.0 billion, to describe procedures for claimants to register and for settlement amounts to be calculated, and to advise potential claimants that the settlement offer required a complete and absolute release. It ended with a mutual statement of respect and amity, now stronger than ever, existing between the people of the Jewish and Catholic faiths.

Ninety days later came the next shocker. The Holy Roman Catholic Church, in the spirit of compassion, respect, and amity as made manifest in the settlement of just ninety days earlier, wished to meaningfully demonstrate its solidarity in the joint roots of these two historic traditions by repatriating to the care and control of the Jewish state, on behalf of Jews the world over, items of their history and traditions that had been in protective care at the Vatican. In her storied past, the Church had collected for safekeeping manuscripts, jewelry, numismatic materials, implements, and items of apparel. In total, over five thousand specific items were to be conveyed to the State of Israel. Among the items was what scholars believed might be the remains of the Ark of the Covenant of Moses' tradition, the second set of tablets whereon were written God's commandments, an iron age knife believed to be that almost used by Abraham in his tortured act of faith, the crown of King David, and, remarkably, remnants of Joseph's coat of many colors. Many of these items had come to Rome during the Templar era, when that organization had secretly mined into the old temple in Jerusalem and had sent everything of religious significance on to Rome. Crusaders had discovered much of the rest in places as far reaching as Egypt, Greece, and Moorish Spain.

In response, the people of Israel, through their government, gratefully received custody of these items, understanding and accepting their solemn obligation to maintain these precious artifacts into perpetuity. It was expected that scholars from around the world would analyze each and every item, but that within a decade, all would be appropriately ensconced in suitable museums for the benefit of Jews and non-Jews alike. This was a great moment in the history of the people of Israel and in the relations of Jews and Christians the world over.

One month after the gift of the artifacts, a short memo was issued to cardinals and bishops for their information and that of others who may from time to time have expressed an interest. The memo explained that the brilliant work of Father Tomas, begun some thirty years earlier and which had culminated in the settlement with the people of Israel, was now at an end. Father Tomas wished to retire from the demands of his office, and to spend the rest of his days working with the poor in an as yet undetermined outpost of faith. He had been granted leave to go on a personal pilgrimage to important Catholic shrines, to renew his faith and recharge his health. It said that Father Tomas had suffered a breakdown as a result of the tragic deaths of two people close to him, those being his lifelong friend Luigi de Parma and his co-worker, the venerable Sister Therese, and that he needed time to revive his soul and his spirit. Catholics were asked to remember all three of these people in their prayers.

Quietly, with no fanfare, overtures were made to the woman now in charge of what used to be the Convent of the Holy Virgin Mary. Mother Church wished to participate formally in the shrine to Sister Therese, and to establish a long-term relationship with the new Women's Institute for Female Equality, and to maintain an office in the facility currently under construction on the property at 2200 O'Neill Street. The woman in charge, Sister Sarah as she had once been known, was emerging as an important power. Ever the pragmatist, the renegade nun responded affirmatively, demanding only that the collective excommunication be recanted by papal decree.

CHAPTER 48

Two years on, the same Florida sun rose on that same Ophrah real estate, but everything had changed. Sarah had gone viral. Devotees abounded, political correctness surrounded, and willful self-serving autocrats astounded. Money flowed in as a torrent from all, some altruistic, more in attempts to export domestic unrest and painlessly align with a popular cause.

Renovations were complete. The place barely resembled its former self with a new private wing, office tower, conference center, and 100-room hostel. The centerpiece was the "Atom"; seven outer pods connecting the central, massive, vaulted, dominating core.

Naming these occasioned horrendous complexity as inclusion of women across all religions rendered almost every symbol and name moot.

Sarah had delegated naming authority and responsibility to a committee of thirty women from around the globe. These women, representing a wide range of faiths and lack thereof, from every corner of the planet, resolved the problem over a weekend in Monaco at a retreat paid for in full by the host nation. The solution came from a physicist who noted the irony that the widely religious number seven equaled the maximum number of electron rings. This rendered an innocuous naming system, connoted purpose, and even provided a workable name for the core. Thus were born Shells K through Q, and the name of the core; "The Nucleus". This nomenclature even permitted inclusion within any given shell of different orbitals, being specific religions and or sects. Assigning Orbitals to Shells was a cute task; what should have been one for the People of the Book had to be three, Hindus and Buddhists brought the total used to five, leaving everyone else to two shells. Taoists and Confucians anchored the sixth. Such diverse orbits as Pagans, Wiccans, Druids, Atheists and Agnostics anchored the last.

Inhabitants of the convent, the nuns, had been moved and relocated, and were gone; all of them but Sarah.

The original convent was now a museum memorializing Therese, and lionizing women across history and geography, whom had been murdered for their faith or status within it.

The guest house Ted had frequented, scene of Sarah's sexual revolt, remained unaltered; Sarah had wanted it razed but circus economics won out.

Today, finally, was the official opening of the Nucleus. Paean to peaceful co-existence across racial, spiritual, and gender lines.

The place reeked of pageantry.

Over three days, delegations from around the globe arrived in a non-stop procession. The town itself was awash in color, fashion and custom, displayed by magnificent women from many cultures and sects. In two short years Ophrah had gone cosmopolitan.

Just over three hundred diverse religious communities were in attendance, sharing in peace and mutual respect. Every continent but Antarctica would attend. The lions and the lambs in peace.

Throngs that heretofore spilled blood now mingled. The entire religiosity of the world condensed to the seven shells. So Sunnis would mingle with Shiites, Sufis, Deists would mingle with many…

Most came with the blessing and support of their men.

In fact, starting eighteen months earlier, when this event was first conceived, The Center, as yet unborn in Earthly form, had assumed divine proportions. First it had been small interest groups, then countries, and finally whole religions joined in; accepted ideals, acquired space, opened Faith Embassies on the campus and in the burgeoning and very affluent town of Ophrah.

In a new and important way, America shared her shining beacon. Six months prior, The Center had received its first official request from a nation to house a formal office. It was a meteoric rise. At its head, a single woman, an ex-nun, mid-wife to peace, a force of nature, and reputed Nobel candidate.

This force had risen at 4 a.m., as was her habit. By five she had taken her exercise and dressed. For lack of time, she snacked on gifts of the Earth during briefing sessions with an increasingly large coterie of inner-sanctum advisors.

Briefed not just on politics and global matters of faith, but also on details of construction, of this pageant, and capital investment. The details of today were plans for tomorrow.

By seven each morning, there were twenty separate sessions. She took no notes, but remembered all. She still called herself Sister Sarah.

Through all of it, the success, the growth, the fame, Sister Sarah found herself more and more alone. Everyone wanted something. Every decision needed to be weighed. There was always an agenda. Everything she did mattered to someone and everyone seemed to watch all the time. So she created the eyes and ears of her mini-meeting counterparts, and became more and more invisible through rigidly maintained privacy and limited access.

She had no life but her work, no contact with the people…the ones she had so adored when Sarah had been the humble nun. She was now removed, important. No longer humble.

Each night before sleep, it was her custom to pray for the soul of Ted.

Ted, the last man she had ever "known," was himself an essential sacrifice to what she had become. A man who might have been venerated but of whom secrets were kept.

There was one companion; her confidante, bodyguard, the former detective and current devotee, Liberté. They had not talked for over a year after that last blowout after the shooting. Liberté had left the force, then Ophrah, and had disappeared.

Then, there she was.

Sarah had been on the construction site; a guard tapped her on the shoulder and said some woman named Liberté wished to see her. They said not a word; Sarah shed tears, there was a silent embrace, and they had been inseparable ever since. Ted was never mentioned then or ever. Liberté never offered, nor did Sarah ask, where she had gone and why she had returned.

It was now 7 a.m. Liberté shuffled files into order. A phone she didn't know to exist rang. Sarah reacted with inelegant haste. The cryptic conversation revealed only that Sister Sarah still kept secrets to which Liberté was not privy.

The call lasted less than two minutes. Sarah stood for an awkward few seconds of silence with slumped shoulders and bowed head portraying duress. Then up came her head, back went her shoulders, and imperious, impervious Sarah was back.

"Where were we?" she asked. The confidante obliged, the moment passed.

Today would be all show.

Five hundred members of the press had called for accreditation. That was winnowed to eighty, to be accompanied by TV coverage operated by the Institute's own production company, already a profit center on its own. Liberté oversaw camera placements since that fit nicely with her prime obligation, which was security.

There were to be myriad interviews with dignitaries, theologians of all stripes, the inevitable visibility whores of politics and Hollywood.

The opening ceremony would be taped in its entirety for worldwide distribution; from the pre-ordained order of arrivals, through filing from the Shells into The Nucleus, peppered with a litany of brief congratulatory orations from leaders of the worlds of Gods and men. A welcome address from Sister Sarah the penultimate event, only the ordered pomp of dismissal marches would follow.

Sister Sarah would be physically present in the "Nucleus" only for the duration of her address.

Twenty minutes after the closing of that session, seven women, each chosen from, and representing delegates of each Shell, were to join Sister Sarah on her private balcony overlooking the complex's inner square. They would greet the public, provide a photo-op, and reinforce the concepts of equality and solidarity even as they reveled in their moment of unique adulation.

Sarah seemed unsettled by the phone call, enough so that she left the device on her bureau.

When nature called Sarah, Liberté seized the opportunity. Two buttons, and the window presented the number as "unidentified." Five more buttons brought factoids, including its registered owner, a trading company of unrecognized name. Liberté replaced the phone, waited anxiously for the "I'm in use" light to fade, resumed her seat, and jotted down details just gleaned.

By Sarah's return all was as it had been. At least from Sarah's perspective.

Innate intelligence and years of training served Liberté well. She could trace things later. For now, secret knowledge was best maintained as such.

"Shall I call your team?"

The Midwife nodded, then turned, "Lib?"

"Yes?"

Sarah came to her, took both hands in hers and said, "I could not do this without you, you know. There is no joy in what I now do. When you returned a little light came back into my life. You are the only person in the whole world that really knows me. That I really trust. You do know that, don't you?"

She who had just come to one more example of how this was a lie simply nodded.

Sarah continued, "From now on, it will be so hard. They all want a piece of me. Everybody! All the time! You're my only real friend. I can't do this without you, Lib." This was followed by a moment of mutual introspection and then a serious, almost weepy, kind of a hug. And then, "Ok, Lib, you've got things to do, and I need to get ready. Can you send them in now?" Liberté opened the door to the entourage: hair stylist, manicurist, dresser, sewer, and speechwriter.

An hour later, after a trip to central control, a tour of security locations, and a fitting with communications ear-piece and transmitter, Liberté returned. She gasped dramatically, causing Sarah to laugh her first laugh during the stress-filled day.

The Midwife was now Empress. Perfect coif. Armani suit of off-white, legs toned slightly by hosiery that ended in tasteful two-inch Manolo black patent heels. And this most unimaginably beautiful brooch.

"Where the hell did that come from?" Liberté asked, while an inner voice intoned caution.

Sarah knew exactly what she meant, "This? A gift. I have had it for a while. It's quite valuable..."

"No shit, Sherlock!"

"I have never thought that I should wear it...until today."

"Well, given the rest of the show, why not I guess."

"Besides, the people who gave it to me asked specifically..."

"That phone call?"

Sarah looked at her sharply but said nothing.

The detective in her knew this was big, but that she had gotten all she was going to get for now. "OK, let's get you out there then. The show is starting, and I want you in our green room for fifteen minutes before you go live. Go ahead now, I'll be right behind."

Sarah stepped through the door and surrendered herself to the forces she had created.

Alone now, Liberté looked around. The phone had vanished. Ex-detective Liberté sat in silence for not more than a minute, then arose with new purpose.

She still clung to the dignity of remorse that she had carried for the past two years, a remorse that had called her back to Ophrah for her true calling.

Sarah was, in every way that mattered, in her thrall, not the other way around. She, Liberté, was now that invisible person behind the throne. Her work could now begin.

Inside and out, forces sniffed, hid, preyed, succumbed. The frontier of feral and civilized a charming ideal but a failed reality.

CPSIA information can be obtained
at www.ICGtesting.com
Printed in the USA
LVOW12s0136050516
486560LV00001B/29/P